◇◇◇◇◇◇◇◇◇◇◇◇◇◇◇◇◇◇◇◇◇◇◇◇◇◇◇◇

Love's Journey

By

Charlotte Kent

The Third Novel in the Series

Captain's Point Stories

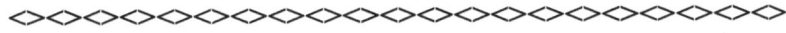

In memory of, Bob, who loved me
Annie Acorn

To my husband, John, the love of my life
Juliette Hill

Charlotte Kent is the pseudonym used by
Annie Acorn and Juliette Hill
when writing their collaborative contemporary
women's fiction/family saga series
Captain's Point Stories

You may contact and/or follow the authors at:
charlottekentromances@gmail.com
@CharlotteKent20

This is Max's fourth starring role in a work of fiction.

The true story of his actual rescue can be found in
Annie Acorn's *Chocolate Can Kill*

The novel, *Love's Journey*, is a work of fiction. Any resemblance to real people or events is completely accidental. A few literary liberties may have been taken when it comes to geographic locations, medical treatments, sailing terms, tidal charts, and helicopter rescue protocols in the interest of creating great literature.

CHAPTER I

Chase and Adrianna Sheffield sipped on the remains of their Monday morning coffee in the sun-filled breakfast room of Montgomery House, her ancestral home and now their common domicile – a large house constructed two centuries before by her sea captain predecessor from granite blocks and slate roofing, with an octagonal tower and formal gardens shaped like half of a ship's steering wheel.

At first glance, the newly married couple appeared to be older brother and younger sister, both having been blessed with dark wavy hair, good bone structure and fine complexions, but his nose was slightly more patrician and her eyes were dark brown to his deep blue ones. Those who knew them well would've said they were mated for life, and they would've been right.

"Listen to this." Chase lifted his eyes from his morning paper, drew his wife's attention, and began to read, "'Your reporter has learned that internationally known, award-winning author John Jeffers and his new bride, the former Susan Chesterton, will be returning today from their honeymoon in Key West to their secluded home in Captain's Point, Maryland.'" He refolded the paper and tossed it onto the table. "How in the world did they find out? Susan only told me last evening, and I'm her law partner."

"Wouldn't Jack have had to file a flight plan with the airport in Key West before flying them back in the helicopter?" Adrianna suggested. "Although, he wouldn't have used his pseudonym. He would've given his name as Jack Jefferson."

"Do you know how sexy you are when you're brilliant first thing in the morning?" her husband asked as he rose from his chair and drew her up and into his arms before planting a long kiss on her lips.

"Don't start anything you can't finish," she teased once he let her up for air. "In fact..." She glanced at the regulator clock that hung on the wall behind him. "You're going to be late if you don't hurry."

For a moment, he met her gaze, the soft look that she loved in his eyes, before he let out a sigh. "You're right," he agreed, "but I'd much rather stay here with you. What's on your calendar today?"

"Otis and I will be busy going over Montgomery Properties' year-to-date report," she told him, knowing full well that her appointment with their property manager to review the business's first three quarters of the year wasn't until after lunch. Hopefully, her husband would find it easier to tear himself away if he believed she was occupied.

Not that either of them needed to work, they didn't, but somehow she didn't view her tall, strong husband retiring in his early thirties as a good thing. He was too much of a mover and shaker to be happy with idle hands, and the thought of her retiring at twenty-seven after all the hard work she had put into earning her degrees made her physically ill.

"And you, you little knave," Chase addressed their Chihuahua-Beagle mix Max, who had just entered the room, tail wagging. "Do you realize how little sleep your mama and my queen got because she had to hold and pet you half the night due to the storm that went through? Why the poor woman looks..." He glanced back at his wife. "Well, actually, she looks beautiful as usual." He returned his stern gaze to the dog. "But it's no thanks to you."

"I have a note right by my mug that reminds me to call Jim once his office opens," Adrianna assured him, referring to her husband's high school track buddy who was now the dog's veterinarian. "Speaking of Jack and Susan, would you want to have them over for dinner and to play cards Saturday evening if they're free?" She brought their conversation around full circle.

"Sure, although I think Jack's sister will be here by then, so we should ask Larry and her as well to round out the numbers." Chase dropped another quick kiss on her lips and then released her, reaching his hand down and giving Max a good scratch behind the ears to show that he bore the dog no hard feelings before leaving them.

Left to her own devices, Adrianna picked up her mug and To Do list, leaving them at her end of the long library table in the couple's home office before joining Otis's wife Penny in the kitchen.

"Saturday's invitation list has grown to include Kate and Larry," she advised the pleasingly plump, middle-aged woman, who was officially employed as their housekeeper, but also filled the role of substitute mother for both of her employers. "Why don't Otis and you join us as well? If we change the menu to spaghetti or lasagna, Jack and Susan can bring Daniel along with them, and they won't have to bother with a sitter. He'll fall asleep on the couch after dinner anyway, and we adults can play cards or just visit."

"What should we do for dessert?" Penny asked.

"I'll make a cheesecake, if you'll do your homemade blueberry and cherry toppings," Adrianna promised.

"Have you told Chase about your plans yet?" the housekeeper asked, attempting to look nonchalant as she folded the dishtowel she was holding and laid it on the counter to the right of the kitchen's oversized farm sink.

"Not yet." Adrianna waited until she once again had the other woman's attention. "I want all my ducks in a row before I go to him with it, so he won't think that I'm crazy."

"You do realize Chase adores you, don't you?" Penny asked.

"Yes, which is why I don't want to disappoint him."

"I'm not sure that's possible, but even so, both partners have to be happy for a marriage to be successful long term," the housekeeper pointed out. "Chase wouldn't want you to spend your days puttering around this big, old house, bored out of your gourd. Otis didn't want me to work after we were first married, but he soon saw that we had a lot more to talk about when I had things to share with him, too. Has Chase said he doesn't want you to move forward once the original properties you inherited are all brought up to snuff?"

"No, my hesitancy is all about me," Adrianna assured her. "What does Otis really think of my idea?"

"Why don't you ask him yourself?" Penny nodded towards the window over the sink. "He's coming through the kitchen garden right now. If you'd like, you two can fill me in completely over a second cup of coffee, and I'll give you my opinion."

"Would you?" Adrianna's expression brightened. "It might help if we had some practice before we go and discuss things with Larry," she referred to an appointment she had scheduled for the next day with her husband's best friend since childhood, who was now the couple's broker besides being Susan's cousin.

"So we're all set?" Otis asked as he entered through the door to the mudroom.

"Larry will see us at ten o'clock sharp tomorrow morning," Adrianna confirmed, hoping that Chase wouldn't think she had gone completely out of her mind when she explained her plans to him the next evening.

At the same moment, Larry Chesterton swirled his desk chair around and relaxed as he watched friends and neighbors walk past his office window that overlooked Main Street in the small, eastern shore Maryland town of Captain's Point, but then his expression sobered as he remembered the previous evening.

He had taken Daniel out for a short walk to give his aunt and uncle a breather, and his footsteps had automatically led him in the direction of Montgomery House. Finding his friends enjoying the sunset from the table in their home's kitchen garden, he had joined them, allowing his four-year-old cousin to run up and down the enclosed garden's paths with Max, thus wearing the child out before bedtime.

Offered a beer, he had accepted, and Chase had gone inside to get it. In his host's absence, Adrianna had leaned forward and asked him if he would be free to meet with her Tuesday morning. Confirming he would be, he had been surprised when she had asked him not to mention the appointment to her husband, since they seemed like the kind of couple who would share everything.

What, he wondered, was she planning? Hopefully, whatever it was, he would be able to avoid a situation in which he found himself lodged between the two of them. Montgomery Properties was one of his largest clients, but Chase was his best friend.

Six hours away, Kate Sinclair searched through the candid pictures of her brother's wedding that were now stored on her computer, smiling at one of Daniel kissing Jack's cheek as she paused on it. Her brother had been right – her new nephew-in-law was a charmer.

A second photo centered on her, and she ran a critical eye over her appearance, before deciding that the blue dress she had chosen for the occasion did, indeed, suit her. A third showed a group of men clustered in a corner. There was Paul Lynch - the good-looking, young minister who had performed the ceremony, Jim Laidlaw – her brother's veterinarian, Larry Chesterton – the bride's cousin and Chase Sheffield – who owned the Sheffield Place Inn where she had stayed and was the bride's law partner. How relaxed and comfortable with each other and her brother they had all been.

Another click and a photo of the wedding couple came into view. Jack – tall, broad shouldered, with dark hair and eyes above his high cheekbones, kind and gentle. Susan – slightly above medium height, blonde, with beautiful blue eyes, long legs and a sweet disposition. She was glad that her confirmed bachelor brother had found someone so nice to love him and love back. He had been without a family, as she soon would be, for far too long.

How could their parents have turned their backs on her brother simply because he reminded them physically of a Cherokee ancestor – a blot on the bloodline in their minds? Well, she was no longer going to be their blonde-haired, blue-eyed darling. Jack was the only one in the family who had ever loved the real her, and it was to be near him that she had originally considered Captain's Point, knowing even as she had made her plans to move there that her parents would sever relations with her, too.

Well, so be it. She was done living a shell of a life, and she didn't believe in their bigotry. Jack and Susan had both made it clear that they would be there for her as she found her way forward, and she knew she could count on them. People like them didn't let you down like others she had known.

A few movements of her finger brought a group shot front and center, and there he was, the man to whom, without his knowledge, she had given her heart just two weeks before - his barely even knowing her or, for that matter, her knowing him. And yet, having only spoken a few words to each other, she knew without a shadow of a doubt that this man was the love of her life. Now, if only her divorce from Samuel Meriweather Sinclair V would go through quickly.

CHAPTER II

"I'm leaving!" Chase shouted at his wife the next morning from the doorway into the breakfast room, somewhat surprised when his words were patently ignored.

Then he remembered that Penny hadn't responded when he had greeted her in passing either, equally strange. A slight wag of the tail Max had curled between his hind legs as he lay shivering on Adrianna's feet provided the only acknowledgement whatsoever of his presence.

Stepping forward, he slid his arms along his wife's from behind, breathing in the scent of her dark waves as he dropped a kiss just below her right ear, pleased when she arched her neck for another before she turned and faced him as she removed a pink rubber plug from the same ear.

"How long does this have to go on?" he again shouted to be heard over the loud noises of a thunderstorm in progress that were filling the room from her MP3 player.

"An hour per day, unless that doesn't work, and then we increase it," she explained in a raised voice. "The idea is that Max will get accustomed to the noise and overcome his fear. I'm not allowed to hold him or make a big to-do over him at all, because that reinforces his belief that something's wrong. Jim believes some dogs react to other parts of a storm such as the drop in pressure, though."

"Then what?"

"We either put him on some type of anti-anxiety drug or live with the problem," Adrianna's eyes filled with concern. "I'd rather hold him until a storm passes than put him on drugs, what do you think?"

"I think I want my queen to be happy in all things, so I'll leave it up to her." Chase pulled his wife into his arms, where he proceeded to kiss her thoroughly, surprised when she averted her eyes when he released her. "Is anything wrong?"

"No," she assured him. "Nothing's wrong, but I would like your opinion about something I've been considering after dinner this evening."

"Sure," he agreed. "Would it help if I knew what it was beforehand?"

"Not at all." She sent him a slight smile. "I don't even have all of the facts myself yet. It's just an idea, and it may not have enough merit to bother you with it."

"I doubt that, but you will have to pay for my time," he teased her as he once again lowered his lips onto hers, this time allowing his desire for her to shine through.

"Promise?" She sent him one of her shy smiles.

"Promise." He gave her another squeeze, filled with an unwarranted need to hold and protect her, and then released her, smiling as she resolutely stuck the pink plug back in her ear and then lifted her coffee mug as if sending him off with a toast.

Three properties away, the sound of her four-year-old son Daniel's feet running along the wide hall that now separated their bedrooms came to Susan Chesterton Jefferson as if it were part of her dream.

"Mama! Jack!" he called as he ran. "Are you awake yet?"

"Come here, Son." She felt her new husband sit up beside her in their bed, loving that he had so easily referred to Daniel in his new role. "Let's not wake up your mom."

"Too late," she muttered the words, even as she smiled at the thought of this being their first morning to awaken as a family in the rambling Victorian that had been Jack's house prior to their marriage. Even the gorgeous ocean view that had meant so much to her throughout her life now formed part of their home.

"I'm here, Mama," her son announced as he climbed onto the bed between her and his new stepfather. "Do you want me to snuggle with you, so you can wake up slowly?"

"I do, if she doesn't." Jack raised the covers, allowing the boy to slide under them. "Why don't you tell us all the neat things you did while we were in the Keys? Then you and I can let Casey and Lady out."

"Can I scoop the dog food into their bowls?" Daniel asked, lining up the start to his first morning in what he often referred to as their big, happy house.

"If you want," Jack agreed, pleased when his new stepson turned and snuggled his small head against his shoulder, "then I was thinking you and I might make some bacon and pancakes for breakfast."

"Blueberry pancakes?" the boy asked.

"Is there any other kind?" His stepfather added a surprised expression to his face.

"Aunt Courtney makes chocolate chip ones," Daniel stated with obvious disgust.

"Ah…" Jack smiled. "The ladies do love their chocolate, don't they? Did you color any more pictures in your book while we were gone?"

"I skipped some and colored a palm tree with a monkey in it, because Grandma said there were palm trees in Key West," Daniel filled them in as Susan managed to open both of her eyes, wondering as she did so how she had connected herself to two morning people.

"Coffee and your view?" Jack kissed his right index finger and, reaching over their son, placed it against her left cheek.

"Please." She sent him a grateful look before she slipped from beneath the covers and headed towards the dressing room and refurbished bathroom he had renovated for her use before he had even proposed.

But then, she paused in the doorway of the former – her blue gown flowing softly around the curves of her body even as it set off her thick, sleep-mussed blonde hair and deep blue eyes in a way that, unbeknownst to her, took her new husband's breath away. "I love you, Jack Jefferson," she said, remaining where she was for the moment.

"I love you, Susie Chesterton." He grinned back at her.

"Me, too," Daniel piped up from beneath the covers, interrupting the litany of things he had done in their absence that he had already gone through twice for their benefit the evening before.

"Come on, you." His stepfather tickled the youngster's ribs. "There's a Golden Retriever and a German Shepherd that are waiting on us to let them out. Go back to your new room and get your jeans on. I'll be there in a jif to help with your tennis shoes."

At almost the same moment, Larry Chesterton balanced a carryout tray, a paper bag and two thick file folders in one hand, while opening the door to his office building with the other.

"One black coffee and one latte." He passed takeout cups to the receptionist and secretary who had been waiting on him, once he was inside. "Adrianna Sheffield will be here at ten. You can send her straight in."

Closing the door of his own office behind him, he crossed to his desk where he flipped on his computer and sipped on his coffee until he was able to access the Montgomery Properties' file. A thorough review told him what he had already known. There was absolutely nothing wrong there.

Adrianna was sharp as a tack, and while her great-aunt had left things in a mess, the young heiress and her property manager had already gone a long way towards insuring the estate's permanent worth. Drawing on the owner's MBA and prior business experience coupled with Otis's knowledge of the property, the two of them had melded into a great team as they had worked side-by-side fueled by Penny's good food and sound common sense. There was no doubt about it, he would just have to wait and see what one of his favorite clients had to say.

Two hundred miles away, Kate Sinclair shut the door on the storage locker that now held all of her worldly goods and most of her clothes. Once she had packed her suitcases, she would be ready for her trip to her brother's in the morning.

Thank goodness her father had insisted on the prenuptial agreement that would allow her to make her transition to Captain's Point without worrying about getting a job in order to sustain her lifestyle. What money she had saved from the household account over the past four years would cover a deposit and several months' rent, and the check that had arrived from her soon-to-be ex-husband the day before would keep her flush for substantially longer than the month between it and the next one.

Still, way down deep inside, she was scared. Had her brother felt this same way when he had left everything he had ever known behind, tired of being treated like a second class member of his own family?

And yet, he had never forgotten her, never ignored her – quite the contrary. Cards and letters, along with small gifts, had come to her from all over the world until, one day when she was fourteen, she had opened a large padded envelope and discovered within it his first novel.

Promptly taking it to her room, she had hidden it from view, cherishing it as if it had been a part of him. Going to bed with a flashlight hours later, she had read through the night as the world as he was experiencing it had opened before her.

Now, it was her turn. Would the world bloom for her, too?

With a sigh, she slid behind the steering wheel of her white Jaguar and turned the key, unaware that when she made her presence known in Captain's Point beginning the next day, she would change the community as those who would greet her had known it irrevocably.

CHAPTER III

At precisely ten o'clock, Larry heard a tap on his office door, which then swung open and revealed Adrianna accompanied by Otis, much to his relief.

"They said we should come on in." The former sent him one of her shy smiles as he stood and hurried forward.

"Of course, why don't we sit at the table since there are three of us?" He remained standing as they took their seats. "Would either of you like something to drink? Coffee, tea, bottled water?"

"I'm fine," Adrianna answered first. "Would you like anything, Otis?"

"Had a cup of Penny's coffee right before we left, so I'll do for a while," the property manager declined the offer.

"Have you heard from Jack or Susan since they got back?" Adrianna asked, buying time as a wave of anxiety washed over her.

"Sure did." Larry's face sobered as he grabbed a couple of legal pads and some pens from his desk and then joined them. "I was waiting at The Cove when they stopped by to pick up Daniel on their way home last evening. Boy was Jack hot!"

"Hot?" Otis looked confused. "At Susan?"

"No, at the paparazzi that had camped out in front of the Key West beach house," the broker filled them in. "Apparently, Jack has had this sort of thing happen before, which was one of the reasons he suggested to Susan that they accept Chase and Adrianna's offer. A private home provides a much better chance of not being discovered."

"So how were they discovered?" Adrianna asked. "Chase and I certainly didn't tell anyone they were there."

"Pen and I didn't either," Otis stated firmly.

"Kate knew, of course," Adrianna pointed out, "but she told me in the car on the way to the wedding that she hoped no one bothered them."

"It wasn't the fault of anyone here in Captain's Point," Larry assured them. "Apparently, Saturday evening they decided to take in a show at one of the local clubs and immediately ran into a scumbag that Jack had met during a sojourn to Monte Carlo. The guy's noted for selling items to gossip columnists, and what happened next was pretty much a sure thing."

"What did happen?" Otis asked, thinking it must have been pretty bad if it had made the mild-mannered author that angry.

"I've never been to the beach house, but according to Susan the master bedroom, kitchen and pool are all in the back, so even though there was a sizeable crowd of photographers, reporters and onlookers, Jack and she hadn't noticed anything," Larry said. "They had slept in, eaten breakfast and enjoyed some quiet time by the pool, before they decided to head to the gym that's in a converted house only two driveways towards town. Susan got ready first and told Jack that she would wait for him on the front porch."

"Oh, no," Adrianna whispered.

"Oh, yes." Larry's face set as his lips thinned before he proceeded with his story, his voice now carrying a hard edge. "My knock-'em-dead gorgeous cousin opens the door and steps onto the front porch in her white short shorts and barely there top – blonde-haired, blue-eyed and long-legged – a perfect innocent looking like a jet-set fashion plate, and the crowd went absolutely wild just as my new cousin-in-law came onto the scene."

"Jack wouldn't have taken too well to that," Otis agreed.

"Not at all," Larry confirmed. "The flashes had startled Susan, and Jack thought she was scared, which was a good thing in a way, because he tried to shield her rather than attempting to beat back the cameramen."

"Which Jack could've done," Adrianna pointed out. "He actually does have a black belt."

"Thankfully, Susan is used to thinking on her feet," Larry continued the story. "According to Jack, she took his hand, held his gaze and headed down the stairs and along the sidewalk as if they were the only two people in the world. The crowd went silent, mesmerized, and the cameramen were so taken aback that Jack and Susan were past them and almost to the gym before they and the reporters knew what had hit them. Luckily, the gym's owner came out onto his porch and kept the crowd at bay, until Jack could hire two off-duty policemen to escort them back and stand guard through the night."

"Is Susan very upset?" Adrianna asked, her eyes filled with concern.

"Hardly." Larry chuckled. "Jack claimed she spent most of the flight back figuring out ways they could sue the reprobates, quoting him case after case from memory."

"Bravo, counselor!" Otis grinned.

"They're not actually going to do anything, you understand." Larry matched his grin. "The only damage occurred to the flower beds, and Jack's already given Adrianna's caretakers enough to get it all replanted. Oops, I wasn't supposed to tell you about that." He glanced at the beach home's owner. "Don't mention that I said anything."

"My lips are sealed," Adrianna promised, "but what about now that they're back here in Captain's Point? Chase has read me two notices from his morning paper that both clearly indicated knowledge of Blue Wolf Manor being Jack's home. Are they expecting to have further problems?"

Larry's face sobered. "Jack said he didn't know, but I could tell he was concerned," the broker shared with them. "He had hoped that Captain's Point being a small town would allow them some privacy. As he put it, it was one thing for the gossip mongers to have an occasional picture taken of him going into a restaurant with a beautiful woman hanging on his arm. In fact, his publisher encouraged it and had occasionally orchestrated them. Now, though, he says he won't tolerate their snapping candid shots of his wife and child, that being a completely different ballgame."

"I would say so," Otis agreed.

"How will he stop them?" Adrianna asked.

"Therein lies the problem, if one does indeed exist." Larry shrugged. "Hopefully, the whole thing will die down soon. Now, what brings you two here to see me?"

"We've had an idea," Adrianna began, and her broker noted that she had clutched her hands tightly together where they sat at the edge of the table. "Actually, it was my idea, but Otis has been nice enough to offer me some encouragement. The thing is, I'm not sure that it's viable, and I wanted your advice and input before I discuss it with Chase later this evening."

"You know I'll help you any way that I can," Larry assured her, sensing the tension coming from her.

"Penny and I are both behind it," Otis spoke up for the side, "but we're not as knowledgeable about some of the costs as we would like to be and you probably are."

"Why don't you just start at the beginning, and we'll see where things take us?" Larry suggested, at which Adrianna gathered her courage and began to lay out her plan.

CHAPTER IV

"Any idea what's up?" Chase asked his wife that evening as he turned their SUV onto the main road and headed them towards Blue Wolf Manor. "Not that it matters, I always enjoy spending time with Jack and Susan."

"Nothing, as far as I know," she replied. "Susan said to come casual and expect family fare served in the kitchen. It's possible that they want to talk with you about what happened in Key West, but she didn't say so."

"Sounds like we're in for a nice relaxed evening." He signaled their turn into the driveway of their destination. "We'll talk about your idea when we get home if you still want to. My first appointment isn't until eleven, and I told Bridgette I might be a little later getting to work in the morning," he referred to his and Susan's secretary as he brought the SUV to a stop, not surprised to see Daniel, Casey and Lady all waiting on the porch.

"They're here!" the boy shouted and ran down the steps. "You're our first company as a family in our big, happy house, and we're looking forward to having you." The four year old greeted his parents' first guests as a married couple, quoting his adults' words slightly out of context as he often did.

"So, how are you liking your new home?" Chase hoisted him up in the air and then carried him into the house, not surprised that Adrianna had already let herself in and announced their presence as was the custom amongst Captain's Point's leading families.

"My room's big enough for the three of us and my toys," Daniel informed him, including the dogs in his count. "It was Jack's room when he visited his uncle before it was mine."

"Oh, well, if it was Jack's room, then it must be mighty fine," Chase stated as he set the boy down, fully aware of the child's hero-worship of his new stepfather.

"We're in the kitchen," Susan called out.

"You two are in luck," Jack informed them, once his wife's law partner had joined them. "We both wanted to have you over to thank you again for the use of your beach house, and Susie has made one of her thousand dollar pies for dessert." He threw his arm around his new wife and kissed her cheek.

"Don't be silly!" she admonished him. "Sometimes I think you bid that much for my box lunch at that charity event just so you would have something to tease me about later."

"Not at all," her husband assured her. "Your company for an hour would've been worth twice that much."

"Now you are being ridiculous." Susan turned to Chase. "What would you like to drink? We're having hot chicken salad, homemade cranberry sauce and Greek-style green beans. Adrianna and Jack are having lemonade, and I'm having iced tea."

"I'll go with the lemonade, too." He took a seat at the kitchen table next to his wife, who was admiring Daniel's latest artistic effort in his thick coloring book.

"This is my place forever," Daniel pointed out the chair that contained a booster seat and was positioned to his mother's left.

"Here we go," Jack placed a baking dish onto a trivet in the center of table. "I'll get the rolls, and we'll be ready to eat."

"So how did you like Key West before your little episode?" Adrianna asked once everyone had filled their plates and enjoyed their first few bites in the comfortable silence often shared by close friends.

"It was wonderful!" Susan beamed at her new husband, who grinned back at her from where he was sitting at the head of the table on Chase's right. "Except, of course, for the fact that Jack wanted to spend all of his hard-earned money on me."

"You, too?" Adrianna turned on her host. "What is it about you men? Chase was throwing emeralds from Tiffany's at me like he had a direct line to Fort Knox."

"They set off your hair," Chase defended himself. "Besides, you had just accepted my proposal when Oliveira's paintings were auctioned, and I was walking on air. There they were, displayed for all the world to see in Tiffany's, and I couldn't resist them."

"Makes sense to me," Jack defended his friend as if any man finding himself alone in New York City would automatically end up in Tiffany's Fifth Avenue showroom.

"And I love both you and them," his wife reached over and squeezed her husband's hand. "Still, Jack and you need to understand that Susan and I would love you two just as much if you didn't bring anything to us but yourselves. What drew Jack's attention down in Key West?" she asked her hostess.

"Designer dresses," Susan shared. "A whole showroom full. He insisted I try on about a dozen, and then he claimed I looked wonderful in all of them. I kept trying to point out that their absence of price tags probably meant they cost a fortune, but he still wanted to buy them all. I finally managed to pare it down to a really beautiful blue one."

"I'd love to see it after dinner," Adrianna said. "Did you have the right shoes to go with it?"

"She didn't," Jack spoke up, his dark eyes twinkling, "so then I had to be told 'No' in the high class shoe shop next door as well."

"I've never bought seven pairs of shoes at one time in my life," his wife stated.

Several minutes later, their hostess stood and began gathering everyone's now empty plates. "Let's have dessert and coffee in the parlor," she suggested over her shoulder as she crossed to the sink.

"May I help with anything?" Adrianna asked.

"No, you two just relax," Jack declined her offer from where he was now loading the dishwasher. "Susie and I have this part down to a science."

Chase stretched his arm along the back of his wife's chair, giving her shoulder a gentle squeeze as he sent her a smile, the look that he reserved for her in his eyes. "We're both lucky in our kitchens," he declared, taking in the warm ambiance of the room. "Adrianna and Otis have already seen to updating the appliances in ours, so we've left it out of our newest renovation plans for Montgomery House."

"Especially since you suggested adding the skylight to the one at our house, when Otis and I were having the roof attended to," Adrianna added, glad that her now husband had spoken up at the time, even though he was then only her attorney.

"I updated the countertop, sink and appliances when I first arrived," Jack filled them in, "and Susie seems content to leave things as they are."

"Perfectly okay," his wife confirmed. "I've told you before that I'm thrilled you've already had everything updated. We share the same tastes, but it would take me forever to decide what I wanted, whereas you seem to know and then make it happen."

"I agree with Jack," Chase announced after he had enjoyed his first bite of dessert a few minutes later, once everyone had reestablished themselves in the large parlor at the back of the house. "A whole one of these pies would definitely be worth a thousand dollars."

"Especially when it meant I got to spend an hour with the gorgeous Susan Chesterton," Jack teased his bride as he matter-of-factly lifted his obviously sleepy stepson onto his lap, where the little guy snuggled against his new stepfather's chest and promptly fell asleep.

"More coffee?" Susan asked, ignoring his comment as she began topping off everyone's cups.

"If you all will excuse me for a few minutes, I'm going to put this little fellow into bed." Jack stood.

Adrianna noticed that Susan's face glowed as she watched her new husband leave the room with their son in his arms. How right she had been to do what she could to bring the two of them together. Perhaps she should keep her eyes open for someone else who could use her assistance in their quest for a spouse.

"It strikes me that you could rent out your husband to distraught parents dealing with bedtime dramatics all over Captain's Point, if Jack has the same effect on other children as he does on Daniel," Chase commented.

"Larry said almost the exact thing when he saw it happen last evening," Susan shared.

"Talk about male bonding," Adrianna said, even as it dawned on her that Larry might be a candidate for her help. "And to think, you were worried that Jack might not want to be burdened with Daniel, who might not adjust well to having a stepfather."

"That was a waste of my time," their hostess agreed as she gathered their dessert plates onto a tray. "Would you like to see the dress now?"

"I'd love to." Adrianna rose and followed her friend along the hallway, pleased to see that Jack was coming down the stairs and would be rejoining her husband.

"Larry filled me in on what happened with the paparazzi," Chase greeted their host when he reentered the parlor. "How bad was it?"

"As those things go, not so awful," Jack stated as his face sobered, "and Susan was amazing!"

"So Larry said."

"I was really impressed," the author continued. "I've gotten accustomed to it over the years, managed to avoid most of it, and let the rest roll off my back, but this was Susie's first time. She handled it beautifully, giving up a photo or two without making any comments."

"I'm sorry it happened at our place," Chase stated.

"It wasn't your fault," Jack brushed off his friend's apology. "If it hadn't been for Jorge spotting us in that nightclub, we would've gotten through without a problem. As it was, your beach house is designed so that the spaces we were using are situated at the back and we weren't bothered by the crowd once we were inside. My concern now is that they'll follow us to Captain's Point, and I won't have them pestering my wife and child. If you think of anything in your professional capacity that might be helpful, let me know."

"I don't blame you, and I will," Chase agreed. "How much of an issue do you think it's going to be?"

"Frankly, I'm not sure," the author admitted. "I know that they're out there, and they know where I live. Right now, I'm praying that some celebrity will do something newsworthy and draw their fire."

"There's only one problem with that," Chase pointed out. "You are a celebrity, and your marriage to a drop-dead gorgeous, totally photogenic woman is newsworthy."

And with that, both men ended their conversation by unspoken agreement as their beautiful new wives rejoined them, for the moment oblivious to the serious concern that hung over them.

CHAPTER V

Kate Sinclair stood at the window of what had been her childhood bedroom in her parents' sprawling house in Virginia and watched her mother drive away for the last time without a single pang of regret. Never had she known a colder woman, and truth be told, her father wasn't much better.

She would place her goodbye letter to them on the foyer table in a few minutes with the certain knowledge that Jacob Jefferson would tee off at precisely nine o'clock the next morning and his wife would show up for her facial at ten, as if nothing disturbing had happened. In point of fact, from their perspective, it probably wouldn't have. Losing a daughter you never had known couldn't possibly hurt you that badly.

Turning back to what had been her room, she attempted to recall happy memories, not surprisingly finding as she did so that all of them revolved around her only sibling - the brother who had teased her, laughed with her, encouraged her and, most of all, loved her.

Closing the zipper on her largest suitcase, she slipped the handles of a smaller bag over its pull handle and picked up her purse – the rest of her suitcases already waiting in the Jaguar's trunk. Propping a white envelope that contained fifty dollars and a thank you note to the daily maid, who had been nice to her during her stay, against the base of the lamp on the bedside table, she declared herself ready.

A few minutes later, she headed her car along the same drive her mother had used, noting as she turned right onto the main road that her mother had turned left – typical of their paths past and present. Well, there were plenty of untraveled highways out there to tempt her, and the road she had been on so far during her life hadn't been all that rewarding.

Two hundred miles away, Jack, Susan, Daniel and their warm home were waiting to receive her – a blessing that her brother hadn't had. How alone he must have felt at this point in his solitary journey. How she hoped to make that up to him now.

"I'm coming. I'm coming. I'm coming," the tires sounded the words as they met the blacktop until she turned onto the interstate and their tune changed to a softer, gentler calling of his name – the man to whom she had given her heart.

Still one hundred and eighty miles away, Larry Chesterton tossed a large mailing envelope into the trashcan under his massive desk, just as he heard a tap on the doorframe of his office.

"Mind if I come in?" Chase didn't wait for a reply, sure of his welcome as he closed the door behind him, strode forward, plopped into a leather visitor's chair and stretched his long legs out before him – relaxed and comfortable with his best friend since childhood.

"Only if you don't mind being in the presence of Captain's Point's biggest fool." The broker tossed the contents of the mailing envelope aside with disgust, a frown spoiling what was normally his jovial countenance.

"What in the world are you talking about?" Chase straightened in his chair.

"This travesty." Larry retrieved the *Most Eligible Bachelors Calendar* that Captain's Point's Chamber of Commerce had printed for the next year as they had for the past forty. "Now that you've gone and married Adrianna, it's just me and a bunch of guys who are still in their early twenties. I look like a thirty-three-year-old anachronism, even if I have locked in December."

"According to my wife, you look like a Greek god with your blond hair and blue eyes." His friend relaxed again. "I believe her exact term was Adonis."

"She really said that?" The broker looked pleased. "But then, Adrianna would only say something nice, while the rest of Captain's Point will probably be laughing at me behind my back."

"Well, then, do something about it," Chase said.

"Like what?"

"Like getting married," his friend suggested. "Believe me, I can recommend it."

"But that's because you've married the best of them, outside of my cousin who wasn't available to me even before Jack Jefferson snapped her up," Larry pointed out. "Besides, between running Chester's and this place, I don't have time to splash my Greek-god looks around, impressing available young women, and I do mean young – all of the ones our age are pretty much taken."

"Then cast your net farther afield," Chase pointed out the option. "There are other places besides Captain's Point. Spend some time visiting Andy up in D.C., and see who you meet there." He referred to Susan's older brother, who worked for Homeland Security and lived in fashionable Georgetown.

"Where would I find time for a long distance relationship?" Larry asked.

"As I recall, it didn't take either Jack or me that much time once we put our minds to it." Chase chuckled. "Pull out your old yearbook and work your way through it. You might just find someone who's available. If not, then ask Susan for some suggestions."

"In other words, you want me to make my humiliation even more public than it already is." A frown once again filled the broker's face.

"You can't have it both ways." His friend shrugged. "Either you decide to spend the rest of your life alone, or you'll have to put yourself out there."

"Thanks for nothing." Larry grimaced. "Now, what did you want when you forced yourself in here and took over my office?"

"I wanted to touch base with you about the other ad hoc spot on the city council that will open up when Charlie Stoddard retires." Chase's tone changed to purely professional. "We need to fill the void with someone who views the future of Captain's Point the same way that we do."

"Granted," the broker agreed. "Do you have any suggestions as to whom we might encourage to run?"

"Only one." His friend grinned. "And the candidate I'm considering should be as clear to you as the nose on your Adonis look-alike countenance."

For a moment, a confused look clouded Larry's face, but then his brow cleared.

"Jack Jefferson!" they said in unison as they exchanged a high-five.

CHAPTER VI

"I've made the guest room bed, put out fresh towels and washcloths in the adjoining bath, and set a basket of unopened scented soaps and lotions on the vanity," Susan counted out the items she listed on her fingers as she entered the Victorian's library cum home office, a crease having formed between her brows. "Flowers – did you remember them when you went to the store?"

"Come here." Jack clicked Save on his laptop and rose from his desk chair, his arms outstretched as he waited for her, neither of them paying any attention to Daniel who was lying on the floor behind the couch in a bright patch of sunlight, coloring in his thick book. "Let's get some perspective before you permanently form a wrinkle in your forehead."

"I know. She's not a foreign dignitary." His wife let out a sigh and relaxed her face as he gathered her to him. "I still want things to go well. Kate's your sister, and you love her. She's taken some brave steps forward in order to get herself here, and I want her to know that we both care about and support her."

"She can't help but know that about you." He sent her a kind smile. "You're sweetness itself. I love you, and she will, too, regardless of how many little touches you do or do not spread around her room." He planted a firm kiss on his wife's lips and then held her close. "The time we spend with her will go better if you can find your way to relaxing into it."

"You're probably right, but it may take another kiss to cinch the deal." She slid her arms around his neck, pulling his face towards hers again.

"I'm in for a third, if you need it," he whispered into her ear as she snuggled her head on his shoulder, not surprised when she offered her face to him again.

"The problem is you have more faith in my abilities as a hostess than I do," Susan admitted as he led her to the couch, where he took an end seat knowing full well that she would curl up next to him. "Also, since you've arranged for Maggie Daniels to do the heavy cleaning, I don't even have that much to do, so my mind is stuck on worrying."

"Number One, Maggie will be here once a week every week from now on," Jack stated. "Wednesday has been her day to be at this house for over twenty years, and I see no reason to change that. You have a career, and we can afford to pay for household help. Otherwise, you'll never have any down time, and I don't want to see you unnecessarily tired and stressed."

"I still say that you're spoiling me again," his wife reiterated an earlier point, "but I do work outside of our home. I'll let you have your way this time, if for no other reason than you'll be the primary beneficiary because I'll have more time to spend with Daniel and you. Besides, I wouldn't want to think that I was responsible for Maggie's income having been lessened. She's a hard worker and does a great job."

"Exactly," her husband agreed before moving on, pleased that she was allowing him to do this for her. "Number Two, my sister isn't someone that you need to worry about, although I can't imagine why you would think of yourself as anything other than a perfect hostess. Chase and Adrianna thoroughly enjoyed their time in our home last evening. Anyone could see that."

"Do you really think so?" Susan's eyes filled with hope. "I was so focused on making sure everything went smoothly that I didn't really notice."

"I can assure you that they did." Jack held her gaze as realization dawned within him. "You've been conditioned to think of yourself as a failure in this area, too, haven't you?"

"Balancing a career as a D.C. lawyer and being a perfect hostess were apparently beyond me," his new wife shared as she averted her eyes, a hint of sarcasm underlying her words as she referred to life as it had been for six years with her ex-husband.

"That was one person's opinion," Jack pointed out, "and I imagine your D.C. guests wouldn't have shared it. You are both gracious and graceful, and you have a real gift for making those around you feel comfortable – not surprising given the parents who raised you and the environment in which they did so. Besides, we make a great team, and I hope any entertaining we do will be a shared venture, including my sister's visit."

"Thank you," she whispered as she rested her head on his shoulder so he still couldn't see her eyes.

"Not good enough, Susie." He pulled away slightly and lifted her chin gently with the back of his finger, revealing that her beautiful blue eyes were awash with tears. "That was then, and this is now – Daniel, you and me. There's no need for your tears anymore."

"No, there isn't." She sent him a grateful smile. "Sometimes they come simply because you're so kind and understanding, and the way you treat me is so sweet when set against what was so awful."

"I love you, Susie Chesterton." He forced the words from his tightened throat, wishing he could magically erase what she had been through in her previous marriage from her memory.

"I love you, too, Jack Jefferson." She once again snuggled against his shoulder as he held her close, and she felt his comforting energy wrap itself around her, healing the hurt that she had carried within her for so long. "Promise me that you'll tell me if I'm doing something wrong or not doing something that I should."

"Better still, I could fill in the void myself," he pointed out. "The biggest difference in our marriage and your time before is that there are two of us actively engaged in this equation, where there was only you beating your head against a brick wall in the former one."

"The biggest difference is that I'm happy and contented married to you." Susan raised her head and sent her new husband a smile. "The two good things that came out of those six years are Daniel and the fact that I now know enough to appreciate you and the way that you love me."

"At least, you were able to learn that in six years." Jack chuckled, lightening the moment. "It took me twenty years to find and recognize the worth of Daniel and you."

"As a wise man once told me the important thing is you learned the lesson." She reached her hand up and ran her fingers through his dark hair where it swept back from his widow's peak, straightening it while unknowingly igniting his desire for her.

"A very wise man indeed." His expression softened still further as he remembered uttering the words she had quoted shortly after their first kiss, pleased when she once again bent her neck and snuggled her head on his shoulder. "And one who will never stop loving you." He rested his cheek against the top of her head and held her still closer.

"Tell me what you think Kate will be feeling based on your own experience," Susan requested. "It will help me to say the right things and better be there for her."

"I'm not sure you can compare us," he began, thinking aloud. "I was fresh out of college and heading into the

Navy, cocky and sure of myself. Frankly, I needed to be taken down a couple of notches."

"I find that hard to believe." Susan looked up.

"Trust me, it's true," Jack confirmed. "Remember, I'd been raised to believe that being a Jefferson meant I was better than anyone else. Still, even with the change of scenery and a bunch of great guys around me, there were times when the fact that I was basically alone in the world would wash over me. If it hadn't been for the pianos that were available to me, I could've become fairly depressed. As it was, they offered me a bridge through the music to some swell friendships, and I learned that there were all sorts of families – those that you're born into and those of your own choosing."

"Kate seems to have already recognized that the Jefferson way as you two refer to it isn't all it was cracked up to be," his wife pointed out, "so basically, it's the loneliness that we'll need to concentrate on offsetting."

"Possibly," he agreed, "and the best way to fight loneliness is to keep busy. My sister has a degree in accounting and successfully completed her testing for her CPA, much to my parents' surprise, probably because I kept asking how she was doing with it. I don't think she ever used her skills, so I imagine it's lapsed or may not have even gone into effect if she was required to also have a certain number of hours of work experience."

"She mentioned that she doesn't need to work, when we were chatting the day she arrived for our wedding," Susan recalled.

"Idle hands won't lead to her being happy and contented, though, will they?" Jack asked.

"Not in my book, but everyone has to make their own choices," she replied.

"True, so really all we can do is encourage Kate, support her in any way we can, and be there to help her pick up the pieces if she makes a wrong decision." Jack gave his wife a squeeze. "I'm glad you'll be here with me. As a woman who cares, you may well see things that I'll miss, and you'll understand more of the ins and outs of Captain's Point, too."

"I'll do my best for both your sakes," Susan assured him as she pulled away. "Now, why don't you figure out what you and your short shadow will want for lunch, while I arrange those flowers before they wilt?"

"Sounds like a plan." He sent her a grin. "But, like you, I may need a kiss to seal the deal."

At which, his new wife slid her arms once again around his neck, more than happy to oblige him.

CHAPTER VII

"You're here!" Daniel was the first to come through the front doorway of the sprawling Victorian and greet Kate when she arrived, not surprising since he had spent the last thirty minutes standing up on the library couch, watching for her car to enter the driveway. "We love you, and I'm going to support you." He flung his arms around her knees and delivered the first hug she had received since she had left Captain's Point almost two weeks before.

"It seems to me that you may knock me over first." She laughed as she reached out her fingers and straightened his tousled hair in much the same way that his mother often did in passing. "How do you like your new room?"

"It's great!" The four year old beamed up at her. "Jack helped me arrange all of my books and toys, and we're reading in the chair every evening."

"How was your drive over?" Susan asked as she joined them and gave her new sister-in-law a quick hug.

"Not too bad," Kate replied, "and it gave me time to put some space between there and here."

"I admire you for what you're doing," Susan stated. "Been there, done that as they say, and I understand the level of courage it takes. Know that I'll do anything I can to help you determine your way here in Captain's Point, although you should find the natives rather friendly."

"Twinkle Toes!" Jack hurried towards them, the last to arrive since he had been playing his violin in the music nook in the farthest corner of the house, when Daniel had shouted his announcement. "It's so good to have you here again." He threw his arm around her and hugged her tightly, the obvious warmth in his eyes underlining the honesty of his words. "What? No trailer hooked onto the back of your car to hold all of your clothes?"

"No, but the car is pretty full." She sent him a sheepish grin. "Frankly, I wasn't at all sure what exactly I'd need."

"And a woman does have to have the right shoes and purses with her as well." Susan sent her a knowing look.

"Exactly." Kate returned her sister-in-law's smile, once again feeling blessed that her brother had found such a nice wife.

"Let's get your stuff all hauled inside before I get too old to make it up the stairs," her brother teased as the new arrival handed him her keys.

"I can carry, too," Daniel announced.

"Do you think you could manage these two?" Jack asked as he pulled two fairly light shopping bags from the floor of the back seat.

"Sure I can." The boy's shoulders straightened.

"Susie, these seem about right for you." Her husband handed her two canvas barrel bags. "And these two for you." He passed two similar bags to his sister. "That appears to have taken care of the light stuff in the back seat."

"Unfortunately, the heaviest things are still in the trunk," Kate whispered in an aside to Susan as they headed for the front porch.

"Good grief, woman, what do you have in these?" Jack called after them, confirming her comment as both of his gals broke out in laughter.

"We are going to enjoy your visit," Susan indicated for Kate to maneuver her load through the front door first.

"If only for the comedic element that I bring to your lives, I suspect," their visitor replied as she started up the broad staircase.

"It's always been my opinion that there can never be too much laughter in one's day," Susan assured her. "I've put you in the larger guest room that's all the way at the end on the right."

"What a lovely room!" Kate paused once she had entered. "With fresh flowers and everything."

"You'll find that you have a view of the ocean from the window seat, and these other windows overlook the front lawn," Susan explained. "This door leads to the connecting bath shared with the next room. I thought you might find this useful, since you would have access to the closets in both rooms."

"I sleep right next door if you get scared in the night," Daniel delivered what he considered to be the most important pronouncement, a serious expression on his face. "If you're really scared, Lady might be willing to stay in here with you, which would still leave Casey with me."

Touched by his gesture, Kate sat down on her heels and drew him to her, surprised by the prick of tears in her eyes. "That's very kind of you," she said, giving him a quick hug. "I'll certainly let you know if I need anything, but let's leave Lady with Casey and you for the time being. I won't know if I'm scared unless I try things on my own first."

"Where would you like these?" Jack came in behind them, two large suitcases in each hand and two smaller ones wedged beneath each of his arms.

"Why don't you put them next to the window seat, and then Kate will be able to use it as a sort of luggage rack?" Susan suggested.

"Good idea," her husband agreed, obviously relieved to be free of their weight despite his well-formed physique. "One more load, I think, if you'll help me, Son," he addressed Daniel, who looked pleased at having been asked.

"I'm stronger now that I'm almost five," the youngster's words carried back to the two women as he followed his stepfather along the hallway to the stairs. "I could probably bring three bags this time."

"Bless his heart!" Kate turned to Susan. "What a good job you've done raising him."

"I only hope that he'll remember my warning about being quiet when he wakes up," her sister-in-law replied. "Each morning that we've been here, he's run along the hall asking if we're awake yet at the top of his lungs. Needless to say, I have been once he's reached us."

"This is it." Daniel announced a few minutes later, the first to return – the strap of a canvas bag slung from one shoulder across his narrow chest as he carried another shopping bag to balance his load.

"Well done." Kate took the one bag, while his mother lifted the other one from him and Jack set down two more fair-sized suitcases in the far corner of the room.

"Promise me that you won't do any clothes shopping until you find your own place." He once again threw his arm around his sister, a grin on his face as he drew his new wife to him with his other arm.

"I almost wish those photographers were here to snap my picture right now." He gave each of them a squeeze. "I'd be the envy of every man in the world who caught a glimpse of it."

At which, the two women once again exchanged knowing glances as Daniel hugged his stepfather's knees, all three glad to be included within this kind, gentle man's sphere of influence.

CHAPTER VIII

"I'm sorry it's taken so long for us to find time to discuss your idea," Chase said as he settled on one end of the library's couch after his wife and he had cooked and enjoyed their dinner later that evening, surprised when Adrianna didn't immediately respond. "Are you irked with me? I assure you that it wasn't a deliberate put-off on my part."

"Not at all." She sent him a tenuous smile and then took a deep breath, gathering her courage. "I'm not really sure how to start our discussion."

"The beginning is usually the best place, and then you move things forward one step at a time," he pointed out as he reached over to where she had uncharacteristically positioned herself at the far end of the sofa and took her hand in his, feeling the need to connect with her.

"It started when we formalized Montgomery Properties as a business," Adrianna began. "As you know, things were a mess, but Otis and I soon put together a plan with Larry's help and your support."

"And did a great job of salvaging for the long term Montgomery House and the other properties you inherited from your great-aunt," he stated firmly. "No one could've done any better."

"Thank you." This time, she sent him one of her signature smiles.

"I'm still not getting any hint of your idea," Chase stated even as he felt the tension emanating from her.

"Otis and I make a great team when we work together as general contractors," Adrianna pointed out, "and we now have a roster of qualified, reliable subcontractors that we've worked with both on the Montgomery Properties' projects and the renovations at Sheffield Place."

"True."

"All that work is now basically behind us." His wife finally met his gaze. "You and I are going to be moving forward with major work on Montgomery House, but Pete Marlborough will be overseeing most of that as our architect. Also, I imagine your intention is for both you and me to be involved with any decisions that come up."

"Unless it's easier for you to just go ahead and make them for us, since you'll be Johnny-on-the-spot, so to speak," her husband agreed.

"I suppose that's what really got my mind working," Adrianna admitted. "I'll be here and available with basically nothing to do."

"Ah…" Chase felt they had finally reached the crux of the matter.

"As you know, I recognize that when I first came to Captain's Point my priorities were a bit skewed," his wife pushed forward. "I had worked hard for my degrees, and I was on career overdrive. Still, I did work hard for my MBA, and I have found working with Otis on the Montgomery Properties' projects to be very rewarding."

"So now you feel like you're going to be at loose ends," Chase interjected.

"Yes." She searched his face. "I've spoken to Otis, and he feels much the same way. There will be some maintenance needs that will inevitably pop up from time to time, but otherwise, things should run along like a top. In the end, I sat down and had a good think about how he and I could take what we have now put in place to the next level, and I came up with my idea. Otis was nice enough to encourage me as to its potential, and we discussed it with

Larry, primarily because we wanted his input about some of the costs we would incur."

"And...?"

"The costs he estimated clearly showed that my idea is viable," Adrianna persevered, "although I would need to draw on some seed money from our joint holdings to get us started. Montgomery Properties is stable, but there hasn't been time for it to accumulate a cash fund."

"There's certainly no reason why we can't do that," Chase stated.

"But you haven't heard my idea yet," his wife protested.

"I don't need to have heard your idea to make that determination," he informed her. "As you yourself put it very well, you're a proven general contractor who has done her homework. Our money is just that – ours, which means yours as much as mine, and I'm always going to be willing to invest in you. Now, explain to me what exactly it is that we'll be investing in, so I can be as excited about it as you are."

"Coming out of the dry cleaners the other day, I decided to do some exploring, and I deliberately turned left instead of right," Adrianna explained. "This brought me into an area that I'm sure had been very upscale once upon a time, but it's now looking rather seedy in some spots."

"Are you talking about the area around Chestnut and Tuttle?" Chase asked. "Mid- to large-sized Victorians, some blocks of row houses, and a bungalow or two thrown in for good measure?"

"That sounds like it."

"Basically, that could be defined as Captain's Point's historic district," he pointed out. "What drew your attention there?"

"The homes looked fairly sound, and most of the yards were maintained," Adrianna replied. "Still, there were a few properties sprinkled amongst them that appeared a little rundown, and a couple of them were listed for sale. The whole area is within walking distance of downtown, which Larry, you, and the rest of the city council have done a great job of refurbishing."

"Compliment accepted." He sent her a smile.

"My idea is that Montgomery Properties should invest in one or two of the more rundown properties, return them to their former glory and then rent them out or flip them, whichever one seems most advisable," his wife continued. "My hope is that this will help to stabilize the historic district, building on what Larry and you have already done. When they've been refurbished with high end finishes, we all thought they would command high end rents, because of their proximity to downtown shopping and restaurants. Once the company has built up its cash reserves, then we would purchase another and another as time and availability allowed."

"Brilliant use of your talents and resources." Chase beamed at her, pleased when she sent him another one of her shy smiles. "We can even handle your closings at the firm, sweetening the pot. Now come here, my queen." He turned slightly in his seat, bringing his left leg onto the couch at an angle that allowed him to lounge comfortably while still maintaining enough space between his long body and the couch's back for his wife to stretch out beside him.

"Are you planning to get your projects listed on the National Register of Historic Places?" he restarted their conversation.

"We've discussed it," she confirmed as she slid herself along the couch.

"Gary Butler, one of our new associates, mentioned when we first met that he had some experience in that area and would enjoy handling more similar petitions," Chase filled her in. "Apparently, having a lawyer involved can occasionally grease the wheels."

"Then we should certainly draw on his expertise," his wife agreed.

"Have Otis and you picked out your first houses yet?" he asked once they were resettled, a more relaxed Adrianna now snuggled within the bend of his arm, her head resting on his shoulder.

"Not yet," she replied. "Larry suggested that we get in touch with Maureen Brownley and get her advice, if for no other reason than she might be able to bring new listings to our attention before they reach the paper." She referred to the mother of her husband's childhood friend, whose nickname was Pug, an ER doctor at the local hospital whose parents owned a real estate firm.

"Good advice," her husband agreed. "Pug's dad is a sound businessman, but his mom is a closet history buff. That area has been her special interest for a long time, and she'll probably be able to put you onto missing details as well as the family stories of the previous owners. I would suggest that you call on Pete Marlborough for historic architectural items as needed, too. He has all sorts of sources available to him."

"You really do like the idea then?" Adrianna's eyes filled with hope.

"Definitely," Chase confirmed, "but I do have one question."

"Yes?"

"You had a great idea that you easily discussed with Otis, Larry and, I would imagine, Penny as well, am I right?"

"Yes." His wife averted her eyes as she again relaxed her head against his shoulder.

"So why did you find it so difficult to approach me with it?" Chase asked. "What made you think that I wouldn't be supportive? Have I treated you like such an ogre?"

"You? Never!" Guilt washed over Adrianna at the hurt in his tone, as she quickly raised herself up on one elbow and cupped his cheek in her other hand.

"Then I don't understand." He swung his leg off the couch and sat up straighter, forcing her to do the same even as he held her gaze.

"It's more about me than about you," she attempted to reassure him.

"Can you explain it to me then?" he asked, this time bringing the back of his fingers to her cheek, gently stroking it, not surprised when she took some time to gather her thoughts, this being her way.

"You're right," she admitted. "I was worried about broaching my idea to you for two reasons."

"Two reasons?" Chase repeated as his mind tried desperately to remember anything he could've done that would have made his new wife so uncomfortable with him. "Haven't I told you over and over that what I want more than anything in this world is for you to be happy?"

"But that's just it." She lifted her worry-filled eyes to his. "How can I know that you really like my idea and aren't just saying so because you're putting my wishes before yours? Getting my way all the time will eventually lead to my being unhappy, because your wants and needs are being left out."

"Do you have any idea how sexy you are when you're so intuitive?" He gathered her into his arms and kissed her thoroughly.

"Chase, really." She laughed when he finally let her up for air. "Are we never going to have a serious discussion without something that I say or do turning you on?"

"Possibly not," he admitted, sending her a sheepish grin as he loosened his hold on her. "As I've told you before, I can't help that you have that effect on me."

"That's okay." She patted his knee. "I wouldn't really like it if you stopped wanting me."

"Okay, let's answer your question," he brought their conversation back on track. "Would it help if you knew that I will always give you my honest opinion before telling you to go ahead with whatever plan of action you have in mind? Of course, the problem then becomes that you won't do something if you think I don't like it."

"Oh, dear…" Her face once again took on a worried expression.

"Basically, we both have to trust that the other will be honest with us when giving their opinions, and then, in the end, we both have to be true to ourselves, don't you think?" He held her close once again, resting his cheek on the top of her head.

"I'm not sure that's as easy to do as it sounds," she admitted.

"Probably not," he said, "so we'll just have to take each discussion that pops up one at a time. Agreed?"

"Agreed."

"So what was the other reason you were uncomfortable bringing your idea to me right away?" He gave her no quarter.

"This one's a little more nebulous," she began. "Basically, I was afraid of disappointing you in several ways."

"Disappointing me?" Honest surprise reflected on his face.

"Yes, for one thing I didn't know whether or not you were expecting me to continue any sort of career, and if you really wanted me not to work now that we're married, then this move would've disappointed you," Adrianna explained. "Also, this whole project will be a major step outside of what has been my previous comfort zone, and anything involving renovations and the real estate market comes with a certain amount of risk."

"Risk that we can afford to take," he assured her.

"Still, you've never failed at anything in your life as far as I can tell," she pointed out, "and I don't want to disappoint you by failing."

"Look me in the eye and hear what I'm saying clearly." He lifted her chin. "I love you. I love everything about you, including your willingness to try new things. If an idea you have at some point doesn't work out, then I will be disappointed with you, but not in you, and I will still love you for trying."

"Chase..." she forced his name past the lump that had formed in her throat as she drew his face down to hers, overcome by the way that he loved her.

"What could I say that would make me deserving of another one of those?" he asked once they separated, a glazed look in his eyes.

"Anything will do." She sent him another one of her smiles.

Whereupon he drew her closer and whispered into her ear, "I love you. I love you. I love you, Adrianna Montgomery Sheffield, and I always will."

"I love you, too." She raised her face once again, allowing his wish to come true.

CHAPTER IX

Relieved by Chase's good opinion of her idea, Adrianna drifted into a deep sleep in her new husband's arms soon after he had taken their kisses to the next level in their bedroom, leaving them both highly satisfied.

Hours later, still asleep, she felt the warmth of a sunny beach on her face and recognized that her head had been resting in the lap of her mother. Pushing her short curls from her eyes, she watched as her father pulled a one-man sailboat from the surf and walked towards them - a broad grin on his face. Leaping up, she ran and threw her short, childish arms around one of his knees, only to be picked up and tossed in the air for her efforts.

"Put me down! Put me down!" She screamed as she laughed, and he did – into the back of a sports utility vehicle that was taking a series of mountain curves much too fast.

"Slow down! Slow down!" Adrianna attempted to shout, but no sound would come out as her mother and father talked gaily in the front seat, apparently oblivious to the danger.

Then their vehicle swerved from the road where, for a moment, it remained suspended in air before it plunged towards the fields far below and her screams merged with Chase's voice calling her name, awakening her.

"Adrianna!" He thrust himself into a sitting position against the pile of pillows behind them as he gathered her into his arms and held her close. "I'm here. It's just a dream."

"Chase…" She burst into tears.

"I'm here," he repeated and held her even tighter as she sobbed into his shoulder. "I love you, and you're okay. We're both okay, although I think you may be scaring our Max."

"I'm sorry." She pulled away, and he lessened his hold as he reached to his bedside table.

"Come here, Max." She hugged the dog, who had been hovering on the edge of the bed, to her. "Mama's okay."

"Here, dry your eyes," Chase said, handing her some tissues. "And you get back in your bed," he ordered the dog. "The excitement's over, although your mama is definitely not okay when she lets out a scream like that in her sleep."

"It was the dream I sometimes have about my parents plunging to their deaths," she explained as her husband plied open her fingers, removed the now soggy tissues and replaced them with a fresh batch. "At the end, I'm in their SUV with them and they won't slow down and we go over the edge and…"

"Don't think about it anymore," Chase stated firmly as he once again wrapped his arms tightly around her. "You're here now with me in our home. You're okay, I'm okay and that ragamuffin over there in his bed on the hearth is okay, even though he's trying hard to look abused since I excused him."

"Is he really?" Adrianna let out a small giggle. "What a sweetheart! Thank you for being such a wonderful husband." She snuggled against him.

"For waking you up when you were screaming beside me?" he asked. "I could hardly have done otherwise. What do you think brought the dream into your head tonight?"

"Possibly our talk about my idea," she suggested. "I was thinking this afternoon that where my parents had spent their lives unearthing houses buried along with the towns of ancient civilizations, I'm now planning on saving historic homes in our own little community."

"An interesting juxtaposition, although you could be right," he agreed. "Maybe the fact that you had a good cry afterwards will help."

"I hope so." Adrianna pulled away slightly, and he noted that her eyes were filled with worry.

"Let me put something else in your mind," he suggested. "I realized as I was going to sleep that I want to pass this along to you."

"Sure." She again snuggled against him.

"When we were talking earlier, you made the comment that I've never failed at anything," he began. "Technically, I suppose you could say that's true when it comes to the major things I've attempted in my life, but if my aunt hadn't died and left me a fortune when she did, I probably would have. I had been keeping things together financially one day at a time ever since Augustus Chesterton died, and frankly, I was running out of steam."

"Susan told me she was appalled at the size of the case load you'd been carrying for so long," Adrianna gave him a quick squeeze, "and I know you've brought on three new associates plus her and still have plenty to keep you busy. I can only imagine the miracles you were pulling off each day."

"I didn't have any choice," Chase pointed out. "Like Montgomery House, Sheffield Place was a money pit, although it didn't have the surrounding buildings and other properties that I could develop. I could've sold it and broken even a couple of times, but for some reason, I couldn't make myself do it."

"Good, bad or indifferent, it had still been your family's home for several generations," Adrianna reminded him. "Believe me, I know how that feels. I would've done almost anything to keep Montgomery House."

"Thankfully, all of that's behind both of us now," he stated, "but my point is that if I had lost everything, I would've failed miserably. Still, it wouldn't have been because I wasn't smart enough or hadn't worked hard enough. It merely would have been a case of no one being able to do the impossible, and you've said yourself that you would've loved me and accepted my proposal, if I'd had nothing but my brains and my hands to bring to our marriage."

"I meant that," she reaffirmed, "and I still say that I would've been glad to be your wife simply because of our love for one another."

"So you can understand that I would still love you regardless as well?" Chase asked.

"Yes, I can," Adrianna agreed. "I put myself through it over nothing these past couple of days, didn't I?"

"Yes, and the next time you start to do so, I'm going to call you on it much sooner," her husband stated. "I can't tell you how hard I've worked trying to figure out what was wrong between us."

"Forgive me?" She lifted her face to his, her eyes filled with hope.

"There's nothing to forgive," he said as he sent her a soft look. "You didn't do anything but worry about disappointing me. Still, from now on, we'll face such moments together."

"Yes, we will," she promised as she pulled his head closer and kissed him, molding her body to his.

CHAPTER X

It was like a game that she wasn't likely to win, Susan thought as she attempted once again to slip from beneath the covers of their bed without disturbing her new husband, who had spent so many years with one eye open and one ear perked while he slept in the wild.

"Are you okay?" Jack asked as his hand found her arm.

"Yes, go back to sleep," she assured him. "Just a thirty-something woman who's given birth making her nightly trip." She picked up his hand, kissed his palm and placed it against her cheek for a moment before she released it.

"I'll keep your place warm until you get back." He rolled towards her onto his stomach, plumping her pillow under his head.

"Feel free." She smiled as she rose and headed through her dressing room to her bathroom with the antique tiles painted with tiny roses that he had picked out especially for her before she had even accepted him.

A few minutes later, she was surprised when she reentered their bedroom to find him no longer lying in bed, leaving his scent that always reminded her of fresh air, sunshine and a splash of his aftershave on her pillow to lull her back to sleep. Instead, he stood at the door to their room, gesturing for her to join him, where he put a finger to his lips signifying a desire for her to remain quiet.

Quickly, she tiptoed to his side, not surprised when he gathered her to him and rested his cheek on the top of her head.

"It's okay, Casey and Lady," Kate's voice carried well along the wide, broad hallway that separated the master suite from their son's room. "I'm only here to help your boy. Daniel, you're having a bad dream, but Aunt Kate is here now. Wake up for me, Sweetheart."

Susan started to step forward, but Jack held her firmly in place. "Leave them be for a minute," he whispered into his wife's ear. "Daniel is Kate's first friend in Captain's Point, and this is a new experience for my sister. Let him work his magic on her."

Pulling back slightly from her husband's embrace, she nodded her head in agreement as a smile graced her face and then relaxed her head onto his shoulder once again.

"You need to go to the bathroom?" Kate asked, the child's previous words having been indistinguishable to the two eavesdroppers. "You usually do that all by yourself, so we should be able to manage it together."

In the doorway of their bedroom, Susan felt Jack's ribcage move beside her as he silently chuckled, and she mock-punched him with her elbow, at which he tightened his hold on her and kissed her thoroughly, both of them working to catch their breath when they finally separated just as the sound of a toilet flushing at the far end of the hall reached them.

"Hold that thought, Beautiful," he again whispered into his wife's ear.

"We survived that fairly well, didn't we?" Kate asked, her voice filled with relief, and received another unintelligible answer from their son as far as her unseen audience was concerned. "Do you want your teddy bear? It looks like one Jack had when he was a boy."

"It is Jack's," Daniel replied clearly. "We're sharing him, and we're calling him John."

"I'm sure John appreciates having a nice friend like you to hug him close," Kate stated, followed by what seemed to be a moment of silence to the couple listening from the other end of the hall. "My, you are a good hugger. I love you, too. Is that how your mom tucks you in?"

"Do you need Lady to walk you back to your room?" Again, Daniel's words came through clearly.

"No, I'll be fine on my own," Kate assured her new nephew-in-law. "I think you're right when you call this a big, happy house. You sleep tight now."

And with that, the newlyweds ducked into the shadows as their visitor's slippers slapped against the broad plank flooring, clearly announcing her return to her room where she closed the guest room door behind her.

"Show's almost over." Jack silently closed the door to the master suite and drew his wife into his arms, where he whispered into her ear before renewing their kiss as previously promised, "Only the grand finale now remains."

"I'm hoping there may even be one of your famous encores," Susan shared once they were back in their bed, no longer the least bit concerned about having disturbed him.

Five properties away, in his large apartment over what had once been The Cove's carriage house, her cousin Larry let out a sigh and closed his much abused copy of Captain's Point High's yearbook from his senior year. Chase had been right when they had spoken earlier, he admitted to himself now. Either he set his mind to being a bachelor for life, or he put himself out there.

Going back through his yearbook, though, had been a waste of time. It had also been a mistake. Everyone he might have found the least bit interesting as a possible candidate for his lifetime partner was either already taken or had left Captain's Point years earlier, including the one he had worked so hard to erase from his mind.

Her picture had been everywhere – with the cheerleaders, the glee club, the dance club and at the prom. He should've known better than to have opened the book, but after all this time, he had thought the hurt healed.

Apparently, once your heart was torn from your chest, the wound festered on, albeit deep beneath the surface.

If he were to find someone now, someone he loved and cared about enough to want to spend the rest of his life with them, they would have to be willing to accept damaged goods, because that was what he now realized he was. Of course, it was possible – not probable, but possible – that the woman he found would be so special she would eclipse all memory of the other who had come before her.

Hanging onto his last thought, he reached over and turned off his bedside lamp, hoping against hope that there really was someone out there whom Fate had marked and set aside just for him.

In the tower suite of Montgomery House, Max perked his ears and satisfied himself that his master's breathing had now deepened with sleep. Rising from his bed on the hearth, he paused and stretched before making his way quietly to his mistress's side of the bed, where he stood on his hind legs and placed his front right paw gently on her hand.

"Your daddy would kill me," Adrianna whispered as she lifted the covers and allowed the dog to join her, wrapping her arm around him in the same way that her husband's was wrapped around her, so that they would've appeared to anyone looking on as three spoons of diminishing sizes nestled in a row.

"He would if he knew." Chase kissed his wife's neck and then nuzzled against it, tightening his hold on her for a moment before drifting back to sleep, a smile etched on his face.

CHAPTER XI

Susan woke softly the next morning, her mind drifting from sleep into semi-consciousness, aware first of her husband's weight on the bed beside her, but not his arms around her. For a few minutes, she enjoyed the absolute luxury of waking up slowly before, with her eyes still closed, she slid her arm along the sheet towards what she expected to be Jack's upper body, but quickly identified itself beneath her hand as a muscular thigh encased in a pair of jeans.

"Don't start anything you won't finish." He chuckled as her eyes flew open with surprise, revealing him propped up against the pillows, his electronic tablet now resting against his tight abs.

"How long have you been awake?" Susan asked as she returned to her back where she stretched first her arms and then her legs in a way that reminded her new husband of a kitten.

"Long enough to let the dogs out, help Daniel to dress and feed the little fellow a bowl of cereal," he stated as he typed a few words into the tablet before hitting Send and then placing the device on his bedside table. "Our son is under orders to play quietly in his room, but how long he will manage it is a question currently drawing mixed options in the betting halls of Vegas. My money is on our running out of time soon."

"And Kate?"

"Not a peep." Jack rolled onto his stomach beside her, immediately lifting the fingers of his right hand and running them through her blonde hair where it lay thick and wavy on her pillow. "I'll never tire of waking up to you in my bed." He gazed down at his new wife, his eyes filled with love.

"Nor will I," she assured him as she reached up and drew him towards her.

"So how would you like to start your day?" he asked, once they separated.

"With a shower, so I can be dressed and ready to fix breakfast when Kate gets up." Susan started to rise, but found it to be impossible, Jack's arm now holding her gently but firmly in place.

"You'll have to rethink that one," he stated. "You, my lovely bride, are supposed to be enjoying the second week of your lifetime honeymoon with me, and I won't have you spending all of your time in the service of others. Kate isn't a guest in the broad sense of the word. She's family, and what's more, we have no idea how long she'll be staying."

"It's still her first morning in our home."

"And she's welcome to join us in our enjoyment of it," Jack pointed out. "Now, how would you like to start your day, my gorgeous wife?"

"Well, put like that…" Susan paused as she gave the matter some thought until a smile spread across her face and she lifted her eyes once again to his. "I do have a request."

"Anything." He brushed her lips with a kiss.

"You remember the first time we met on the boardwalk," she began.

"The moment when I fell in love with you, yes." He rolled onto his side and drew her to him.

"You took my breath away," she shared, her voice soft, "and when I met you later at the market, you did it again to the point that my mind went completely blank and I made a fool of myself."

"A beautiful and completely charming fool," he corrected.

"What you don't know is that I returned to the boardwalk a little while later to meet Larry for dinner, and I heard you playing Massenet's *Meditation*," she filled him in. "I had never experienced the piece played so beautifully, and the way you stood at the end of the pier with the sunset spreading above you was magnificent. How your music called to me! And yet, it frightened me, too."

"I scared you?" Jack tightened his hold. "Playing my violin?"

"Not you, your playing." Susan struggled to explain. "I heard in it the call of my mate, and I knew I couldn't resist you if you chose to pursue me. At the same time, though, I never wanted to put Daniel or myself in a position where we could be hurt again, so I was afraid of what my reaction to you might mean for our futures. How perfectly you had to love me to overcome all of that!"

"I'm thankful that I measured up." He cupped her face in his hands and kissed her gently. "So how does that pertain to your starting your day?"

"If you don't think it will disturb Kate, I'd like for you to retrieve Daniel and bring him in here, along with his coloring book or something else quiet for him to do. Then I'd like to drink my morning coffee you bring me in bed, while you play your violin for the two of us."

"I've never done a coffee concert in my jeans and a jersey." He dropped a kiss on the top of her head and released her. "One mocha coffee, one short male complete with coloring book, and one violin concert coming up, Mrs. Jefferson."

"I do love being on my honeymoon with you!" Susan let out a satisfied sigh.

"Glad to hear it." Jack chuckled. "I can assure you that no one else is going to get a chance at spending one with you."

A few minutes later, he returned with Daniel in tow, a mug in one hand and his violin case in the other. "Close the door so we don't wake up your Aunt Kate," he reminded his stepson who complied before climbing onto the bed.

"Can I listen with you?" Daniel asked as his arms slid around his mother's neck.

"If you'll sit still, so I don't spill my coffee." She patted the sheet beside her.

"Any special requests?" Jack asked as he waxed his bow.

"No, I'm open as to the program," Susan stated. "What a luxury this is!"

"That's the idea." Her husband positioned his violin and began playing *Plaisir d'amour* by Martini, his eyes holding his bride's as he finished the tune, softly singing the Anglicized words '*I can't help falling in love with you.*' in his rich baritone as he did so.

"Lovely," she breathed when their room fell silent. "Simply lovely."

"I agree." He blew her a kiss before once again placing his bow on the strings, only this time he was interrupted by a light tap on the suite's door to the hallway.

"Aunt Kate!" Daniel hurriedly crawled to the end of the bed, slid off and ran to welcome their visitor, who appeared before them in her pajamas, an anxious look on her face. "We're having chocolate coffee and a concert," he greeted her.

"I heard the music," their guest explained as her glance flicked from her brother to her sister-in-law. "Am I interrupting something private, or may I join you?"

"You can sit in Jack's place." Daniel took her hand and pulled her forward, as Susan sent Kate a smile and patted her husband's side of the bed, closing the deal.

"I haven't heard you play in years," Kate addressed her brother as she curled against what would normally have been his pillows. "I hope you don't mind." She turned her attention to her sister-in-law.

"Not at all," Susan assured her, reaching over and giving the other woman's hand a squeeze. "The more the merrier, as long as we can keep things informal. Would you like some coffee to go with your music? Jack has things set up in the gym right next door."

"I can get you mocha, French vanilla, or dark roast," her brother offered, "and we have hot chocolate available as well."

"French vanilla." Kate made her selection. "I feel so pampered."

"Isn't it wonderful?" Susan agreed. "I'm not a morning person at all, and your brother bringing me coffee in bed makes a difference to my whole day."

Once Kate had been served and had enjoyed her first sip, Jack returned to his violin, this time choosing to play *Clair de Lune* by Debussy.

Susan closed her eyes and prepared to let the music flow over her, but her husband only played a few bars before stopping.

"What's wrong, Peanut?" he asked as he again set aside his instrument, before taking a seat within reach of his sister on the bed where he gathered her into his arms, her shaking shoulders clearly indicating that she was crying.

Susan started to rise, but Jack reached out a hand and stopped her.

"I'm sorry," Kate apologized, her words muffled by his shoulder. "That song was the last thing you played in your room before you explained you had joined the Navy and would be going away." She drew back and wiped her eyes on her sleeves. "You took all of the love with you and left me alone with them, and it all sort of washed over me just then. I don't think I've felt loved since, except for your letters and the times you met me for lunch or dinner someplace. That is until I showed up here for your wedding."

"And now we all love you," Daniel piped up. "Would you like me to hug you, too?"

"Would you?" Kate held out her arms to the child beside her. "You give such good hugs."

"He does, doesn't he?" Susan passed her arms around both of them, not surprised when she felt her husband's wrap around hers as well.

"Group hug!" Jack announced.

"Family hug," his stepson corrected from where he was somewhat buried in the crowd.

"When did you get to be so wise, Tiger?" Jack asked, sending his wife a proud smile.

"I was born me," a small voice responded from the bottom of the heap.

"I never knew you were so unhappy back then." Jack sat up straighter and took his sister's hand. "Why didn't you tell me?"

"Because there wasn't anything you could've done about it," she explained. "Even I knew you couldn't tell the Navy that you had to be released because your kid sister, who had two living parents, needed you and was having a meltdown, and then you began writing your novels. They were wonderful, and I lived for each new one, rereading the old ones until the next one would come and I could see even more of the world through your eyes – people and places that I would never meet or want to visit, but somehow they became treasures when wrapped in your words."

"I felt the same way when I read them," Susan shared. "I would never want to hike along a snake infested swamp, but your brother's description of the story told by the lines that appeared on the face of the old man who was their guide in *Jungle Places* made me wish I could've met him."

"Exactly." Kate sent her sister-in-law a smile. "You do understand, and by then, I was almost through high school and hoped that college would be better."

"And wasn't it?" Jack asked, still upset that he had failed to see his baby sister's needs.

"Somewhat," she said, even as she picked nervously at a loose thread on one of her pajama top's buttonholes. "I no longer spent evening after evening alone with only the constantly changing maids in that huge house, but college comes with its own trials and tribulations as you know. The best part was that by then you had left the Navy and made it a point to see me more often, especially during the time when you were at Harvard. Anyway, I'm here now, feeling very loved and wanted, so why don't you play us another piece?"

Recognizing there was nothing he could say that would change the past now, Jack dropped a kiss onto his sister's nose before turning to his new wife. "This one's for you, Susie." He kissed his finger and reached over Daniel, touching her cheek before he once again retrieved his violin.

Whereupon, he slipped into the notes of Massenet's *Meditation*, glad to know that at least this piece had taken him along the right path and had won for him his Susie and their Daniel.

CHAPTER XII

After a simple breakfast of fruit and a croissant, Kate joined her brother and his wife in their home gym, where she put herself through a grueling routine in an effort to relieve some of the tension that seemed to have taken up residence within her. Now, three hours into her morning, she stood in the shower in the bathroom off her temporary bedroom the nozzle set on massage and allowed the hot water to pound the tightness from her shoulder muscles.

How welcome they had all made her feel. And yet, she kept embarrassing herself in front of them with her tears. Was she really that unstable after what she had been through?

Believing the water to have done its best, she turned it off and reached for one of the oversized fluffy towels that Susan had provided for her, once again filled with a sense of gratitude for the blessing of such a nice sister-in-law. Wrapping the towel around her, she headed to the bedroom and donned a pair of jeans and a comfortable sweatshirt before she applied bare necessity makeup and brushed her thick, curly hair into a ponytail, Jack having explained that casual was the order of the day.

Laughter came to her from the front lawn, and she looked out the window just as her brother glanced up and gestured for her to join his family below. Hurrying to comply with his wishes, she came upon them in time to see Lady leap into the air and snatch an orange Frisbee that had been destined for Daniel's waiting hands. More interested in the birdlife that filled the shrubs along the house, Casey paused in his explorations and sent her a wag of his tail.

"Now we can play teams," Daniel announced as he ran forward and grasped her hand.

"Guys against the gals?" Jack suggested.

"I'm game if that means Lady's on our side." Kate laughed as her eyes met Susan's.

"Sounds fair to me," her sister-in-law agreed, but then her face lit up as a Mercedes SUV pulled into the drive.

"Cousin Larry!" Daniel ran forward to greet the new arrival, who promptly tossed the excited youngster into the air once he had disembarked.

"How're you doing, Charger?" Larry asked. "I haven't seen you for a couple of days, so I thought I'd come and check on you."

"We're doing great." The boy hugged his legs around his cousin's waist. "Aunt Kate agrees with me that this is a big, happy house." But then his voice dropped to a whisper as he cupped his small hand around the side of his mouth. "She cried during our violin concert this morning, but I hugged her and now she's okay."

"Glad you were there for her." The broker met their visitor's blue eyes as he moved forward to join the group, even as he wondered what had been wrong with her. "I see that you've arrived safely."

"Yes, and I've been pampered ever since." Kate returned Larry's smile, wishing she had taken more care with her hair and makeup.

"Now we can play three teams," Daniel announced.

"I'm not sure your cousin will want to chase after a Frisbee in those clothes," Kate pointed out.

"No, Daniel's right, I'm in." The broker removed his suit coat and laid it carefully atop a large azalea bush, thinking as he did so that no upstart woman was going to replace him in the boy's affections.

"Isn't that an Armani?" Jack whispered in an aside to his wife. "Is he nuts?"

"I think you're right, and he's wearing dress shoes, too." Susan's eyes widened as she lifted her right shoulder in a slight shrug.

"So who's on what team?" Larry pressed forward.

"Two teams or three?" Jack looked to the ladies.

"Let's do three teams," Daniel once again stated his preference for the higher number.

"Kate and I are a team," Susan claimed her partner.

"That leaves Daniel and Lady for you and me to choose from." Jack indicated for Larry to take his pick.

"Daniel hands down." The broker placed his hand on the boy's shoulder. "You're not sticking me with a dog."

"Lady and I may surprise you." Jack sent him one of his slow grins. "Susie, you and Kate go first since we men have a height advantage."

Taking her cue, Susan picked up the orange disk and sent it floating towards her partner, only to have it intercepted midair by Lady, who outran Daniel for it, dodged Larry's attempt to retrieve it and passed it back to Jack, who immediately spun around and sent it flying back towards the dog where she was already waiting twenty feet away.

"I think we may be in trouble," Kate called to her sister-in-law as Lady once again made her way successfully back to her owner.

This time, though, Susan managed to grab Jack's throw, although she strongly suspected that he had deliberately pitched slow. Trying to get off a quick toss, her aim suffered, and Larry intercepted the Frisbee before it could reach Kate.

"Heads up!" The broker sent the disk towards Daniel, who caught it, but Lady easily snatched his return toss.

Slowly the scores climbed, surprisingly even, although Susan found herself more and more convinced that her husband was working hard to allow his sister and her to win.

"Three way tie," Jack announced. "Ladies' throw. Let's make this sudden death, and then I'll start lunch. Daniel has requested a cookout, Larry, and I'm assuming you'll join us."

"Wouldn't miss lunch with The Champ for anything." The broker sent his pint-sized cousin a smile.

Everyone took their positions, Jack remaining near Susan as Kate felt the pressure build within her, reminded of a time years before when she had failed to catch a fly ball, losing a game for her team as her brother had been watching. Not that he had been upset with her, quite the contrary. He had greeted her at the sidelines with a bear hug and had then treated her to a chocolate-dipped cone on the way home.

Still, he had done everything he could as they had tossed the Frisbee back and forth to give Susan and her a winning advantage, and she wasn't going to disappoint him again. Preparing to jump high, she took her stance and drew in a deep breath as her sister-in-law released the orange disk that seemed to float towards her in slow motion, as it cleared first Daniel's and then Lady's heads leaving Larry, who stood somewhere behind her, as her only competition.

Recognizing it was time, she thrust herself off the ground, stretching her right arm into the position where she managed to clasp the Frisbee's rim in her grip just as Larry's fingers partially covered hers. But then, the world seemed to turn upside down, her body crashing into his and knocking them to the ground as he grabbed her to him, breaking her fall.

"Humph!" The broker's breath left him as his back struck the ground to the sound of a seam ripping, to be followed only a moment later by Kate's body dropping hard onto his front.

For a few seconds, both of them lay still – Larry somewhat dazed by Kate's head having connected with his jaw, the blow softened by the thickness of her ponytail, and Kate lying with her eyes closed, enjoying the feel of his strong arms around her and the scent of his expensive aftershave.

"Cousin Larry!" Daniel was the first to find his voice as he ran towards them, Lady already busy licking the broker's cheek. "Is Aunt Kate hurting you?"

Suddenly aware of the way his blood was coursing through his veins due to the nearness of the woman in his arms, Larry quickly reassured the little guy. "No, although you Jeffersons play rough. Girl, you'd better be careful how you get off of me." He relaxed his hold on his opponent.

Finally mobilized, Susan started forward even as she met her husband's laughing gaze.

"I'm not sure how to score that one." He reached out his hands, pulled his sister off his cousin-in-law and passed her onto his wife to make sure Kate was okay, and then extended a hand to the man who still lay on the ground. "I don't hold out much hope for those pants," Jack stated, relieved that Larry himself appeared to be no worse for wear once he was standing.

"They'll certainly need a trip to the tailor's and dry cleaner's, and the shirt's bound to be grass-stained." The broker sent him a rueful look as he rubbed his bruised jaw. "Thank goodness this suit came with two pairs of slacks. I think the point should go to Daniel and me purely on the basis of my humiliation."

"No way," Susan disagreed. "I'll testify in any court of law that Kate had a grip on that Frisbee first, and you should've left well enough alone."

"Will you still stay for lunch?" Daniel asked as he slid his hand into Larry's.

"Absolutely, I wouldn't renege on a promise now, would I?" Larry picked the little guy up and retrieved his suit coat from the azalea bush.

"Come in, and I'll lend you some exercise pants and a sweatshirt," Jack led the group towards the front porch. "Susie's made a huge bowl of her potato salad as well as baked beans to go with the burgers if that makes you feel any better."

As the others continued their comfortable banter, Kate brought up the rear where she lifted the back of her hand to her face as if to brush away a stray wisp of hair and breathed in the hint of Larry's aftershave that had been transferred there, thinking she might never wash that particular spot on her body again.

CHAPTER XIII

Larry woke up the next morning grateful that the two aspirin he had taken before he had gone to bed had enabled him to sleep like a log, but then he tried to move. Every muscle in his body ached, and his entire backside felt bruised. Wishing that he actually was a log and could simply remain still on the floor of a nice pine woods somewhere, he edged himself painfully into a sitting position with his feet on the floor.

The good news was that he worked from home on Fridays. The bad news was that he still had to negotiate his way to his kitchen and study. What had he been thinking?

Bending slowly forward, he rested his head in his hands, his elbows propped on his knees, certain that the bruise that had already formed on his jaw the evening before had spread even larger during the night. Hopefully, by the time he arrived at Montgomery House the next evening, it wouldn't be too obvious in the soft lighting of the Sheffields' home. All of this because he had let a little slip of a girl – no, a woman – get under his skin. Remaining a bachelor all of his life wasn't looking nearly as bad.

For a moment, he closed his eyes and let his mind replay the scene - his leaping up to snatch the Frisbee, feeling his fingers close over hers, and then that horrible moment when he realized they were falling and he had abandoned the orange disk and grabbed Kate to him instead.

Most women would've screeched their heads off, but not Jack's sister. No, sir. She had lain perfectly still, and he had been afraid for a moment that despite his best efforts she might've been hurt. Thankfully, she had merely had the breath knocked out of her in the same way that he had.

There he had lain, clutching her to him like some sex-crazed teenager until Daniel had run towards them and snapped him out of his stupor. He couldn't even remember what he had said to her, something completely inane he was sure. After the thrust of her body against his, he had expected her to seem like dead weight lying there, but she had been light as a feather stretched atop him, her waist so slim beneath the loose sweatshirt she had worn that it had surprised him.

"I'm sorry," she had mouthed the words as he had passed her on his way into the house, and he had attempted a smile, but had grimaced instead as his jaw muscles had given a painful reminder of the recent hit they had taken.

And once he had changed into Jack's casuals and rejoined the group on the patio, she had quickly risen from her chair, a slight blush on her cheeks, looking up at him shyly from beneath her long lashes.

"Thank you again for what you did to keep me from being hurt," she had said, despite the fact that he had made himself look like a complete fool. "Let me get you one of Jack's beers from the fridge."

Daniel had even whispered into his ear later that Aunt Kate was sorry she had hurt him.

There was nothing for it. He would have to find some way to make it up to her. Hopefully, she would be at Chase and Adrianna's dinner, and he could find out how he could be of the most service to her. In the meantime, he wasn't sure that he had enough aspirin still in the bottle to get him through what he could only assume was going to be a very long day.

As Larry stood, letting out a loud groan, Kate tapped on the doorframe of her brother's library cum office in Blue Wolf Manor, a short distance along the main road leading into Captain's Point.

"Hey, Pumpkin!" Jack glanced up and sent her a smile. "It's about time you made an appearance. Have you had your coffee yet?"

"Not yet, but I can get that myself." She took a step forward. "Would you have a minute, or are you writing?"

"Not the question you should ask," he stated as he clicked on Save. "There's rarely a moment when I'm not writing somewhere in my brain. Why don't we talk in the kitchen? I'm about due for a refill." He picked up a mug from his desk and followed her across the hall and into the large, airy room where they came upon Susan and Daniel icing a sheet cake.

"I want to thank you both again for allowing me to visit so soon after your wedding," Kate began once the three adults were all seated at the table.

"We're anxious to see you settled in your new home." Susan reached out and patted her sister-in-law's hand. "You need to feel anchored, and we're looking forward to having you placed near us on a permanent basis."

"I've enjoyed the past two days with you, but it's time that I start searching for my own place." Kate turned to her brother. "I've never looked for a home on my own, and I wondered if you had any suggestions – types of housing, areas to look in, things to avoid."

"Are you planning on renting or buying?" he asked.

"Renting until I'm more familiar with the area and know what I want to do with myself, unless you think that's the wrong way to go." Kate looked from him to Susan and back.

"I think you're on the right course," Jack agreed, "but as to areas where you should look, Susie would have a better idea than I would."

"Frankly, I have no idea," his wife surprised them both. "I've never had a need to look for housing in Captain's Point, and even if I had, there's been some new development in recent years. Larry would know more where to look. Would you like for me to give him a call?"

Kate hoped her face didn't show her dismay at her sister-in-law's suggestion, calling on the broker for assistance after the way she had humiliated him the day before had not been her intention at all.

"Why don't we all pile into the SUV and go for a drive?" her brother suggested, saving her from having to make a response. "It's been my experience over the years that in small towns, folks often just put out a sign and let word of mouth take it from there. We can also make a note of any apartment complexes or condo developments we spot while we're out, so Kate can give them a call when we get back. We could stop in at Chester's for lunch once we're finished."

"Daniel would get a kick out of that," Susan agreed, "especially if we finish off lunch with some gelato."

"Would there be any chance of finding anything on the internet?" Kate asked.

"Why don't we see?" Jack rose from his chair. "I'll give you a spiral notebook as well. They can be really helpful when you're making a move."

The internet search revealed that two apartment complexes had vacancies, and Kate made careful notes of their addresses and phone numbers, even though the visual tours of the rooms showed the properties in question to be fairly outdated.

"I texted Larry, but he didn't have any leads," Susan announced as they all regrouped in the foyer. "He said he would keep an eye open, though."

"You'll like Chester's," Daniel addressed Kate as he slid his hand into hers. "It's Cousin Larry's restaurant."

"Actually, Larry shares ownership with his parents who live in Florida," Susan filled them in, "although they rely on him to manage the place in their absence."

"I thought Bill Graham was the manager." Jack opened the front passenger door of the Mercedes for his wife, sending her a grateful smile when she insisted that her sister-in-law take her place so their guest could have a better view as they toured the town.

"He is, but Larry's mother insists that Bill be given only limited authority," Susan explained as she buckled her seatbelt, her voice taking on a hard edge. "It puts a terrible burden on Larry time wise, and it isn't at all necessary. Bill's a hard worker, and Larry says he's quite competent. That's Aunt Gertrude, though, always with a finger in the pie that she hasn't baked."

Jack sent his wife a sharp glance, this being the first time he had ever heard her utter a derogatory comment about anyone other than her ex-husband, but found her gazing calmly out the window as if she hadn't said anything out of the ordinary. Perhaps, her opinion was so spot on that it was shared by everyone, he surmised as he started the SUV's engine, thinking as he did so that it sounded as if his and Larry's mothers would get along well – not a recommendation in his book for either one of them.

"Will Cousin Larry be at Chester's?" Daniel asked.

"Possibly," his mother answered, "but I wouldn't count on it, because he doesn't know that we're coming."

"We can still hope," her son stated firmly in his adult way, as he opened the picture book she had passed to him.

"Yes, we can." Susan bent and kissed his cheek.

While in the front seat, Kate concentrated on familiarizing herself a bit more with the lay of the land in Captain's Point, even as she, too, hoped that Daniel's wish would come true.

CHAPTER XIV

The weather had turned cooler overnight, and Jack found himself wishing that he had put on a jacket as he stood and knocked on the door marked Manager at the first apartment Kate had located on the internet. The single concrete block building had at one time been painted white, but now appeared as a light gray, with streaks of rust emanating from leaf-filled gutters along the roof's edge that added nothing to recommend the six apartments that sat devoid of landscaping in the middle of a blacktop parking lot filled with potholes.

No one answered, and with a sigh of relief he turned away and shook his head in the negative as he returned to the SUV. "It may be the Taj Mahal inside, but there's a dirty curtain that's seen better days hanging in the manager's window," he advised his passengers as he fastened his seat belt. "I think you should cross this one off your list."

"I second that," Susan agreed from the back seat.

"Aunt Kate can stay with us forever," Daniel added his two cent's worth.

"Part of me would love to stay with you forever." Kate smiled at him over her seat's back. "That way, I could receive all of your wonderful hugs that I wanted on any given day, but when you're grown-up, it's important that you spend some time on your own."

"Why?" Daniel asked as his eyes widened. "Won't you be lonely?"

"I may be occasionally, but that's when I'll get in the car and enjoy a visit with you," Kate reassured him. "Other times, though, I'll be learning some adult lessons, like what's important to me and how I want to spend the rest of my life – a little like school, only you have to do it on your own."

"It still sounds lonely," Daniel insisted, "but I'll be supportive when you live in your apartment, just the same."

Kate found herself unable to respond to this sign of affection, the words sticking in her tightened throat, so she concentrated on the neighborhood through which they were passing. What a sweetheart the little guy was, she thought, even as she noted the lawn sizes were shrinking and many of the homes looked like they could use a paint job in addition to some needed repairs.

"I don't think I've ever been in this part of Captain's Point," Susan stated, "or at least, if I have, I don't remember it looking like this."

"We're a little further off the beaten path," Jack acknowledged. "I wonder if this is one of the areas that Steve McKinney was telling me about after church a couple of weeks back. If so, I see why he's concerned." He signaled a right turn onto a somewhat busier four-lane, divided highway and then, one block further along, again turned right into a mid-sized complex of plain, rectangular apartment buildings that boasted red brick exteriors.

Three young men lounged against a seen-better-days sedan set atop concrete blocks midway along the edge of the parking lot and watched through narrowed eyes as the Mercedes passed, one of them choosing that moment to blow a series of smoke rings in Kate's direction.

Reflexively, she turned her face from the window, meeting her brother's worried expression with eyes widened with concern.

"If this is the best Captain's Point has to offer in the way of rental properties, then I think Daniel's right," Jack reassured her. "You can stay with us or in one of my other properties forever. New York and the farm aren't that far away."

"Absolutely." Susan reached forward and patted her sister-in-law's shoulder. "Daniel and I stayed with my folks at The Cove for over six months before your brother took us under his wing, and I'm not ashamed of it. That's what families do for one another when one of their members has a need."

"We Jeffersons stick together, just like the Chestertons," Daniel made his position clear from behind his large picture book.

"Why don't we investigate the area just past the main harbor that's seen some new development in recent years?" Jack suggested as he swung the SUV back onto Main Street.

"New sounds like it may be more what I'm looking for," Kate agreed as she relaxed once again in the plush leather seat, overwhelmed by the love and support that surrounded her.

Two blocks off Chestnut Street on Tuttle Avenue, Jewel Parkerson stood at her dining room window that overlooked a small bungalow and wrung her hands. How had her lovely life gone from so good to so bad in only three short years? First, her Bruce had died, then the economy had turned sour, and now her friend Sarah's house wasn't being maintained by the young couple who had bought it.

With a sigh, she turned away from the sagging gutter and cracked window that had been her focus and ran her eyes around the formal dining room and cozy front parlor viewed through a wide arch that formed the main living space in her own larger home. A bright, airy kitchen, full bath, and ample family room completed the downstairs floor plan – too much space when she included the three large bedrooms, her sewing room and two more full bathrooms upstairs. Still, Bruce had purchased this home for the two of them before they were married, and leaving it would be like leaving him, even though he was now waiting for her to join him at Captain's Point Cemetery.

Well, he would have to wait a while longer, Jewel lifted her chin. She was, after all, only fifty-four years old. Not that Bruce had received his promised three score and ten, he hadn't. Dr. Thompson had warned him that he needed to cut back, relax, and lose a few pounds, but her husband hadn't paid enough attention. Now he was gone, and she was facing alone her own appointment this afternoon, concerned about the words she would hear.

At least, whatever news was coming in her direction would be delivered in a kind way from a handsome young man. A vision of thick, blond hair, deep blue eyes, a firm jaw and a pleasant smile filled her head, and unlike her Bruce, she would follow whatever advice was offered to her.

Two more aspirins and a hot shower had loosened Larry's muscles enough for him to consume a bowl of cereal and make it into his home office without too much trouble, a large mug of coffee in tow. His leather desk chair proved again that it had been worth the money spent on it as it provided support exactly where it was needed, and relief filled him as he made slow, but steady progress through his work day. He wasn't going to let the side down.

But then, the phone rang.

"Larry Chesterton," he answered as he always did when working from home.

"I wanted to remind you that you have an appointment here in the office at three," his secretary stated. "Is there anything you need me to get ready before you arrive?"

"No, I'm on top of it," he replied. "I'll see you then. Thanks, Glenda." He hung up the phone and swung his desk chair around, enabling him to look out over the ocean as a single thought filled his head.

Bummer…

CHAPTER XV

Full of crabmeat and sides from Chester's, Daniel had fallen asleep in his stepfather's arms as he was carried inside and now lay snuggled beneath the colorful quilt on his bed. Frustrated, Kate had announced that she was going to take advantage of the dancer's bar her brother had had the foresight to install in his home gym in hopes of a future visit from her and had excused herself. Thus, Jack and Susan found themselves alone on the couch in their home's library, where she had curled up beside him in such a way that she could raise her head from his shoulder and face him.

"I want to thank you for being so supportive of my sister in the car." Jack stroked his wife's thick hair.

"Don't be silly," Susan stated in her matter-of-fact way. "Neither of us could've looked in a mirror if we had allowed her to move into either one of those places. Even if it was all she could afford, which it isn't, she's totally unprepared for life in that kind of environment. Quick as a wink, she would land in a situation that she couldn't handle."

Jack let out a sigh. "You're right. It was different for me as a man, and while it was restrictive, the Navy did provide a buffer period during which I could determine my priorities."

"She'll just have to stay here until she finds something – a rental house or one of the new condos that isn't completed yet." Susan lifted her head. "I want you to see me say this. I'm fine with that. Really, I am. I would think less of you if you didn't offer our home to your sister until she can get on her feet, and Daniel would probably never speak to you again."

"He has latched onto Kate, hasn't he?" Jack chuckled. "What an old soul he is."

"Frankly, he reminds me of you and vice versa," his wife pointed out. "Both of you seem to want to draw people under your wings. I'm just glad we were among your finds. I love the way you take care of us, always making sure that our needs are met and paying attention to every detail."

"Maybe, just maybe, that's because I love the two of you so much." Jack brought his lips onto hers, kissing her thoroughly before she snuggled against his shoulder and let out a small sigh of her own.

"I can't believe our two weeks are almost over," she said. "Why didn't I take three?"

Jack started to say something, but closed his mouth instead, thinking it best not to point out that she didn't have to work at all if she didn't want to.

"It isn't that I don't want to go back to the firm, I do, but I want to stay here with you as well," she shared her thoughts. "Of course, if I did stay with you, then you would never find the time to write, I would miss my legal work, and both of us would be sick of each other and miserable within a short period of time."

"I would never be miserable because you were here in the house with me full time," Jack stated firmly, holding her closer. "Never, but at the same time, I do understand what your law practice means to you. I say we take it a year at a time or even a day at a time, until we find the level that works best for both of us. I am going to talk with Adrianna about my position, though. It makes sense on so many levels, and I think you should talk to Chase about both of you working from home on a regular basis. Larry does it, and it should work out for the two of you now that you've hired those new associates."

"You're right," Susan agreed, "and I've told you before that I think Chase will go for it. The good news is that all five of us, six including Kate, have so many options. All of us worked hard for what we have at some point in our lives, but so do lots of other people who never manage to achieve our level of success. Luck and the fact that money goes so much further in a small town like Captain's Point has given all of us an advantage."

"The best news of all is that you found it in your heart to agree to my proposal, Susie Chesterton." With his hand he lifted his new wife's face once again to his.

At the same moment, Larry lowered himself gingerly into the manager's chair behind the huge desk in his office on Main Street, singularly unaware of how lucky he was to have options.

"Can I get you anything?" A worried expression had planted itself on Glenda Bank's normally placid face, her grey eyes gazing at him from behind a pair of thick lenses.

"A cup of coffee would be nice." Her boss grimaced as he reached for a file. "The aspirins I took before leaving home should kick in soon. I can't believe I was such an idiot. Jack would've lent me a pair of tennis shoes, or I could've even gone barefoot. Leather soles and grass simply don't play well together."

"I've known you since you were born, and this is the first time I've seen you do something this silly." His secretary shook her head. "Let's hope that you've learned your lesson."

"Yes, ma'am." He sent her a sheepish grin. "Coffee?"

"Coming right up." She turned and left him as he glanced at the time displayed on his computer's screen.

Jewel Parkerson would be there in just a few minutes, and he wasn't looking forward to their meeting. How could Bruce have been so foolish? Of course, the man hadn't known he was going to die, but still...

"Here you are." Glenda set a small tray within easy reach of Larry's right hand. "I brought you a couple of Sissy's brownies as well."

"You're a saint, but then you know that." He grinned as he reached for one of the chocolate squares, noting the chopped nuts and thick layer of buttercream icing that took them up a notch. "Tell Sissy she's earned at least four brownie points."

"That girl's head is full enough of herself as it is." Glenda's lips narrowed into a slim line as she let the pun pass. "Even if she is a whiz on her computer, you see where she is today."

"No, I didn't notice her." Larry took another large bite of the first brownie, which had proven itself to be as delicious as it had looked.

"She isn't here, that's why," Glenda stated. "Came in this morning, dropped a container of these on my desk, zipped through her work and announced pretty as you please that she was taking the afternoon off."

"Was she needed?" Larry took a sip of his coffee, preparatory to moving on to the second brownie. "She would've assumed that my uncle and I would both be working from home today."

"That's not the point," his secretary held her position. "What if Anders or you had needed her? She didn't ask for the time off, she just took it."

"Has she done this often?"

"Two Fridays out of the last five, and I do my reports on Friday afternoon each week," the older woman pointed out. "If one of you wanted something done pronto, then I would have to refuse or leave my reports until Monday, which would start our whole week off on the wrong foot."

"Keep me posted, and I'll keep track of it," Larry promised, not wanting his secretary upset.

Glenda let out a small sigh. "I suppose that's the best we can do, given the circumstances." She patted her boss's hand where it lay on his desk in the same way that she had when he had lost out to Chase for anchor position on the relay team back in high school. "You enjoy your other brownie." She managed a smile and then left him.

By himself, he searched for a phone number on his computer as he munched on the chocolate treat. Sissy, he decided, was worth keeping if for no other reason than her baking abilities, although her talents might be more appropriate to Chester's.

The sound of traffic on Main Street announced the arrival of his client, punctual as usual. Quickly, he wiped his somewhat sticky fingers on the napkin that his secretary had thoughtfully provided and reached for the appropriate file, making sure as he did so that a clean legal pad and pen for Mrs. Parkerson's use were readily available in case she needed them.

"Jewel, how nice to see you!" Glenda's professional voice carried back to him as she hurried forward to greet her longtime acquaintance. "Mr. Chesterton is ready for you."

Thirty minutes later, the antique doorbell at Blue Wolf Manor disturbed the audience of an impromptu piano concert being given by Jack Jefferson for his three most ardent fans.

"I'll get it." The pianist abandoned the keys and headed for the foyer, Daniel following a close second.

"Goodness!" Jack took the large bouquet of red roses from the hands of the florist's assistant who was almost hidden behind them. "This is a surprise."

"It's flowers!" Daniel ran along the hall to the parlor in order to keep the women informed. "Bunches and bunches of flowers!"

Being two normal females, both Susan and Kate immediately rose and followed Daniel to where Jack was now closing the front door – an arrangement of two dozen red roses having taken up residence on the bombe chest next to him.

"You shouldn't have." Susan reached out her hand towards the flower nearest her.

"Glad you think so," her husband said as he threw his arm around her. "These aren't for you, my lovely wife. They're for Kate."

"Tell me they aren't from my ex." His sister's eyes narrowed.

"I didn't look." Jack pointed to a small envelope. "Take a peek."

Her fingers shaking, Kate released the envelope from its holder and removed the tiny card, at which her cheeks filled with pink before she passed the missive to her brother.

"My, my!" His eyes met his wife's as he grinned and then read.

Welcome to Captain's Point and congratulations on a fair win!

Looking forward to getting to know you better,
Larry Chesterton

CHAPTER XVI

"Jewel!" Larry greeted his client as if she were a queen and gestured for her to take one of the comfortable leather visitor's chairs, noting as he did so that Glenda had closed his office door behind her when she had left them. "The pad and pen on the desk in front of you are yours to use if you feel the need for them at any point during our discussion."

"Thank you." She took the offered seat, lifted her chin and worked to sublimate the emotions that were swirling inside of her. "I'd like to say a couple of things before we get started if I may."

"Certainly," he relaxed in his chair and gave her his full attention.

"My Bruce was a good man," she began, a hesitancy underlying her words. "I loved him, and he loved me from the day we first met in grade school. Even so, like everyone else, he had his faults. He didn't know how to slow down, which contributed to his no longer being with us, and he was too trusting, which is why we're having this conversation. I know the news isn't good." She sent him a wry smile. "You're a nice man, and you may think it best to soften the blow. I would prefer that you not hold back in any way. Understanding the true nature of my situation is the first step in my journey forward."

"I agree." Larry straightened and pulled several printed sheets from the file before him, but retained them in his hand for the moment. "May I say in addition that I can see clearly why Bruce found it so easy to love you for so long, or would that offend you?"

"Compliments meant never offend." She took the document he held out to her, and then reached into her purse for her reading glasses. "As you know, Bruce always handled our money, so I'm not sure of the protocol in such situations. Do I read this through first, or do we go over it together line by line?"

"We can proceed in whichever way will make you most comfortable," he assured her. "Which would you prefer?"

"Why don't you lead me through it," she suggested.

"As you know, your husband left everything to you as his surviving spouse," Larry began. "Over the years, Bruce had done a fairly good job of setting up your finances in such a way as to insure a comfortable retirement for you both, but then, he began to deviate from his more conservative patterns."

"You're talking about the real estate development consortium that Gerald Tate was putting together through the bank," Jewel interjected, her tone taking on a hard edge. "Bruce tried to back out of his commitment once he realized that there was so much opposition building amongst community members such as Chase Sheffield and yourself, whose opinions we had always admired, but he was contractually obligated to keep our funds invested for five years."

"Exactly." Larry sent her a smile. "I'm glad you bring that understanding to the table. The good news is that you own your house outright. The bad news is that Bruce liquidated a fair number of what we commonly refer to as blue chip securities and borrowed against his life insurance in order to fund that commitment. In a few years, you can begin to draw against your husband's social security, if you need to, although as your financial advisor I would recommend that you hold off on that as long as possible, allowing it to attain its maximum benefit before you begin to draw against it."

"So, basically, I own my home, but I don't have much income to speak of." Jewel looked up from the document she had been studying. "And, of course, I've used up most of the insurance payout during the past couple of years."

"Page three is a monthly budget I've put together based on your current commitments and the income the remaining securities will provide at this time," Larry filled her in. "As you can see, there's a shortfall of approximately four hundred per month. As far as our office has been able to determine, there is no certainty of your ever receiving any income from Tate's development scheme."

"What are my options then?" his client asked.

"Option one would be to sell the house, invest the resulting cash and downsize your living arrangements, either by purchasing a smaller property for yourself or renting," Larry explained. "Option two would be to secure some sort of employment that would cover the shortfall. Do you have any computer or other skills?"

"Not really." Jewel shook her head in the negative. "I married Bruce right out of high school and never worked outside of our home, except to do some minor volunteer work at the hospital as a pink lady. Are there any other options you could suggest?"

"There is one other possibility we were able to confirm," Larry stated. "Because of the area in which your home is located, you can secure a license to take in a boarder or boarders, if the layout of the house lends itself to something of this nature and you're willing to do so. You'll find the figures at the top of page four that show the amount you would need to charge in order to cover the increased insurance costs and taxes, while still retaining an amount sufficient to meet your needs. Would something like that appeal to you?"

"I would prefer to take in a boarder over selling the home Bruce bought for us," his client said. "Would there be any way that you could stop by the house one day next week and give me your opinion as to how I could best go about it, given the floor plan of the home?"

"I'm not an architect, but I'm certainly willing to give you my opinion," Larry agreed as he scanned his appointment book. "Would eleven o'clock Tuesday morning work for you?"

"I'll look forward to seeing you then." Jewel removed her reading glasses and returned them to her purse. "In the meantime, I'll study these documents further."

"Is there anything else you'd like to ask while you're here?"

"Only one thing." His client's fingers clutched the edge of his desk so hard that her knuckles whitened. "In your opinion, will I be able to recoup any of the funds that my husband invested in Gerald Tate's real estate scheme once the five years are up?"

"I can't state positively, because only time will tell," Larry began with a caution, "but given the growing concern among Captain's Point's residents when it comes to large scale development, it would be my professional opinion that you can only expect to withdraw a small percentage of the funds that were initially invested."

"Thank you for your honesty." Jewel rose from her chair as did Larry, who managed to walk her to his office door without any visible signs of his discomfort. "I'll look forward to seeing you on Tuesday."

Once he had passed her onto Glenda's capable hands, he returned to his chair, glad for both its supportive comfort and the fact that he hadn't had to reveal his personal opinion of Gerald Tate to the widow the other man had robbed, all within the boundaries of the law.

CHAPTER XVII

Elizabeth Chesterton straightened and surveyed with a practiced eye her well-tended rose garden in the walled area behind her home that was known locally as The Cove. But then, she caught a glimpse of the roof overlaying her nephew Larry's apartment above the home's extensive garage that had formerly served as the carriage house, and she let out a sigh. If only those one cared about were as easy to watch over and nurture as a garden, she thought.

At least now Susan and Daniel were happily ensconced in Blue Wolf Manor with Jack. Anders and she couldn't have designed that man better if they had tried. Chase and Adrianna were made for each other, too, and even though technically Chase hadn't been hers to fret about, she had done so with vigor. It was pure pleasure to see him mated for life to such a fine young woman.

Only three individuals remained within her sphere of influence who might still need a small push, if they were to achieve the kind of happiness she had enjoyed throughout her married life with her Anders. On second thought, maybe there were four. It wouldn't be right to forget the new addition to their group, and Jack deserved any help she could give him with his sister.

Still, her primary concern was her nephew, and frankly, if she were honest with herself, she had been hitting her head against a brick wall for years over that one. There was no doubt about it. Candy Jones had damaged Larry badly when she had turned her back on both her hometown and him, claiming she preferred to seek a career in show business. For years, the boy had nurtured the hope that the girl to whom he had given his heart would return, but she hadn't.

Neither, of course, had she made a success of herself in Hollywood, although according to information shared by Candy's older sister during a rare visit back home, her sibling had offered her wares on every available casting couch in her efforts to achieve it. Eventually, the long-legged blonde had made her way to Vegas, where she had remained on the back row of a dance troupe until a small-time wheeler-dealer had convinced her to live with him, keeping her barefoot and pregnant for a number of years, but never marrying her as far as anyone knew. She supposed the hussy had gotten what she deserved for having hurt their Larry so badly, but still, as a mother she hated to think about the children who had resulted from Candy's self-centered decisions and the lack of reasonable guidance they must have suffered in the intervening years.

Well, there was one thing she could do for her nephew. She could bring pressure to bear on Anders' brother, as soon as her sister-in-law and he arrived at The Cove for Thanksgiving. It was time that pot-bellied couch potato stood up to his wife in a way that would improve the quality of their son's life.

At the same time Elizabeth arrived at this conclusion, her friend Penny Plunk turned to the window over the sink in Montgomery House's large kitchen and looked with eyes awash with tears upon her young employer, who had just returned with Max from his afternoon walk. How hard this must be for Adrianna, she thought, as she noted the younger woman dawdling as she approached the house. Still, the next few minutes had been inevitable ever since the girl's great-aunt had died and no longer needed her own constant ministrations.

Oh, well, she had enjoyed a long run as the Montgomerys' housekeeper, Penny let out a small sigh as her fingers caressed the recently installed granite countertop in front of her. She would miss all of the new appliances, the skylight that had brightened the kitchen and the sense of being part of something worthwhile. Somehow, she would have to figure out what she wanted to do with herself going forward.

"We're back," Adrianna announced as Max and she entered from the mudroom, breaking through her housekeeper's reverie, completely unaware of the direction the older woman's thoughts had taken.

"So I see." Penny added a smile to her face.

"Did you get my note?" Adrianna asked.

"Yes, and we're ready to go."

"I'm sorry about the extra work for tomorrow night's dinner party." His owner unhooked Max's leash from his harness. "I thought I'd never get the numbers right. First, I asked Jim Laidlaw to join us when I took Max to see him, and Bev Lockhart seemed a logical choice to pair with him. They get along well, don't you think?" The matchmaker in Adrianna shone from her eyes.

"They always seem to," Penny replied, thinking to herself that one of them would probably be more excited about the pairing than the other.

"Next, I decided it would be a good idea to have Pete Marlborough and Julia Henderson over socially," the budding hostess referred to the historical architect that her husband and she had commissioned to do major work on Montgomery House that was scheduled to begin shortly and his firm's interior design consultant. "I thought it would be nice if I got to know them a little better before we break ground on the addition. I met Pete occasionally during the renovations at Sheffield Place Inn, but I've only met Julia once briefly. This way she can get some sense of my design style before we work together.

"Then, when she accepted and he was tied up with a family commitment, we were left with an extra female.

Luckily, Paul Lynch was available." Adrianna remembered the relief she had felt when the young associate minister, who rented the former caretaker's cottage on the property, had accepted her invitation.

"On the way back, I stopped in at Artful Soul to sign up for one of Arthur's watercolor classes and found Edwina there visiting with him, and you know the rest." Her eyes twinkled. "Do you think we should begin to think of those two as a real couple? I mean, at their age?" In her mind, she pictured the elderly twosome – he, the first person to rent one of the new retail spaces now available in the property's former carriage house and she, the renter who lived in the former Montgomery House dependency - clutched in a passionate embrace.

"Otis mentioned that they were meeting for lunch almost every day in the gazebo when the weather was still nice," Penny shared what information she had, "and I've never heard of cupid enforcing an age limit."

"Do you think I should make some brownies in addition to the two cheesecakes?" Adrianna asked.

"It wouldn't hurt if you're in the mood, although I'm not sure they'll be needed," Penny responded, wishing they could move on to the matter she cared about most.

"Would this be a good time for you to take a break?" Adrianna opened the cupboard door next to her. "The wind off the water was a bit nippy today. We could take some mugs of tea into the library and enjoy a chat in front of the fireplace."

"That would be nice." The housekeeper added water to the large teapot that always stood ready on a back burner of the professional grade stove. "A cup of Yorkshire Gold would go down well about now. Would that do for you, too?"

"Sounds great." Adrianna removed her thick sweater and hung it over a hook in the mudroom, then washed her hands and prepared a small plate of iced cookies she had baked earlier as a treat for Chase.

A few minutes later, both women settled themselves on the couch in front of the gas fireplace that was rapidly turning the high-ceilinged library into a cozy retreat. But then, Adrianna rose, crossed to the long library table that served as the couple's home office desk, and returned a moment later with two legal pads and two pens, handing one of each to her housekeeper, who now found herself confused.

"I thought we might both want to take notes at some point," her employer explained as she retook her seat, a crease marring her normally smooth brow. "I don't believe I've ever been so nervous about approaching someone as I am with you about this. I should start by saying I hope you'll be completely honest with me, and I know I speak for Chase as well when I say that we both value your contributions here at the house and always will. Otis and you are so much more than employees to us. You both help fill the roles left vacant by the deaths of our parents. You're part and parcel of what makes Montgomery House seem like home, and we wouldn't want either of you to be unhappy because of us."

"Otis and I care about Chase and you the same way," Penny assured her, even as she still wasn't certain where this unexpected conversation was now taking them. "I'm thrilled with my upgraded kitchen, and having you young people to work with has livened up both of our lives."

"Still, I've wondered if you might not be bored at times," Adrianna stated. "I'm sure Great-aunt Martha kept you much busier than we do, especially since Chase and I enjoy cooking some of our meals and I like to bake both as a treat for him and for relaxation. Then it hit me that you might be glad to have an opportunity to work with Otis and me on our new project. You live and breathe the home improvement and cooking channels now that we've installed a television in the kitchen, and no one understands a cook's workflow needs any better than you do."

"Let me get this straight," Penny said. "You've asked me to meet with you this afternoon because you want me to serve as some sort of kitchen design consultant on your home improvement projects in the historic district?"

"Only if you would enjoy doing so and don't think it would be too much of a burden on you." The worried look returned to her employer's face.

"Oh, my dear, I've been such a fool!" The housekeeper laughed. "I thought you were going to terminate my position or at least cut back on my hours, because I do have some time on my hands when we have a week in which you two don't entertain. Instead, you're offering me a chance to do some really rewarding work and draw on my expertise, such as it is."

"So you'll do it?" Adrianna beamed at her.

"Absolutely!" Penny's eyes sparkled.

CHAPTER XVIII

Thinking herself lucky, Kate slid her car into a just vacated marina parking slot located right in front of Long and Short. Despite the fact that her sister-in-law's hair always looked marvelous, she was a little nervous about her first appointment with Bitsy Long Wilder, the beauty parlor's owner. The dinner at Montgomery House the next evening would be her first major social event since arriving in Captain's Point, and Susan's cousin was sure to be there. No doubt about it, her hair needed to look its best.

Disembarking, she was struck by the fact that this, too, marked a first – her opening excursion on her own as she began her new life in Captain's Point, although it hadn't been any big deal to find her way here. She had merely turned right as she exited her brother's driveway, driven past Chesterton Farm, where Susan had grown up, Montgomery House, the Sheffield Place Inn, where she had stayed for the wedding, and The Cove, then taken the next right to the marina. The shop itself backed onto Chester's, so it had been a simple matter for Susan and herself to arrange an appointment as they had walked from her brother's SUV to the restaurant at lunchtime.

Straightening her shoulders, she added a confident look to her face, crossed the sidewalk and opened the door to the busy shop.

"Kate!" Edwina Foster, her diminutive form dressed uncharacteristically in jeans and a powder blue T-shirt that set off her silver hair and blue eyes, greeted her as she entered. "How nice to see you out and about. Are you beginning to feel more at home here in Captain's Point?"

"So far, it's proven to be everything I hoped it would be," she replied, "although I'm still looking for a permanent residence for myself. Jack and Susan have made me feel very at home and Daniel's a jewel, but I don't want to outstay my welcome."

"I'll let you know if I hear about anything suitable," Edwina promised. "Let me introduce you to my grandson's wife Ginny." She drew the new arrival towards the row of plush pink chairs that flanked the front window, indicating a blonde-haired woman about Kate's age. "And this is Lucy, my great-granddaughter."

"What a beautiful baby!" Kate expressed her honest admiration at the picture perfect six month old, even as a wave of sadness at her own lack of a family passed over her. "And that's a precious outfit as well."

"Ginny, this is Kate, Jack Jefferson's sister that I've mentioned," the older woman completed the introductions.

"Mrs. Foster, Hilda is ready for you now," a young woman dressed in the pink uniform worn by all the shop's employees spoke up.

"I'm Kate Sinclair," she checked in.

"Bitsy's new one." The receptionist glanced down at a large appointment book spread atop the antique desk that acted as a front counter. "She's finishing up with Mrs. Madison now. If you'll take a seat, I'll let her know that you're here. Would you like a cup of tea and a cookie while you wait?"

It was then that Kate noticed that both Ginny and Edwina held oval-shaped, pink glass dessert plates with a pink teacup set atop one end.

"The tea is British Afternoon, and the cookies are delicious," Ginny filled in the new arrival, having noted the hesitant look that had appeared on her lovely, heart-shaped face.

"Then I should certainly take advantage of your offer – sugar, no lemon, please." Kate smiled at the receptionist as she took the chair next to Ginny's, then turned to address her new acquaintance. "Fancy my finding one of the few people I know in Captain's Point here at Long and Short on my first visit, and now Edwina has introduced me to you two as well." She reached out a finger to Lucy, who promptly grabbed it and steered it towards her mouth.

"Careful," Ginny warned her. "She's teething. Jason's grandmother is fairly new to Captain's Point, too, you know. She flew here from Chicago to visit us, just before Lucy was due, and we convinced her to move to the area. She's been a great help to me these past few months, and…" The young mother glanced quickly around as her voice dropped. "She's even found a wonderful man to spend time with. In fact, I think he's taking her out to dinner this evening."

"Are you talking about Arthur?" Kate asked, bending her head a bit closer. "I met him when I drove over for my brother's wedding. He's a charming man, but I hadn't realized they were a couple in the real sense." Her mind filled with a picture of a tall, elegant, gray-haired gentleman with kind, faded-brown eyes.

"Jason and I aren't sure they are," Ginny shared, "but there's a sort of glow emanating from Edwina that wasn't there when she first arrived. Wouldn't it be neat if they were to get together at their age? Oh, no, it looks like Bitsy's finished with Mrs. Madison. If you're free, why don't you come and have lunch with Lucy and me on Monday? That way, we can have a real chat."

"I'd love to." Kate was struck again by how friendly everyone in Captain's Point seemed to be.

"Let's say eleven-thirty, because I'm never sure when Lucy will set our lunchtime," Ginny suggested as she pulled a small spiral notebook and a pen from her purse and jotted down her address and phone number. "Jason and I moved here not too long before I gave birth, so I'll be looking forward to getting to know you better."

"Ms. Sinclair?" A buxom blonde about Susan's age, who was wearing a rose-colored version of the shop's uniform, approached them. "I'm Bitsy Wilder. I see Janice has your tea ready." She indicated the receptionist with a nod. "Feel free to bring it with you."

"See you Monday." Ginny sent Kate a bright smile, before the latter turned and followed the shop's owner between too oversized potted plants and into the main service area beyond.

A little over an hour later, Kate opened the door to the shop, pleased with her wash, cut and curl, now secure in the knowledge that Bitsy would keep her well-informed about events in Captain's Point going forward.

The sun heading towards the horizon straight ahead momentarily blinded her, and she reached into her purse for her sunglasses as she took a step forward, immediately feeling the impact of a sizeable body knocking into her right side.

"Excuse me!" She glanced up, embarrassed, only to feel warmth of a blush flood her cheeks as she met the twinkling, deep blue eyes of Larry Chesterton, who was once again clutching her to him in an effort to keep her from falling and hurting herself.

"Trust me, as light as you are, it's absolutely no trouble at all for me to keep doing this, if you feel the need for it." He chuckled. "My! Don't you look nice!" He retained a light grip on her right arm as he released her slightly, his face reflecting his honest admiration.

"On the other hand, this looks rather painful." Kate lightly touched the bruised area on his jaw with a fingertip.

"It's not as bad as it looks," he assured her. "Your ponytail provided a buffer."

"Thank you for the lovely roses," Kate said, pulling herself together. "They were a nice surprise."

"It was the least I could do after causing you to fall," he stated.

"Oh, no, that was my fault entirely," she disagreed. "I feel like I should do something to make it up to you."

"Then join me as my guest for dinner, if you're free, and we'll call it even." Larry worked hard to keep the eagerness from his voice, suddenly filled with a desire to spend the evening with the woman before him. "Call my fair cousin and your brother, and tell them you're going out on the town."

"Okay," Kate agreed, hardly able to believe her good fortune, "although I think I'll keep them guessing as to whom I'm with. It will give them something to talk about in my absence."

"Let's step around the corner into the shade." He guided her beyond the beauty parlor's doorway, and then pulled his own phone from his pocket, selecting the number for Montgomery's restaurant and turning slightly to allow her some privacy while she made her call, keeping his own voice down so as not to ruin her plans. "Raoul, Larry Chesterton here. Is the Montgomery table free this evening or has my erstwhile friend claimed it for himself and his bride? ... Excellent, I'd like to reserve it for myself then. My lovely guest and I should be there in about half an hour, if the time works for you."

"That's put the fox among the hens." Kate grinned at him a moment later. "I believe you may be a bad influence on me."

"Possibly, but having a little fun at Chase and Susan's expense has been almost a religion to me since I was no more than a sprout," he responded. "Now, of course, your brother's been added to the equation by extension."

"Makes sense to me." She accompanied him around the building, not surprised when he slowed as they approached Chester's doorway.

"If you'll bear with me for a few minutes, I was coming here to check in with my manager when I bumped into you," Larry said. "Then we can start on our way to a much quieter venue."

Wondering where he was taking her on what she now thought of as their first date, Kate couldn't help but note the respect with which Bill Graham greeted him, even as she remembered Susan's comments earlier. Certainly, adding a stopover at the restaurant on his way home from work each evening would get tiring after a while, not to mention the time it took away from other possible pursuits.

"Have you met Jack Jefferson's sister Kate?" The object of her thoughts addressed his restaurant's manager.

"Earlier today, actually." Bill sent her a grin. "I trust you enjoyed your first experience at Chester's."

"Very much so," Kate assured him, glad she had spent some time in her brother's gym and then joined her sister-in-law for a jog afterwards.

The two men proceeded to take care of their business, even as Larry returned smiles and waves from various patrons, who lifted a crab leg here or a cornstick there in greeting to him, and Kate took advantage of the opportunity, examining the restaurant from a different perspective than that of a diner. Immaculately clean for its type, the décor was pleasant, the seating well-arranged and the wait staff attentive. No wonder Chester's was the success Susan claimed it to be, since she herself could speak to the food being delicious.

"That should do it," Larry brought his conversation to a close beside her. "Thanks again." Placing his hand on the small of her back, he opened the door for Kate and then steered her left along the boardwalk.

"I've reserved the coveted table at Montgomery's for our use this evening," he explained as they took their time, sauntering along, Larry still nursing his back in a way that he hoped wasn't too noticeable and Kate hoping to stretch out the moments. "Martha Montgomery originally owned the restaurant, but after Adrianna inherited everything, she wisely sold it to its long-time master chef and manager John Thornburg who insisted, along with Chase, that she should retain first refusal of the best table in the house to help maintain the cachet of the place. They're not using it this evening, so I claimed it for us, although we could've crashed their party if they'd planned one. We would've been welcome to do so."

"I'm sure we would've been as close as Chase and you are," she acknowledged.

"Bound to be," he pointed out. "We were practically raised in the same cradle."

"I've never lived this near the water," Kate shared, taking in the view to their right, "but I'm beginning to understand why my brother has always been so drawn to it."

"Wise man, your brother." Larry paused and allowed his gaze to take in the Atlantic Ocean spread out before them. "We're all glad he's chosen to make Captain's Point his permanent home, and now you have, too." He threw his arm around her shoulders and gave her a quick squeeze, before releasing her and once again heading them towards their destination, his steps lightened by the thought that even Chase would agree he was putting himself out there this evening.

CHAPTER XIX

"Mr. Larry!" Raoul greeted the attractive couple with a broad smile. "You have not graced our humble establishment with your presence since your cousin's wedding, and I see that you have Mr. Jefferson's beautiful sister with you this evening as well. Now, let me think…" He held up an index finger. "Miss Kate, is it not?"

"Imagine your remembering my name, when you only met me for a few seconds over two weeks ago," Kate expressed her honest surprise.

"It is a gift." The maître d' shrugged his shoulders and bent his head slightly in a gesture of humility, even as he retrieved two leather-bound menus from behind the reception desk and led them towards the elevator that would carry them to the second floor.

"I believe the sunset will be exceptional this evening." Raoul signaled for a waiter to fill their water glasses and indicated for the couple to take their places on the large banquette that provided the Montgomery table's seating. "Enjoy your meal."

Left alone, Kate opened her menu, while Larry took a sip from his water glass and then followed suit, relieved to have something to do that would cover up the nervousness that now filled him.

"What would you recommend?" his date, because that is what he now recognized she was, asked him, lifting her beautiful eyes to him full of trust in his ability to recommend a suitable selection.

Clearing his throat, he glanced rapidly over the main pages, his mind having gone completely blank as to the items offered that only a few minutes before he could've recited from memory. Surely, it hadn't been that long since he had taken a member of the opposite sex other than Susan out for a social dinner, but then, he found, he couldn't even remember the last time he had done so.

"We should each start with a cup of cream of crab soup, and John's special offerings have never let me down," he began. "I've often enjoyed the crab-stuffed snapper as well as the trout. Tonight, I'll probably go with the steak and lobster myself, both because I missed lunch and as a way to celebrate having such a beautiful dinner companion with whom to share my meal." Immediately, he wished he could take back the last part, thinking it had sounded too corny, although his companion hadn't seemed to notice.

"I'll go with the stuffed snapper, since you recommend it." Kate closed her menu as their waiter arrived, introduced himself and took their order, noting that her date appeared to be quite comfortable as he selected a high end chardonnay to accompany their meal.

"This is nice." Larry settled his sore back against the seat.
"The view is marvelous." Kate's eyes traveled to the bank of large windows that encompassed the extended turret in which their table sat overlooking the ocean.

"The sun actually sets behind the restaurant, of course," Larry filled her in, "but Raoul was right. The cumulus clouds floating around in the sky should make for an extraordinary sunset."

For a minute, the two of them enjoyed what he thought was a comfortable silence, but then, he noticed that Kate was twisting and untwisting the corner of her napkin in her lap. Sitting side by side on the banquette, he easily placed his hand over hers as he drew her eyes to him. "Is there something wrong?" he asked.

"I'm not sure," she admitted, her beautiful crystal blue eyes full of worry before she averted them. "I've never been in this position before, and I don't want to embarrass you."

"If you're in some kind of trouble and could use my help, then a little embarrassment would be a small price to pay for my being able to fulfill your need," he assured her. "I hope we're going to be good friends for a long time to come, and we're practically relatives, so let's not stand on any ceremony."

Their waiter choosing this moment to deliver their cups of cream of crab soup, Larry lifted his hand from hers and picked up his spoon, thinking she might find it easier to discuss whatever was worrying her if he gave her a little space.

For her own part, Kate enjoyed two spoonfuls before speaking. "I'm remembering to be careful because Daniel told me this soup stains," she shared, sending him a small smile.

"But that isn't what's troubling you." He finished off his last bite and pushed his cup and its saucer forward slightly.

Kate took her time and finished hers as well, before honoring him with a reply. "Raoul made me think when he referred to me as Miss Kate a few minutes ago. I'm not sure whether or not I should point out that you're having dinner with a married woman." A hint of pink tinged her cheeks. "Divorce papers have been filed, and there never was a real marriage. Still, technically, I'm married."

"Ah…" Larry sent her a kind smile. "I can see where that might put you in a difficult position. If it makes you feel any better, Susan filled me in about your divorce after the rehearsal dinner, when the two of us were waiting while Jack thanked John Thornburg. She's very proud of you for having the courage to leave what's his name, and I imagine you won't find a stronger supporter anywhere, since she's been through something similar herself."

"Your cousin's been wonderful." Kate's eyes filled with honest appreciation. "My brother's a very lucky man, and believe me, he knows it. The fact that he's won Daniel as part of the bargain is an added treasure."

"Daniel's done well there." Larry's expression sobered. "His birth father has proven himself to be a real jerk, and there isn't a Chesterton breathing who isn't relieved that the boy has Jack to mentor him."

"The little guy's very attached to you, too," Kate pointed out. "I saw the way he ran over to greet you when you drove up yesterday, and he was disappointed not to find you at Chester's, when we went there for lunch."

"Still, a boy his age needs a father figure in his home, someone who can react instantly at the moment something happens." Larry smiled at the waiter who had just placed a large platter in front of him. "And they don't come any better than your brother."

"I can agree with you on that one." Kate picked up her fork. "This looks delicious."

Larry nodded his approval of the wine and waited until they were once again alone. "As to your original concern," he picked up their conversation, "I agree with my cousin. It took a lot of courage to make the decisions you've made, and I'm glad you've decided to join us here in Captain's Point. I hope you'll consider me your friend, and a short term legal issue shouldn't be allowed to get in the way of good friends enjoying each other's company as far as I'm concerned."

"Thank you," Kate almost whispered, keeping her eyes on her plate as she blinked back sudden tears.

"No, thank you, for overcoming your doubts and agreeing to have dinner with me." He reached over and gave her a quick hug. "Now, I insist you give that stuffed snapper its due, while we both enjoy this gorgeous sunset that is rapidly spreading itself before us."

And with that, he dipped a succulent bite of lobster into the tiny dish of drawn butter, thinking that he might actually enjoy finding his way in the new world of out there, particularly if Jack's sister would agree to be his frequent companion.

CHAPTER XX

Feeling relieved by Larry's easy acceptance of her current situation, Kate followed his command and enjoyed a few more bites of her snapper, while at the same time appreciating the rose, pink and gold display the sunset was providing.

"So tell me about yourself." She paused between bites and glanced her dinner companion's way, recognizing that, with the exception of her brother, every man she had ever known had liked nothing more than to talk about himself.

"There's not much to tell," he replied. "Except for my time at Yale, I've spent most of my life here in Captain's Point, surrounded by family and friends. Thanks to my uncle's generosity, I've spent my professional life doing something I enjoy in a non-pressured environment. In addition, I keep tabs on Chester's for my parents. Chase and I also share a common interest in Captain's Point's future, so both of us serve as city councilmen. We're hoping to convince your brother to take an active role in that going forward, but keep that under your hat, if you will, until we approach him about it."

"I will," she promised, even as she wondered what her privacy-loving brother would think of such a suggestion.

As she separated another bite of snapper, Kate couldn't help but compare the humility that shone forth from Larry's description of himself with the cocky rendition of his accomplishments that would've poured from her ex's mouth. The former's words were made even more notable by what had been left unsaid – the Phi Beta Kappa he had been awarded at Yale per Susan, the fact that he was brilliant when it came to helping others with their investments, no mention at all of his own share in the ownership of Chester's.

"That reminds me." She set her fork down for a moment. "My father insisted on negotiating a pre-nuptial agreement that has left me with a fair number of securities. The thing is, I never liked or even respected the shifty-eyed broker my ex and his family used – his primary recommendation being his golf handicap as far as I was able to determine. Would you have any qualms about reviewing my finances with me, given that we are, as you said, almost relatives?"

"I'll be glad to take a look at them for you," Larry replied, "and as for your being practically a relative, almost everyone I work with professionally is either a relative or a friend, due to the very nature of Captain's Point. It raises the bar a bit from my standpoint, but then, even in a huge metropolis, all clients would deserve the best I could give them." He pulled a card from his wallet and handed it to her. "Give Glenda a call Monday, and she'll fit you right in. Let's give you some peace of mind in that area as soon as we can."

"Thank you, I will." She slipped the card into her purse, struck again by his kindness. "So, if you don't mind my asking, why haven't you ever married? You have so much going for you – good looks, a good income, a nice smile." Quickly, she retrieved her fork, thinking she had revealed too much of herself.

"Feel free to continue." He chuckled, but then his expression sobered. "It isn't that I have anything against marriage. The right woman at the right time simply never came along. Perhaps, that's the downside of living in a small town. Your options are somewhat more limited."

For a few minutes, they ate in silence as his mind wandered back in time to a long-legged blonde in a cheerleader's outfit and hers considered the limited sphere of acceptable options that had been provided within her parents' country club culture.

"What do you do in your spare time?" she asked, wishing to provide him with an easy flow of conversation in return for being his dinner guest.

"Spare time?" He laughed. "What's that?"

"No, seriously, what do you enjoy during your down time?" she persisted.

"I spend time with my family first and foremost – sharing a meal, playing cards, working a puzzle together or just conversing," Larry stated. "I read almost anything I can put my hands on, listen to music, work out and, if the weather's right, I sail or do some deep sea fishing. Chase and I have a longstanding rivalry going in the single's race that occurs each year as part of Captain's Point's Annual Regatta, although I have a feeling your brother may put a wrench in both of our ambitions this coming year."

"That he might," she agreed with pride. "Jack's sailed all types of boats over the years."

"I know he's glad to have you here with him." Again, Larry found himself reaching out his hand and giving hers a quick squeeze.

"I'm afraid I may be overstaying my welcome," Kate stated, but hurried to add, "not that either one of them has said anything, you understand. Still, Jack and Susan are on their honeymoon, and there I am. Unfortunately, our joint efforts to find me a suitable place to live have so far been unsuccessful."

"What exactly are you looking for?" he asked, intrigued.

"That's part of the problem, I'm not really sure." Her lovely eyes met his as if seeking the answer in them. "Jack agrees that I would be wise to rent first, and I took my clothes and some smaller belongings from my married home, but no furniture. I had thought a furnished apartment, but none of the ones we saw so far were right for me."

"I often hear about opportunities of all sorts as an offshoot of my work," Larry shared. "I'll certainly let you know if knowledge of something you might like comes my way."

"I'd appreciate it." She sent him a smile so filled with gratitude that he wanted to hug her close and tell her everything would be okay, but wisely refrained.

"I've told you all about me, so it's your turn," he pointed out.

"There's really not much to tell." With her fork, she drew a circle in her mashed potatoes. "I grew up, loved for all the wrong reasons and not given much valuable instruction as to how to live a fulfilling life. I majored in accounting at the University of Virginia and even passed my CPA exams, but I never used my skills, except by keeping the charitable accounts for some of my women's groups, so all of that has been wasted and is now out of date. I married the man of my mother's dreams, and you know how that turned out."

"Tell me about your marriage," he said, suddenly wanting to know, while at the same time remembering how much Susan had said it helped her to share with him.

"You have to understand that there have always been two parts of me – the part that was raised to be one way by my parents and the part that was heavily influenced by my brother – both diametrically opposed." Her eyes filled with an intensity that startled him. "Being several years older than me, Jack managed to escape while I was a preteen. Still, he kept in touch and made it a point to instill in me certain values that were underlined and are reflected in his novels. Basically, he taught me three things in particular – true love existed, a real family was important and a woman should save herself for the man she married. I imagine the latter was his way of protecting me in his absence, but I took it to heart."

"Sounds like he led you along the right path," Larry interjected.

"I couldn't have told you this as concisely before I left my ex," Kate continued. "It's only been during these past couple of weeks that I've managed to gain so much perspective. My parents' side of me led me to seek a husband and family amongst the limited group of acceptable families around which I'd been raised, much to my detriment. I believed myself to be in love with my husband. He was handsome, admired by his peers, able to provide for me, and he could be charming. He pursued me as if I was the Holy Grail, and I was flattered. Looking back, I can see that I was in love with love and not him."

"You really have done a lot of self-examination," he spoke up. "Susan did, too."

"Making a major life-changing decision does that to you." Her shoulders shrugged slightly. "Anyway, saving myself for my husband had been a waste of my time. My groom was so drunk on our wedding night that I don't think he even noticed. Frankly, I'm not even sure he knew it was me he was with. He certainly wasn't particularly gentle or caring. Two weeks later, we attended a party at his parents, and towards the end of the evening he left with an ex-girlfriend – also now married – and didn't return. My mother-in-law showed me to a guest room and explained in no uncertain terms that men would be men and Sinclair men in particular were passionate beyond the means of any one woman to please them."

Larry felt his throat constrict as he was suddenly filled with an overriding desire to make love to the woman beside him – not in a wildly passionate way, but rather encompassing her in a slow, soft, gentle lovemaking through which he could somehow replace the hurt she had endured with faith in another man's virtue. Part of him wondered if Jack or even Susan knew the totality of what Kate had been through.

"Anyway, after that night, I moved my things into another bedroom, the Jack part of me having taken over," Kate continued softly beside him. "My husband was welcome to spread his passionate desires anywhere that he wanted, but not any longer with me. I expected him to be angry, but instead, he seemed relieved. I kept myself busy with various charitable pursuits, and he worked hard at his golf game. Then, one day, I woke up, realized I was wasting my life and determined to end the marriage." She lifted her eyes to his full of questions.

"Not one day too soon," he assured her. "Your brother was right. True love exists, real family is important, and your husband was a fool not to value the higher prize that you awarded him."

Their waiter picking this moment to hand them each a dessert menu and retrieve their plates, neither one of them was required to converse further, although both of their thoughts continued even as they read through the choices in the tiny leather portfolio.

She wondered how different her life might have been if she had met the man beside her four years earlier, and he realized the memory of the woman he had once loved had been well and truly eclipsed, at least during these past few minutes, by the woman beside him.

CHAPTER XXI

Waking first Saturday morning, Jack slipped from beneath the covers and closed both doors to his dressing room before turning on the electric toothbrush in his bathroom. Feeling a bit more himself, he returned quietly to bed, stretching out for a comfortable think as he rejoiced in the presence of his beautiful wife sleeping beside him, but then his mind returned to the first night they had spent together right here in this room.

Once again, he berated himself for not having guessed beforehand what awaited him based on things he had already known of her previous marriage. What he could've done, though, he still didn't know.

Thank goodness her ex lived far enough away that they would never cross paths, his hands clinched into fists, but then he consciously relaxed them. The important thing now was to make his Susie's life so different from what she had known during her time with the jerk that she would never think so little of herself again.

At first, he had thought her to be merely shy. After all, he had spent most of their courtship holding his need for her out of sight as he had concentrated on helping her to heal from her divorce in an effort to clear the way for her heart to open to him. Only during the two short weeks prior to their marriage had he allowed his desire for her to shine forth, letting her see the depth of his passion, and no one could say that she hadn't responded in kind as he had kissed her and held her close, wanting his ring on her finger before he pressed further.

Their wedding guests gone and the October evening unseasonably warm, they had changed into casual clothes and taken an opened bottle of champagne and two flutes onto the balcony off the bedroom they would now share. Here they had stood at the rail arm in arm, sipping their drinks, recalling special moments from their day, and following the progress of the lighted ships on the ocean spread out before them even as they had picked out constellations from the myriad stars above. And then, he had placed their crystal glasses on the pine table behind them and had taken her into his arms, whereupon she had frozen.

"What's wrong, Susie?" he had asked, holding her close.

"I am," she had responded, her face averted as she had drawn back slightly. "You're a man of the world, but I've only shared a bed with one other man and, frankly, I wasn't very good at it. I should've told you before, but you ignited such a flame in me that I thought with a fresh start…" She had lifted one shoulder in a small shrug. "Now, though, I'm not sure that I've been fair to you."

For a moment, he had remained silent as his emotions had run the gamut from shock at the words he had just heard to a desire to get into his SUV and track down the man who had left his sweet Susan so damaged. Finally, he had controlled himself enough to keep his voice calm. "Exactly what do you mean when you say you weren't any good?"

"I mean I was inexperienced – in point of fact, a complete innocent, and I never managed to move much beyond that point, leaving Bill less than satisfied with the results of our…efforts." She had hung her head, embarrassed, and if he had been in a position to place his hands around her ex's neck, he could've easily killed him, his anger at that moment had been so intense.

"And this was somehow your fault?" He had managed to speak gently to her, finding it almost unbelievable that he was having this conversation with a healthy, beautiful woman. "Did you talk about what he wanted or needed?"

"Bill said I should read up on the subject if I didn't know how to please him, and I did," she had met his gaze, her beautiful eyes awash with tears. "None of the things I tried seemed to help."

"Forget about Bill. How did you feel about your times together?" he had asked.

"I had come to that part of our marriage with no clear expectations beyond expecting it to be pleasurable," she had stated, obviously uncomfortable with the conversation. "It was okay at best."

Forcing himself not to think about what she had suffered through when it had been at its worst, he had taken her shoulders gently in his hands.

"Hear me loud and clear, Susie," he had insisted, wanting there to be no doubt as to his position. "Everything about you arouses me - from the touch of your hand, to your grace as you move around me, to your beautiful face and the curves of your body. You hold your child in your arms, and I want to take you in mine. You laugh, and my heart sings. Surely, you haven't been blind to my desire for you these past couple of weeks."

"No, you've made your intentions quite clear," she had replied, managing a small smile, "which is why I had allowed myself to hope that maybe I could do better with someone as kind and gentle as you are." And then, her beautiful eyes had widened with fear – not of him, but of his expectations.

"I can tell you from now until eternity that everything you are and you do is exactly as I would want it, and you might still not believe me." He had drawn her to him. "May I make a suggestion?"

"Yes, please." She had relaxed in his arms and looked up at him with eyes now filled with hope.

"Let's take this one step at a time," he had proposed, "but understand it's important for both of us to enjoy this journey. As a man of the world, as you put it, I can tell you truthfully that for me knowing I'm giving you pleasure will enhance my own a hundredfold. We've shared a lot about our inner feelings with each other in a very short time. This is one area where that sort of communication is critical. Are you with me?"

"Yes." Her chin had lifted slightly.

"Do you trust me to lead the way?"

"Oh, yes!" Her eyes had filled with her love for him. "I trust you completely."

And then, he had carried her over the threshold from the balcony into their master suite. "I promise nothing but pleasure awaits you at my hands in this room," he had said, kissing her lightly before setting her down and heading her gently towards her dressing room.

Quickly, he had slid into his robe and turned the one light that was on down to low before he had drawn back the drapes from the room's windows, remembering the full moon and the stars still shining outside. Positioning himself halfway between the bed and the room's entrance, he had stood, not at all sure what awaited him, until she had opened the door to her dressing room and stepped forward, taking his breath away with her loveliness.

"You're so beautiful," he had forced the words past the lump that had formed in his throat, for a moment forgetting all else. "I love you with everything that I am, Susie."

"I love you, too." She had sent him a shy smile.

Reaching over, he had turned off the lamp, sending the room into semi-darkness.

"And the love of his life entered their room, a vision in blue, everything a woman could be or ever would be, and every fiber of his being called to her," he had begun writing their story as he had held out his hand.

"And the love of her life stood before her, tall and strong, and every fiber of her being called out to him," she had responded as she had stepped forward and placed her cold hand in his, and he had drawn her to him and kissed her, at first gently, then questioningly and finally with the strength of his full passion as he had felt her responding at each point in kind.

"He held her in his arms, loving the feel of her soft skin on his lips." He had bent and kissed her neck. "Even the scent of her called to him." He had slid the thin strap of her gown from her shoulder and had kissed the spot where it had lain, pleased when he had felt her light shudder of pleasure in response.

"And she came to him, shy and timid, but knowing she could trust this man from whom she had never known anything but love and kindness, and she gave herself up to him, believing that in his bed in this place she would know pleasure for the first time." She had slid her arms around his neck, and he had slowly danced almost in place with her to the music he had set playing softly in the background earlier, allowing her to feel his body pressed against hers through the thin cloth, signaling his desire.

"I want to make love to you more than I've ever wanted anything in my life," he had whispered into her ear, meaning every word of it, and she had pulled his face down to hers as a soft moan had escaped from her throat, clearly indicating her need for him through her kiss.

Filled with desire, he had lifted her into his arms and laid her onto their bed where he had played her body with the same tenderness that he brought to his violin, pleased when he had sensed the notes singing within her as they had both risen to a crescendo.

Later, as she had lain in his arms their having played through an entire symphony, he had heard her sigh of contentment even as he had been sure of his own.

"I had no idea such pleasure existed," she had said, her voice filled with awe. "How cheated I was before, but then, maybe it isn't your experience that made it so different, but rather the way that you care for me."

And he had felt so full of love for his bride at that moment he had thought he might burst. The joke, though, was on her ex who had cheated himself out of the pleasure that he, as her new husband, had enjoyed these past weeks sharing their bed with his Susie - her confidence in her own sexuality restored - the best lover by far that he'd ever known because of the responsiveness, love and trust that she brought to their relationship.

The object of his thoughts chose this moment to awaken, obviously surprised to discover him propped against the pillows watching her sleep.

"Have I died and gone to Heaven?" he asked. "There's an angel in the bed next to me."

"Not as far as I know." She stretched lazily in the kittenish way that he loved. "I can, though, attest to the fact that you were alive and kicking between nine and eleven last evening."

"That wasn't kicking, my dear," he said as he pulled her to him and kissed her, clearly expressing his desire. "Pay a bit more attention this time."

"Silly!" She gave herself up to the pleasure she knew he would give her.

"Mommy! Daddy!" Daniel's footsteps could be heard as he ran along the hall towards their room. "Are you awake yet?"

"I'm afraid you'll have to take a rain check on your offer." Susan sent her new husband a wry smile, even as she watched his face for his reaction to having been called Daddy – a term Daniel had called forth for the first time the past evening.

"There you are!" Jack greeted his stepson, obviously glad to see him. "What took you so long?"

"Casey and Lady slept in," Daniel advised them in all seriousness as he ran forward and gave his mother a hug.

"Come here, Bud." Her new husband gestured for their son to come around the bed, as Susan found herself wondering yet again how anyone could think waking up at seven-thirty represented a long, lazy lie-in.

"I'll be back," Daniel assured her over his shoulder as he hurried to obey. "I have to help Jack with his exercises." He grinned as his new stepfather lifted him off the floor and positioned him along his own long length, chest on chest, and then proceeded to bench press his small body aloft as the child stretched out his arms and held his legs in a swan dive position. "One, two, three…," Daniel counted, "…eighteen, nineteen, twenty."

"Whew! Promise me you won't learn to count much further anytime in the foreseeable future." Jack gave his human barbell a bear hug. "Now what are we missing?" he asked.

"Family hug!" Daniel's face lit up as his stepfather rolled him onto the mattress and pillows between his two adults, who kissed him on opposite cheeks as he wrapped his young arms around their necks. "Oh, no!" he exclaimed, releasing them and sitting up. "I forgot. Casey and Lady said they both have to go out."

"Bet I'll have my jeans and tennis shoes on before you will," Jack issued a challenge.

"No you won't." Daniel crawled to the bottom of the bed and slid off. "Mama already set mine out."

Left alone once again, Jack calmly rolled over on his side facing his new wife. "I think I'll concede this one to our son." He threw his leg over hers and drew her to him, kissing her long and deep in a way that ignited a sure flame within her. "You should know that I won't forget to cash in that rain check this evening."

"I'll look forward to it." She smiled up at him, and then placed her hand on his arm as he rolled away and sat up, drawing his attention back to her. "Thank you for making Daniel and me so happy this morning."

"It wouldn't have been fair for me to have kept all the happiness floating around in this big, old house to myself." His face filled with joy at her words as he stood and reached for his jeans.

CHAPTER XXII

Pete Marlborough thrust his arms into a clean sweatshirt, ran a comb through his thick auburn hair and wished with every fiber of his being that he was going to the Sheffields' dinner party instead of his nephew's first birthday party. Not that he didn't love his nephew – his whole family for that matter – he did. Now, though, his designer would be on her own with Adrianna, and there was no telling what she would say.

No, that wasn't true. He pulled himself back to reality. Julia Henderson was a consummate professional. He would say that much for her. Over and over, she had amazed him with the depth of her knowledge. Her passion for historic design was as strong as his for the architecture that had originally housed it, and he could only describe her ability to pull a room together as extraordinary.

Still, there was something about her that irritated him, even as he liked her as a person – had done ever since her family had moved into the house next door and he had become best friends with her older brother in the third grade. Maybe he should've made some sort of excuse when Wayne had asked him to hire his kid sister as a favor only seconds after he had mentioned his business had grown to the point that soon he would need to bring on a designer.

No, that was ridiculous. He once again argued with himself. Julia had satisfied every client she had worked with, and it would've been stupid for him to have denied his firm her talent, merely because of his feeling a minor sense of irritation in her presence. Maybe, if he took a step back, he could figure out what was causing it and resolve whatever it was in such a way as to make their working relationship flow more smoothly in the long run.

Resolutely, he picked up the large gift bag that contained the set of multi-sized, colored building blocks he had bought for his nephew and headed on his way, feeling better now that he had a plan in place for addressing his issues with his designer going forward.

Unaware of her employer's thoughts, Julia Henderson took a last look in her vanity mirror before setting out for Montgomery House. Pete hadn't needed to remind her that the stakes were high on this newest project, but that was his way, always looking over her shoulder as if he couldn't quite trust her abilities. Part of her was relieved that he had declined the invitation, while part of her wished he was going to be there this evening.

She straightened her shoulders in an effort to shore up her confidence, even as she remembered the way Pete had made it a point to tell her at the end of the previous day that he knew he could count on her. Something in his expression had reminded her of that long ago summer evening before she had started in middle school, the one when he had chosen her over Steve McKinney for his team during a backyard game of kickball – an act of unselfish kindness on his part, because both of them had known at the time that it meant his team would lose.

Still, he hadn't forced her to endure being the last one chosen yet again – the only girl on a street whose homes were filled with nothing but boys. Sometimes, she wondered how much her career path had been driven by the hours she had spent listening patiently to his explaining first this and then that type of architecture as they had sat in a group of kids on someone's front porch. Pointing out to her various examples in the homes along Chestnut, he had gone beyond their exteriors, bringing their past alive by making up stories about members of previous generations' lives, and she had hung on his every word.

A quick glance at the small crystal clock on the vanity confirmed that she needed to get moving, and Julia headed to her bedroom where she tied a fringed, olive green shawl over her cream sweater, setting off her blunt-cut, chestnut hair and her amber eyes. Gold ball earrings and a carefully placed pin completed her look to her own satisfaction. If clothes made the man, she thought, then such an outfit as she had chosen for this evening's dinner would hopefully make her appear as a successful professional woman.

The bad news was that Pete would be absent. The good news was that Adrianna and Chase were genuinely nice people.

Edwina Foster fastened the clasp of a cloisonné pin on the collar of her powder blue blouse and then stepped back so as to get a full view of herself in her cheval mirror. Yes, she thought, she would do. She glanced at her platinum dress watch, confirmed that Arthur would be knocking on her door at any moment and slipped into a gray cashmere sweater that Ginny had gifted to her on Saturday. How talented her grandson's wife was!

Unwittingly confirming Edwina's estimate of his time of arrival, Arthur disembarked from his Buick and headed towards the Montgomery dependency's door, a small bouquet of white roses in his hand and a plan in his heart. Tonight, he reaffirmed to himself, he was taking Edwina's and his relationship to a new level, but then his shoulders sagged. If only, she didn't kill him for doing so!

In the two bedroom duplex that had been hers alone since her husband had been killed by a drunk driver, Bev Lockhart slid the wand of a soft-colored gloss along her lips and attempted a smile. Not that she didn't appreciate an invitation to go out, she told herself, she did as long as she wasn't the only single female to Jim Laidlaw's single male presence.

In the three bedroom ranch in which he had been raised, Jim hurriedly splashed on some spicy aftershave, ran his fingers through his damp hair and shrugged himself into a thick, cream-colored, Irish-knit sweater. Bev would probably be at the dinner tonight.

The last time he had seen her socially had been at the Animal Shelter's charity event, at which he had won her box lunch for a bid of five hundred dollars thanks to Jack Jefferson's intervention. Afterwards, Jack and Susan had asked Bev and him to join them, thereby avoiding an hour of awkward moments for which he had been grateful.

Such an overt attack was not the way to successfully approach his matrimonial target. He knew that for a certainty after all of these years. Hopefully, there would be at least one other single female at tonight's dinner, someone he could engage in conversation, thus giving Bev a bit more of the space she still needed. The tortoise, he reminded himself, had won the race over the hare.

In the renovated caretaker's cottage on the other side of Montgomery House's former carriage house, Paul Lynch ran his used hand towel around the bathroom sink, tossed it into a plastic laundry hamper and reached beneath the vanity for a clean one. Adrianna had asked him to keep an eye on Jack's sister's enjoyment during the evening, and he had agreed, glad to do so.

He had appreciated Kate Sinclair's company, the few minutes he had spent with her at Jack and Susan's rehearsal dinner, and he was looking forward to getting to know her better. Renting the cottage, when it had become available, had been one of his best moves when he was newly arrived in Captain's Point, providing him some welcome opportunities for social interactions with nice people in the community.

In his oversized apartment over The Cove's former carriage house, Larry's thoughts wandered back to the previous evening as he reached for his keys. "Are you going to tell them who you've been with?" he had asked Kate when he had held her car door open for her.

"I don't think so." She had sent him a grin. "A woman should always keep an air of mystery about her."

Well, one thing was for sure as far as he was concerned. Tonight, he would be openly taking up most of her time. Kate Sinclair was intelligent, attractive and, most of all, fun, and then there was that gentle sadness deep in her crystal blue eyes – a sadness that called to him each time he was with her, much to his surprise.

"Beautiful!" Jack said softly from where he lounged against the doorframe of his wife's dressing room. "Are you still enjoying playing house in your special girlie room?"

"Absolutely!" She beamed over her shoulder at him. "I've never felt any more feminine in my life than when I'm in these two rooms." She nodded towards the bathroom beyond with its antique, rose-painted tiles. "Would you help me with this please?" She suspended a gold chain from her fingers.

"Actually, I was hoping you would prefer to wear this." Jack pulled a signature Tiffany's box from behind his back and strode forward, flipping the lid open to reveal a pendant comprised of a single pink diamond surrounded by smaller white ones that matched her engagement ring.

"Oh, Jack! It's lovely." She returned the other necklace to her jewelry drawer, her fingers trembling as she accepted the box.

"Here, let me fasten it for you." He took the platinum chain, and she lifted her blonde waves to make his job easier. "There." He bent and kissed her still exposed neck on the sensitive spot just beneath her right ear. "Happy two week anniversary, my sweet wife."

"You're going to spoil me one way or the other, aren't you?" She sent him a smile.

"You can count on it." Briefly, the memory of the designer dress shop in Key West filled his mind, but he shoved it aside as he gathered her into his arms and kissed her, before tightening his hold. "Unfortunately, our son and my sister are waiting for us downstairs. Otherwise, I would suggest that we phone our regrets and stay here making mad passionate love in our bed."

"There are moments when I think I could be happy, just you and me in our master suite for the rest of our lives." She lifted her fingers to his cheek. "But then, we would both miss Daniel and Kate and my folks and our friends rather quickly, I would imagine."

"Possibly..." He made a good attempt at looking as if he needed to think that one through, then planted another kiss on his wife's lips before releasing her. "At least, I know for sure that I'm escorting the loveliest woman of them all to the ball."

"And I know that I'm accompanying the handsomest, most wonderful man." She took his arm.

"What's in your bag?" Kate asked downstairs as she pulled the top edge of Daniel's canvas shoulder bag towards her where she sat on one of the kitchen chairs waiting.

"My coloring book, some crayons and one of my storybooks," her new nephew replied. "I'll be the only child there, so I have to behave because it's an honor," he quoted his mother, "although I'm welcome to sit in Jack's lap and rest my head on his chest whenever I want."

"From what I've seen since I arrived for my visit, you shouldn't have any trouble behaving," she assured him, "but if you find you're concerned about your ability to do so, feel free to stick by my side for a while."

"I love you, Aunt Kate." He threw his arms around her neck.

"I love you, too, Sweetheart." She hugged him back, hoping as she did so that her brother and sister-in-law wouldn't mind too much her sticking like glue to one of them in the same way, if she felt herself getting into trouble.

In the large kitchen of Montgomery House, Adrianna, Penny and Chase worked like a precision team as they put the finishing touches on the evening's dinner, while Otis completed the set-up of a drinks area on a side counter.

"Serving buffet style was the right idea with this many people," Penny stated as she surveyed the stacked plates, napkin-wrapped cutlery and trivets that ran along the over-sized granite island.

"Thank goodness the dining room table seats fourteen," Adrianna pointed out. "I'm afraid I got a little carried away with the invitations."

"I don't know." Chase threw an arm around his wife and dropped a kiss on her forehead. "They're all nice people, and Montgomery House can certainly handle fourteen guests at a time with room to spare."

"Fifteen when you count Daniel," Adrianna reminded him. "Jack's promised to bring his booster, and I've placed one of the breakfast room chairs on my right."

"That should work fine," Otis stated as he placed the lid on a leather-wrapped ice bucket, just as a young voice called forth from the foyer. "We're here, Uncle Chase and Aunt Adrianna!"

Daniel, it seemed, had arrived with his elders in tow.

"Show time!" Chase winked at Adrianna. "Now, relax and enjoy yourself as much as our guests are going to, my queen."

CHAPTER XXIII

"I hope it's okay." Jack entered the kitchen right behind his stepson, carrying the boy's booster seat in one hand and a flat, insulated bag in the other. "My bride insisted that Daniel and I throw together one of our warm Brie appetizers to bring along with us."

"I put the dried cherries on top," Daniel announced proudly. "Jack poured the maple syrup on afterwards, and Mama sliced the Granny Smith apples to use instead of crackers."

"Sounds delicious!" Adrianna gave the little guy a quick hug. "Let's set it up right here on the end of the island, so everyone can help themselves while Penny's homemade rolls are browning."

"The maple syrup makes a marvelous addition," Susan stated from where she was rapidly arranging thin slices of apple around the lip of the shallow bowl that held the Brie.

"Am I seeing things, or has Jack been following Chase's example?" Adrianna asked her best friend as she nodded towards the diamond pendant that shone against the background of Susan's cashmere sweater.

"Hopefully, it's merely a phase that new husbands go thru," her friend confirmed her suspicions. "It's lovely, though, isn't it?"

"Not nearly as lovely as its wearer." Jack dropped a kiss on his new wife's cheek, just as the door into the kitchen garden could be heard opening through the mudroom.

"Knock, knock!" Arthur's pleasant baritone called out. "Three guests sliding in through the back way."

"I brought some of my spiced nuts for everyone to enjoy after dinner." Edwina handed a crystal bowl to Adrianna. "I've always found that most men can't resist them."

"I certainly can't." Paul Lynch eyed the warm Brie. "And this looks delicious as well."

"Help yourself." Penny added a stack of snack plates to the already laden island, quickly fanning some cocktail napkins alongside them.

"I sprinkled the cherries, and I only ate two." Daniel smiled up at the young minister. "Would you like for me to show you how to do it?"

"Bitsy certainly did a nice job with your hair," Edwina addressed Kate, who had just accepted a glass of Pinot Noir and a compliment from Otis about how much he liked her argyle-design sweater with its muted tones of blue and gray.

"Tell me I'm not the last to arrive," Larry demanded from the doorway leading into the foyer, quickly taking in the sticky condition of Daniel's fingers and scooping his young cousin up in time to save his own khaki pants from their assault. "Let's rinse off those digits of yours." He carried the little guy to the kitchen sink, sending a smile in Kate's direction that she missed.

"Heading your way with two lovely ladies in tow," Jim called from the foyer as he herded Bev and Julia, who had arrived in separate cars at the same time as himself, towards the wonderful aromas wafting from the kitchen. "You haven't let Larry wolf down all of the best bits, have you?"

"Unfair!" Larry returned Daniel's feet to the floor. "I haven't even taken a first bite."

"Well, you should." Kate handed him the small plate of Brie she had just prepared for herself and a napkin. "This is a real treat, and someone who's in as great a shape as you are can risk the calories. It won't take me but a second to serve myself another."

Penny placed three sheets of homemade rolls into the oven that was still new enough from Adrianna's original renovations to the kitchen to please her each time she used it, and Otis waited until his wife closed the door and then handed her a glass of wine to sip on before dinner.

"To our host and hostess!" Arthur lifted his glass, drawing everyone's attention at precisely the moment he chose to drape his other arm around Edwina's dainty shoulders, relieved when she didn't draw away from him, leaning briefly against him instead as she lifted her own glass.

"How have you been enjoying your stay in Captain's Point?" Paul addressed Kate in an effort to fulfill his promise to Adrianna.

"I love it here already." Her eyes shone as she lifted them to Larry's face where he stood behind and slightly to the minister's left, still reveling in the compliment he had received from her on his build. "Everyone's made me feel very welcome."

"You can thank your brother for that," Jim teased her. "He threatened us all with his black belt skills the evening of Susan's and his rehearsal dinner."

"Shame on you." Kate sent Jack a look that closely resembled one her sister-in-law had used with Daniel earlier in the day when he had run through the downstairs of Blue Wolf Manor shouting at the dogs to hurry up or they wouldn't catch the bad guy they were after.

Chase popped another Brie coated apple slice into his mouth, savored the moment and then reached for another one from the plate he was sharing with his wife, murmuring into her ear as he did so, "Everyone seems to be having a good time."

"Where did you find such a beautiful shawl?" Bev asked Julia where the two women had taken up residence near the doorway to the butler's pantry, all the unattached guys now grouped around Kate.

"I had to go all the way to Baltimore for this one," Julia admitted, "but I've since discovered that you can purchase them online." She proceeded to share the name of the high end store that carried them.

A musical ding announced that the rolls were ready, and Chase donned an oversized pair of oven mitts and began removing two large baking dishes of lasagna from the smaller double ovens that were located on the far wall.

"Hot dishes coming through," he announced as he carried them to the island and set them on the waiting trivets.

"I have the dressings." Adrianna placed several bottles near an oversized bowl of tossed salad at the same time that Penny added a huge basket of warm rolls to the assemblage.

Noting that everyone gathered were members of his church, Paul murmured to Chase, "Would you like for me to bless the food?"

"Sure," his host agreed and heads bowed as the young minister cleared his throat and drew their attention, then thanked God for the meal set before them and the hands that had prepared it.

Reluctantly, Arthur removed his arm from Edwina's shoulders once the Amen had been said all around and stepped back to join the younger men, where they had positioned themselves in a way that would allow the women to go first.

"Ladies…" Chase gestured for Bev and Julia who were closest to the salad to begin serving themselves. "You'll all find that we're set up in the dining room."

One by one, everyone filled a plate and made their way through the butler's pantry.

Larry was pleased to note that Kate's name card had been placed next to his and sent her a smile that this time she received. Pug, an ER doctor friend, had recommended that he try some over-the-counter heat patches to ease the persistent soreness in his back, and even though the bruised area now resembled a patchwork quilt beneath his sweater, the broker had found some relief. The purple area on his jaw was beginning to yellow as well. All in all, Larry thought as he took his seat next to the woman whose company he had enjoyed so much the previous evening, it looked as if he was in for another great time at Montgomery House.

Penny set two additional baskets of warm rolls on the table and then returned with a well-laden plate, quickly joining her husband midway along the side that extended from Adrianna's left and put them across from Larry and Kate.

Except for an occasional "This is delicious" or "Please pass the rolls," the room maintained a comfortable silence for a few minutes as everyone concentrated on giving the meal its due. Gradually, quiet one-on-one conversations developed between neighboring diners, and Larry turned to Kate.

"You said last evening that you had a degree in accounting," he began. "How do you plan on using it now that you've moved here?"

"I really hadn't given using it any thought," she blurted out, surprised by the question. "You'll be able to tell me more when you review my portfolio, but I don't believe I'll have to work."

"What will you do with yourself, if you don't?" Larry's eyes narrowed.

"Would you mind passing me the butter, Twinkle Toes?" Jack addressed his sister not having heard his friend's question, and Kate obliged by handing him the narrow dish.

"Twinkle Toes?" Larry's eyebrows lifted a notch.

"Aunt Kate's a dancer," Daniel advised him from his other side. "Jack put a ballerina bar in our gym just for her."

"A dancer…" Larry dropped his eyes to his plate, lifting another bite of lasagna that he no longer wanted onto his fork.

What a fool he had been. Was he completely without judgment when it came to women? First Candy and now Kate, both dancers without an ounce of sense in them.

He looked across the table to Penny and quickly engaged the comfortable, middle-aged woman he had known all of his life in conversation, completely missing the hurt look that had sprung into Kate's eyes.

"What kind of dancing do you do?" Paul Lynch asked in his gentle voice from her other side.

"Not much anymore," she admitted. "When Jack was still living at home, I had every young girl's dream of becoming a ballerina, although he soon saw to it that my musical talents, such as they were, went in quite a different direction. In college, I took a few courses in modern dance, mainly out of general interest, and I still like to use a bar to do stretches and exercises simply because I find it a good way to keep my figure after wonderful meals such as this one."

"Well, they've kept you in great shape," the young minister replied, but then the thought entered his head that this might have been too personal a comment to make to a new member of his congregation.

Ignoring Bev, who had turned her back to him once seated and engaged Chase in conversation, Jim addressed Kate, "Jack told me when I was checking out Goldie at the stable this morning that you're having some trouble finding a place to rent on your own. If you need any help with your search, let me know."

"Thanks, I will." She sent him a smile, wishing that the offer had come from Larry and not him.

For a moment, the table fell silent as everyone finished off their last bites, and then Daniel piped up, "Aunt Kate loved it when you sent her all the florist's roses." He directed his comment to his cousin Larry. "My mama said she'd never received so many at one time, and Jack said he'd certainly never sent two dozen at once to a woman in his whole life."

For the first time in his four years on the planet, the broker wished that his short cousin wasn't present, feeling the warmth of a blush, even as he watched the cheeks of the woman on his right redden. "I felt I owed your aunt something for having pulled her to the ground like I did," he sought to explain without thinking, digging the hole he now felt himself to be in even deeper.

"They were lovely, and I appreciated them," Kate murmured as she toyed with a small bite of tomato and a wedge of cucumber that remained on her plate. "It was a wonderful gesture."

Diagonally across the table, Jim opened his mouth to comment, but Larry cut him off short. "Don't even think about it, my friend," he stated in a tone that caused both Susan and Adrianna to glance up sharply.

Relieved when Penny and his hostess both stood – the latter announcing that if everyone would help by carrying their plates into the kitchen, dessert would be self-serve from the island – Larry hurried to comply, wondering as he passed through the butler's pantry, his plate in one hand and a now empty bread basket in the other, how he could ever have thought that this evening had the potential to be another great time at Montgomery House.

CHAPTER XXIV

Late the next afternoon, Larry sat poised on the edge of his bathroom's Carrera marble vanity top and applied yet another heat patch to the one remaining area on his back that still bothered him. Finished, he stood and faced the mirror he had utilized only a moment before.

"What in the world is wrong with you?" he asked his reflection, still struggling to release himself from the memory of the hurt in Kate's eyes as Jack had been herding his family through the front door of Montgomery House the previous evening.

How had he gotten so far off the beaten path? Somewhere along the way, he had allowed the devastation of Candy's rejection to eat away at his insides until it had turned him into the person he now was – a person who could cause pain to someone like Kate, who had never been anything but wonderful to him.

Now he was so far gone that he didn't even know what he had done that had hurt the woman with whom he had only intended to spend a nice evening. Not knowing the cause meant that he couldn't even begin to make it up to her, although one thing he knew for sure. He would not be sending her another two dozen roses. This was personal between them, and he needed to apologize with actions as well as words.

How was he going to face her? There wasn't even time for her hurt to dissipate before he approached her again. Jack had asked Chase, Adrianna, the Plunks and himself to join them for an informal early supper this evening, wanting to get advice from Otis about something and making himself available to Chase and Larry, since they had expressed an interest in talking.

Maybe it would be best for the women of Captain's Point going forward, if he remained a bachelor for the rest of his life. After all, if he couldn't sit beside a sweet, gentle woman like Kate for an hour without hurting her, what kind of husband would he make? As bad as it was to see hurt caused by him in a woman's eyes, how would it be to watch a wife's love for him die?

Determined, he switched off the bathroom light and returned to his walk-in closet, where he donned a white shirt, his favorite jeans and a navy blue sweater, his thoughts still churning in his head. He supposed he could pretend he was sick and beg off, thus allowing Kate space from him that she might appreciate, but then he wouldn't have the opportunity in which to determine where he'd gone wrong and possibly begin making it up to her.

Catching a glimpse of himself in the full-length mirror that hung on one wall, he straightened his shoulders and attempted to remove the reflection of his inner anger at himself that he discovered glaring forth from his face. No woman would find herself attracted to a man who appeared as off-putting as that.

Taking a moment, he attempted a grin, found it lacking and settled for a slight smile. Now, if only he could maintain this look past the first few seconds in Kate's presence. His gaze softened as he remembered how she had handed over her own appetizer plate for him to enjoy the previous evening, unselfish and caring.

Well, she deserved better than he had given, and somehow, someway he was going to make it up to her.

In the largest guest bedroom in Blue Wolf Manor, a glimpse of motion to her left caused Kate to glance up and discover her brother lounging in the doorway.

"You look nice." He sent her a proud smile. "That navy blue sweater really suits you."

"Do you think so?" she asked, for some reason less sure of herself than usual. Perhaps, it was because of the implied criticism in Larry's comments the previous evening, censorship that had escaped her understanding.

"You're a beautiful woman, Kate." Jack's face filled with concern as he crossed the room, took a seat on the bed and patted the place next to him, indicating for her to join him. "Has your marriage to what's his name damaged your self-confidence that badly?"

"Yes and no." She sat on the spot next to him and leaned her head against his upper arm, seeking the comfort from his strong presence that had always been there for her. "Being unloved for so many years certainly didn't help it, but I've gotten my head around the fact that I was set up for a false marriage all along. Nothing I could have done would've changed that. It's more what's happening now."

"I thought you were happy here with us." Jack wrapped his arm around her and held her close.

"I am," she sought to assure him. "No one could've made me feel any more loved and welcomed than Susan, Daniel and you have. I feel like I'm part of a family for the first time in years."

"I can understand," Jack shared. "It's the same way for me. Being with Susan and Daniel day in and day out is magical."

"But this is your future, your family, and I can't and shouldn't stay here forever," Kate explained. "Maybe I hoped for too much too soon from Captain's Point or maybe it's me, but I feel like I'm butting my head against a brick wall, whenever I leave your comfortable home and find myself in mixed company. I'm never sure that I'm doing or saying the right things. What mattered to me when I was younger doesn't do so now. I've rejected the road I had chosen, and I can't find any signs that say

Future. The one path I had taken a few steps along now appears to be a dead end. Part of me is frustrated, and part of me is scared."

"You know that Susie and I are both here for you, don't you?" her brother asked. "Anytime, anyway that we can be of help to you, let us know."

"You've always been there for me, and Susan's made it clear from day one that she understands better than most the position in which I now find myself," Kate reassured him. "I can't imagine how hard it must've been to move on from her marriage with Daniel in tow. Then again, I see his sweet face, and I understand how looking at him would've also given her a reason and the courage to put one foot in front of the other."

"And in the end, they both found me," Jack pointed out, "and now all three of us are the better for her choice."

"Life's hard, though, isn't it?" Kate asked. "Life in the real world is full of possibilities, but it also has its share of pitfalls. I don't want to end up in the wrong place again. How did you reach the point where you were comfortable that you were on the right path?"

"The same way that you're going to have to, I'm afraid." Her brother tightened his hold. "Through the School of Hard Knocks. You're going to make mistakes, Kate. It's part of the growth process, and all you can do is learn from them, brush yourself off and move on. Keep your eyes open and watch – really watch – how those you admire live their lives, the choices they make, and their approaches to Life's challenges."

"Daddy?" Daniel could be heard running up the stairs.

"In here, Son," Jack called.

"Mama wants to know if there's anything she should do to get the hamburgers and hot dogs ready for you to grill." Daniel stood in the doorway, catching his breath with Casey and Lady panting behind him.

"Tell her I'll be right down to take care of them," his stepfather advised him.

"You two better hurry up, or you'll miss the party," Daniel threw over his shoulder, his footsteps now heard by them as he ran along the broad hallway.

"Where does he find all that energy this late in the day?" Kate asked as an aside.

"I don't know, but we'd better get down there." Jack released her, stood and led the way as they followed the little guy downstairs and headed straight for the kitchen just as the doorbell rang. "Can you answer that?" he asked.

"Sure." She switched gears, now left alone in the foyer, but then she paused. Taking a deep breath, she gathered her strength, added a smile to her face and stepped forward, the single outline against the cranberry glass clearly stating that it was Larry who awaited her on the other side of the door.

CHAPTER XXV

"I see you received the navy blue sweater memo, too." Kate's smile brightened as she unlocked the front door and opened it to their first guest. "Did you forget your key?"

For a moment, she wondered if this greeting, too, had been somehow wrong, as Larry sucked in his breath, his eyes taking her in from head to toe.

"You look stunning!" He finally forced the words past his throat, his eyes once again moving from the blonde curls she had pulled up and back from her temples, along the form-fitting, cowl-necked cashmere sweater draped at her waist with a gold chain belt, to the navy and gray tweed pants that completed the picture before him.

"You don't look so bad yourself," she replied, feeling suddenly shy as she strove to lighten the moment. "Is that for me?" She indicated a small brown paper bag he held somewhat extended towards her in his hand.

"Not unless your name's Susan, I'm afraid." With an effort, he pulled his eyes from her slim waist and again faced her. "My cousin called and asked me to bring a jar of my aunt's homemade bread and butter pickles along with me."

"I've been looking forward to those." Kate took a step back, realizing he was still standing on the porch. "Jack's been carrying on about them ever since I arrived."

"I don't think you'll be disappointed." Larry entered the foyer, but then paused before heading to the kitchen in such a way as to block her from closing the door. "I want you to know that I'm really glad you've joined us here in

Captain's Point," he blurted out as he suddenly found it difficult not to lift her chin with his finger and kiss her. "I don't believe you'll be disappointed with those who live here over the long term."

"Everyone that I've met so far has been wonderful." She sent him a smile, even as she was aware of the heat emanating from his body as he stood so near, the scent of his high end aftershave that now filled her dreams wafting towards her.

"I guess I'd better get these to the kitchen." He shifted the bag slightly, but made no sign of moving.

"Susan and Jack are probably waiting for you to join them." She couldn't take her eyes away from him.

"Cousin Larry!" Daniel ran through the doorway from the breakfast room, breaking the spell. "Mama made an extra large bowl of potato salad because she knows it's your favorite."

"I'll have to remember to say thank you then, won't I?" Larry sent Kate a wink and lifted the little guy onto his own hip. "What have you and your furry friends been up to today?" He nodded towards Casey and Lady as he headed with his short cousin towards the kitchen.

"We ate breakfast and, after church, we colored in my book and we helped Mama peel the boiled eggs and...," Daniel proceeded to list the major activities from his day as Kate followed along behind, having left the door unlocked for the Sheffields who had just turned into the drive, wondering how she had ever doubted that Larry liked her.

"Did you forget the code?" Susan asked as she took the pickles from her cousin.

"No, I accidentally left my keys at your mom's when I stopped by for these before I walked over here," he explained.

"Montgomery House contingent has arrived," Chase called from the foyer. "Heading towards the kitchen from which wonderful aromas are emitting."

"We brought you some homemade applesauce." Otis set two quart jars on the counter. "This one is plain, and this one has cinnamon. They're for you all, not for tonight. We've been eating the stuff all day."

"No one was forcing you to," Penny stated. "In fact, I distinctly remember Adrianna telling both Chase and you to get out of the kitchen if you couldn't stop tasting."

"Guilty as charged," Chase admitted, "but at least, I can claim that I've been starved for good old-fashioned home cooking for a long time."

"That's right, leave me to take the heat all by myself," Otis complained, even as he sampled one of the bread and butter pickles that Susan had just added to a large divided tray of appetizers.

"If you guys want to join me outside, we can get these started." Jack hoisted a cookie sheet layered with hand-pressed burgers, Italian sausages and hot dogs high enough to pass it over his wife's head. "Grab a beer or a soda from the fridge in the mudroom on your way by, if you want one. Son, why don't you stick with us guys? You can throw the Frisbee for Casey and Lady and give them a few minutes of exercise."

"I'll bring it out to you." Kate bent down and whispered into Daniel's ear.

A minute later, she made her way down the steps to the outdoor kitchen, Daniel's knit jacket and hood in one hand and the Frisbee in the other. "Your mom thought you should put this on now that the sun's beginning to set," she explained as she zipped him up and handed him the orange plastic disk.

"What is it about sunsets here in Captain's Point that makes them so beautiful?" Kate asked as she paused beside Larry.

"I'm not sure they're any different than anywhere else," he replied. "It may only be that we notice them more due to our slower pace of life."

"If that's true, then it's yet another reason why I made the right choice when I decided to come here." She breathed in the scents of pine and salt air that her sister-in-law had shared earlier in the day always signified to her that she was home.

"I think I'll see if Susan can use any help," Larry stated, taking a step towards the mudroom entrance, but Kate quickly reached out a hand and stopped him.

"No," she said, her eyes averted. "I'll do it. You stay here with the men."

Now what had he done? Larry dug his hands into his jeans' pockets. He had helped his aunt, Susan and Courtney with heavy lifting in the kitchen for years. Surely Kate hadn't thought he had meant that she should go in his place, or had she? Was she that sensitive? Maybe the fault for the hurt look in her eyes the previous evening hadn't been all his.

At the eastern edge of the spotlight lit lawn, Daniel pulled back his arm before thrusting it forward, and the conflicted broker watched for a moment as the orange Frisbee lifted into the air before he stepped closer to the grill, where the other men were gathered.

A minute later, Jack slammed the grill's lid down, dropped the spatula he had been holding onto the granite countertop, and began running at breakneck speed towards the pine woods shouting, "Daniel! Daniel!"

Chase and Larry exchanged quick glances and immediately surged after him, not knowing what was wrong, but understanding intuitively that there was power in numbers.

Left by himself, Otis retrieved the spatula and checked on the grilling meat, certain of only one thing as the younger men disappeared into the woods. There was no longer any sign of either Daniel or his small pack of dogs on the lawn, the abandoned orange Frisbee lying in the grass near the entrance to the path that led through the woods to Chesterton Farm the only sign the boy had ever been there.

CHAPTER XXVI

Jack slowed as he entered the pine woods, his footsteps muffled by the needles covering the path beneath him, then paused as he neared a bend and signaled for Chase and Larry to be quiet behind him.

"You shouldn't have done that." Daniel's childish voice came clearly from around the corner, accompanied by a deep rumbling.

Was Lady growling? Jack wondered with amazement, never having heard the dog growl.

"My daddy and I don't want pictures of my mama taken and put out there for everyone and their uncle to see," Daniel quoted Jack's words to whomever he was addressing.

Was his son speaking to one person or a group? Jack shifted his weight forward, took a silent step and shifted his weight again until the small group came into view.

"Give me the camera," Daniel insisted as he extended his hand and Lady's growl deepened.

Quickly, Jack took in the fact that there was only one young man cowering before Daniel and his pack and that Casey's hair was raised clear along his spine and onto his tail as he stood with his short owner's hand on his neck. Placing his own hand behind his back and holding up a single finger to let Chase and Larry know what they were facing, he strode forward.

"So, what do we have here, Son?" He took a position behind the little guy. "Lady, sit!"

The German Shepherd immediately complied, but her growl continued as Casey followed suit, settling into position in such a way that his oversized body blocked the stranger's access to his small owner.

"This man took our picture, and I knew you didn't want that," Daniel announced, his left hand now on his hip, his right hand still extended. "I told you to give me your camera."

"You can have the camera," the photographer's youthful tenor quavered, "but this is my first time to use it, I spent everything I had on it, and I don't want to drop it. Frankly, I'm afraid to hold it out to you." His eyes remained locked onto Lady, who was occasionally raising her top lip slightly on one side, revealing a couple of sharp canines as an adjunct to her deep-throated warning, just in case the intruder wasn't getting her message.

"Come!" Jack spoke the single word, and Lady took up a position by his right knee, her opinion silenced by her master's hand on her head.

"Give me the camera." Daniel repeated firmly, and this time the photographer complied.

"Can I have it back?" The young man addressed Jack, a pleading look in his eyes. "I don't even have an assignment. I just took a chance after I read in the *Washington Post* that you lived here in Captain's Point. I thought if I sold a couple of freelance shots it might open a door for me."

"That depends," Jack replied. "Now, Daniel will be careful with it, while I make a phone call. The Shepherd's never hurt anyone, but I'm not offering guarantees. I'm duty bound to let you know that I'm a certified black belt and my skills are up to date. One of the two gentlemen behind me holds several state wrestling and track records, and the other one, while equally honored athletically, would kill you with his bare hands if you harmed even one hair on this boy's head. Do I make myself clear?"

"Yes, sir," the photographer almost whispered his reply as his eyes widened. "All I wanted was a couple of photos. The boy came after me. I didn't drag him in here."

"That's a point in both of your favors." Jack pulled his phone from his jeans' pocket and selected a number on speed dial. "Chuck? Jack Jefferson here. I'm sorry to bother your family and you on a Sunday evening, but my son, two of my neighbors and myself have cornered an intruder on my property despite the No Trespassing signs you and I posted earlier this week."

In front of them, the young man's shoulders sagged.

"A single car, no siren, no flashing lights, one deputy should be enough," Jack continued. "You can probably guess which two neighbors are with me. ... Five minutes will be fine. We'll be waiting in front of the house. Oh, and Chuck, thanks for the personal touch here."

The photographer emitted a low groan, as he whispered under his breath, "My dad's going to kill me, and my mom will be so embarrassed."

"You shouldn't upset your parents," Daniel offered a bit of advice. "Parents are your best asset."

Larry found it hard to keep the sides of his mouth from twitching as he recalled the moment when he had said the words that his short cousin was now quoting.

"Daniel, I'll take the camera now." Jack returned his cell phone to his pocket and held out his hand. "Could I ask you to go back to the house with Casey and Lady, and would you please request that Mr. Otis stays in the kitchen with the ladies and you until we men come back inside? I know they'll be safer with the dogs and the two of you to protect them."

"Will you be okay without Lady?" Daniel asked.

"I think the three of us will be fine, now that you've collared our trespasser for us." Jack gave the little guy's shoulder a gentle squeeze. "Don't forget to pick up the Frisbee on the way in."

"Casey and Lady, heel!" Daniel slipped past the men and headed along the needle-strewn path towards the rambling Victorian, a dog on either side, his small shoulders straightened, his head held high.

"We'll give him a moment, and then I think, Chase, I'd like you to go first, this gentleman can go second with me by his side, and Larry can bring up our rear, if you don't mind."

"Sounds like a plan," Chase agreed, his dark blue eyes locked on their youthful visitor, until Jack indicated for him to go ahead.

Slowly, the group made their way across the wide expanse of lawn, just as Chuck Ward steered his car onto the driveway of Blue Wolf Manor.

"Evening, gentlemen." The burly sheriff disembarked from his clearly marked vehicle. "I see you have things under control." He opened the door to the cage-enclosed back seat. "My better half took the kids to a movie, so I decided to take this call on my own. One of the deputies can deal with him once we reach the station." He gestured for the photographer to get in and closed the door behind him before turning and raising an eyebrow to the waiting men.

"Thanks for coming so quickly." Chase held out his hand, shook the sheriff's, and then excused himself so that he could assure Adrianna he was okay.

"Same here, Chuck." Larry slapped his old friend on the shoulder. "We always have been able to count on you to come through in a pinch. I'll calm any fears Susan may have until you come in," Larry addressed his host and then left them as well.

Gesturing to the sheriff, Jack walked with him a few feet along the drive. "This is the camera he was carrying." He handed it over. "I'm sure he's left some sort of transportation nearby – a car, motorcycle or something. You might want to make sure that whatever he has with him is retrieved. I'll cover the costs. He's just a kid really. Make sure that any pictures he's taken of my family, the house or me are deleted and then give him the camera back with a warning. Send me his full name, address and phone numbers, if you will. We've probably scared him to death, but he has initiative, he's been polite, and he did no real harm, except for the photos. I'm going to contact a friend of mine in D.C., if our friend cooperates with you, and see if I can get him a shot at some sort of starter position that will keep him out of such situations in the future."

"Not sure I'd be that generous to him myself," the sheriff stated.

"Let's just say that I'm paying things forward." Jack turned back towards the house, indicating the matter was closed. "I'll get in touch with you tomorrow." He held out his hand. "Thanks again for being on call."

"Not a problem." Ward shook the offered hand and then opened his vehicle's door, not surprised when the author waited behind them on the driveway until they cleared his property.

Meanwhile, in the home's kitchen, worry and relief had vied for position.

First, Otis had appeared with news of what was happening outside, soon persuading the women to stay put and let the younger men handle whatever was going on.

Next, Daniel, Casey and Lady had arrived, much to everyone's relief - the former full of what came across as a tall tale, both dogs panting in their excitement as they sported what could only be described as huge grins.

"Everything's okay," Chase sought to reassure them, when he made his entrance, quickly passing an arm around Adrianna and drawing her to him. "Just a young kid trying to snap some shots of our boy here with a new camera, but Daniel soon put him straight."

"Way to go, Cuz." As he entered the room, Larry exchanged a high five with his short cousin, who sent him a grin in return.

"I must say you have your animals well-trained." Chase put his hand on the boy's shoulder that immediately straightened further. "I'm impressed with the way you three work as a team."

"Are you okay?" Kate asked Larry, her back to the room, her voice soft. "Otis said the three of you went tearing across the lawn after Daniel."

"At least, this time I managed to keep myself from falling backwards onto the ground like a fool." Larry smiled down at her. "Daniel had everything under control by the time we got there, and Jack had arranged beforehand for the sheriff to be on call in case something like this cropped up. It didn't hurt either that your brother noticed something was wrong only a few of seconds after I had seen that everything was alright."

"Still, I'm glad it's over and that you're fine." She shifted more to his side, even as she lifted her worried eyes to his, and reflexively he threw an arm around her shoulders and gave her a quick squeeze.

"Where's my buddy?" Their host's broad-shouldered frame filled the doorway to the mudroom.

"I'm here, Jack!" In his excitement, Daniel flung himself at his stepfather, who waylaid his trajectory, hoisting the child off the ground in defense of his own knees, only to receive an almost throat-choking hug around his neck.

"Son, I'll never be more proud of you, if I live to be two hundred." Jack sent a relieved look to his wife, even as he returned his stepson's embrace. "You did a great job out there of supporting the side."

"That was easy to do," Daniel stated calmly as he released his tight grip, a serious expression now taking up residence on his small face. "Casey and Lady were right beside me, helping me out, and I knew Uncle Chase, Cousin Larry, Mr. Otis and you were all watching my back."

At which every woman in the room blinked back tears, and all of the men averted their eyes.

CHAPTER XXVII

Susan rinsed the soap from her face, patted it dry and met her own worried eyes in her vanity mirror. What in the world was wrong with Jack?

Once Daniel had finished eating his dinner, her husband had risen from his chair at the other end of the table, retrieved their son and set him on his lap. Two minutes later, Adrianna had pointed out that Jack's chest had once again done the trick. He had excused himself and taken the now sleeping Daniel upstairs to put him in bed, while she had suggested the rest of them should adjourn to the large parlor, thinking her husband might entertain their guests with some music once he returned.

Instead, he had dropped into the large armchair just inside the room's doorway, where he had grown quieter and quieter as the evening had progressed, his wonderful energy seeming to have somehow imploded inside of him. Perhaps, he had outdone himself when he had run so fast towards the woods, beating both Chase and Larry there despite their being five years his junior, much to the two retired track stars' chagrin. Then again, maybe he had caught some kind of bug and hadn't wanted to complain in front of their guests.

Quickly running a comb through her hair, she hurried through her dressing room, but then carefully turned the doorknob, so as not to disturb her husband if he should have already fallen asleep. This effort on her part, she soon discovered to have been a complete waste of time as he wasn't even stretched out on their bed, and it took her a moment to locate him where he was seated on the couch at the other end of the room – elbows on his knees and his head in his hands.

"Why are you sitting here like this?" she asked softly as she sat next to him, surprised when his head jerked up as if he hadn't even been aware of her approach.

"I thought it would be best, until..." His face filled with anguish. "You have to understand, Susie, that I don't know how to do this. I'm totally out of my element."

"Do what?" she asked, completely confused.

"Whatever it is that you'll want me to do when you're angry," he explained. "I've never seen you angry before, so I don't know what to expect. I figured you might want me to sleep on the couch, so I plopped down here, but then again, you may prefer to have it out in the form of some sort of argument."

"Whoa!" She held her hands up, her face reflecting her honest surprise. "Let's step back a minute. What did I do that gave you the impression I was angry?"

"It's not about anything you did," he answered. "It's about what I didn't do, and you're too much of a lady to have given any hint about how you felt while our guests were here. Still, now that they're gone, you have every right to feel the way that you do, and I'm prepared to accept whatever's coming as no more than my due."

"Jack, Honey, I have no idea what you're talking about." She took his strong hand in her slim ones. "Now why don't you start over?"

"Are you telling me that you're not angry with me about the photographer?" His face filled with the same hope that had shone forth from Daniel's months before when she had announced her son wouldn't be punished for breaking a rather ugly vase quite by accident.

"Of course, not," she stated firmly. "Why would I be? At least, you had made arrangements in case something like that happened. Larry said you had Chuck Ward's personal cell number on speed dial and had already spoken to him about our possibly needing his assistance, while I had buried my head in the sand and hoped your concerns were unfounded here in Captain's Point."

"Unfortunately, there are a few crazies everywhere," Jack stated. "I've even had them try to get into my house, which is why I had an alarm system installed here. Two summers ago, one of the teenaged girls in the tour group I was leading on an excursion out West actually stripped herself naked and stretched out on the couch in my cabin to await me."

"That must've surprised you." Susan worked hard to suppress a smile.

"It would've," he agreed, "and more to the point, it might have proved costly, once I'd spurned her advances. Luckily, I had promised one of the female guides the use of an extra topographical map I had in my pack, and I gestured for her to enter the cabin first. She took one look and stood still in the doorway, telling me to sit on the steps behind us for a moment."

"I'm glad she was there for you," Susan said, "but I still don't understand why you thought I would be angry at you over something you didn't cause and couldn't help, especially when you responded so quickly. Larry said it hadn't been more than seconds after Daniel threw the Frisbee for Lady that you shouted out his name and went running towards the woods, so you hadn't been negligent in watching out for him."

"But I hadn't kept you two and Kate out of harm's way either," Jack made his point clearer. "What you must think of me. I failed all three of you today, and if you're sweet enough not to be angry at me that's okay, because I'm angry enough at myself for the both of us."

"Then I will tell you what I think," she said, as she curled up next to him and rested her head on his shoulder while still maintaining a hold on his hand, understanding his need to know. "I look at you, and I see the man who cared enough to take my child and me both under his wing, who prepared for what appears to have been the inevitable, and who rushed to the aid of our son when he needed you – not, I might point out, for the first time. Let's not forget your having flown a helicopter along a cliff, so that Chase could pull Daniel off a ledge, turning both of you two wonderful men into world-class heroes."

"You're never going to let me live that one down, are you?" Jack sent her a crooked smile.

"Never," she maintained, "and let me add that I see the man Daniel ran to and hugged, the man who said exactly the right words to leave our child confident in his abilities as opposed to scared of what might await him going forward, the father who had already given our son the tools that he needed to get him through the experience."

"I wish you could've seen the little guy on the attack, demanding that the fellow turn over his camera because we didn't want stray pictures of you getting about," her husband said, pride sounding in his voice. "There he was, standing as tall as a four-year-old boy can - Lady baring her teeth and growling on one side of him and Casey's hair standing up all the way along his back to his tail on the other side. It was amazing!"

"I'm assuming you don't think this will be our only incident." Susan let out a small sigh.

"Probably not," he admitted. "Marrying me may not have been the best move you ever made, Susie."

"Now that I won't have," his wife straightened, her voice firm. "Don't ever say that again, or you will see me angry. You're the best thing that's happened to Daniel and me or ever will, and I won't stand by and let you take the blame for some idiot's inappropriate actions, just because you're talented enough and worked hard enough to become famous. If there wasn't a market for the periodicals that are full of such stories and pictures as these folks are after, none of this today would've happened."

"Still, we need to sit down tomorrow and have a serious discussion about how we're going to protect ourselves and, especially, Daniel going forward." Jack held her gaze.

"We don't need to discuss anything," Susan stated. "I have perfect faith in your superior ability to put together some sort of viable plan to maintain our privacy as much as possible. You have previous experience with this sort of thing, and I don't. Besides, you're much better at getting things done than I am. If you want my opinion of what you come up with or my help in deciding between two options, I'll give it, but I'm perfectly willing to leave Daniel and myself in your capable hands."

"Thanks for believing in me despite what happened today," Jack said. "Most women would've sent me packing or at least confined me to sleeping here on the sofa." He bent his lips to hers.

"Most women are fools then." She nestled against him once they separated, before exhibiting her own practical side. "Besides, I'm not sure this couch is long enough for you to stretch out on, even if I did feel like relegating you to it."

At which, they both shared a laugh before he hugged her to him even tighter.

CHAPTER XXVIII

Jack lay on his stomach breathing in his Susie's sweet scent from her pillow as she made her nightly trip and then returned to his side, prepared to take her once again in his arms as she lifted the covers to rejoin him. This time, though, she surprised him. Instead of snuggling against his body and nuzzling her head into his shoulder, she continued her arms around his neck and clung to him.

"What's brought this on, Baby?" he asked as he tightened his hold.

"A dream – a nightmare really – a will-o'-the-wisp that's now gone, but left a bad taste behind."

"I'm here with you," he whispered into her ear, "and Daniel's right along the hall all snug in his bed in our big, happy house as he would say. Even Kate's tucked in for the night." His lips brushed her temple.

"Promise me that you'll never tire of Daniel or me and throw us away," she begged, and he responded reflexively, rolling her onto her back and throwing his right leg over hers, so that he could look down at her beautiful eyes in the semi-darkness, even as he wished he could remove her longstanding pain that led to the pleading look he found there.

"I recall promising to love you in good times and bad until death do us part," he stated, his voice having taken on a throaty quality. "Let's see if this will help you believe way down deep in your heart that I'm in this forever."

Then he brought his lips down to hers and kissed her long and hard in a way that spoke of his naked desire, quickly igniting hers for him as well into the bargain. And as he brought their lovemaking to its final triumphant close sometime later, he clearly stated, "I love you, Susie Chesterton, and I claim you as mine for all time."

For a few minutes, they lay still, each catching their breath, their fingers entwined where he had held her hands against the pillows. But then, to her pleasure, he released her and cupped her face in his hands, touching her lips lightly before kissing her forehead, her eyelids, and the tip of her nose.

"I love you. I love you. I love you," he whispered repetitively, once for each new place his lips brushed on her body, as he aroused her desires yet again, this time showing her clearly the depths of his emotions as he made love to her so sweetly that only her arousal kept her from crying at the sheer beauty of the moments he was creating for them.

Later, as he gathered her once again into his arms for sleep, he whispered against her temple, "No other man will ever have a chance to know you and hold you in these ways, Susie Chesterton, not as long as there's a breath left within me. You have my oath on that, here and now."

"Thank you." She snuggled against him, her heart filled with gratitude for this man and the way that he loved her as she let out a contented sigh and nuzzled her head against his shoulder as was her habit. "I love you, Jack Jefferson, and I will as long as there is even one breath left within me."

"You'd better, woman." He chuckled as he tightened his hold. "Although, truth be told, I wouldn't mind proving myself to you yet again."

The alarm signaling it was Susan's first day back to work woke them both too early the next morning, and as his wife struggled to open her eyes, Jack's hand found the soft skin of her stomach, immediately bringing forth yet again his desire for her. Reaching around and drawing her closer, he brushed her lips with his, kicking his need up another notch, even as he wondered why he was doing this to himself.

How could his Susie not know how much he loved her, when a cold strike of water first thing in the shower had become a necessity for him ever since the first morning after their wedding? Not that she wasn't available, she was, giving herself up to their lovemaking eagerly, but there were limits to what he would ask of her.

Unaware of his thoughts, Susan chose this moment to mold her body to his, for the first time becoming aware of his need for her to which she responded in kind. With a moan, Jack rolled her onto her back, but then raised his head and asked, "Won't you be late?"

"I don't care." She drew his face to hers. "You're number one in my world, and we're still on our lifetime honeymoon, remember?"

A while later, he whispered into her hair. "I love you so much, Susie. How am I going to let you leave me and return to the real world after that?"

"You could go back to sleep," she suggested.

"Not when you have my hormones raging like they are now," he chuckled. "I haven't felt this much need since I was seventeen."

"Perhaps, you should share." She rolled them onto their sides and kissed him greedily, refusing to even acknowledge his attempt to pull apart and remind her of the time as her hand found his waist and then made its way up his broad chest, a maneuver that rocketed him further along their path to a successful completion.

"I feel very wanton." She chuckled in his arms, once they lay together twice satisfied.

"I've always believed that wantonness had its place." He grinned back at her. "Now, though, you'd best be getting started, or Chase Sheffield will be wanting my guts for garters."

Taking his advice, she reluctantly headed to the shower, surprised when she returned to their bedside before she had finished dressing to find not the morning coffee she had expected, but Jack still lying as she had left him.

"Are you okay?" She sat on the edge of the bed and ran the back of her fingers along his cheek.

"I may be getting old." He half-opened his eyes. "These two rounds this morning have brought me to my knees."

"I'm not surprised." A smile graced her face as a sense of awe filled her, the power she had over him in this one area now clear to her for the first time. "Do you realize how many times you've satisfied my unreasonably demanding desires in the past twenty-four hours? If I were you, I'd be thrilled my wife was leaving for work, if for no other reason than it would provide an opportunity to replenish my strength."

"I'm not thrilled you're leaving, but I do need sleep." He squeezed her hand briefly and once again closed his eyes as she stood and headed for her dressing room, returning a few minutes later to find him rolled onto his right side, sound asleep with her pillow clutched in his arms like an oversized, out of shape teddy bear, his face nestled against it in such a way as to enable him to breathe in her scent.

Rounding the bed, she brought her fingertip to her lips and placed it against his cheek, even as she realized seeing him this way had shown her as nothing else had that this kind, gentle man would never tire of her unless she herself did something terribly wrong to him. How would she ever be able to leave the house knowing the depth of his love and his need for her as she now did?

Not wanting their son to disturb her husband's rest, she softly made her way along the hall to Daniel's bedroom, surprised to find his bed still mussed, but nonetheless empty, Casey and Lady both curled in sleep on their own oversized dog bed where it lay in front of the hearth. Tiptoeing across the hall, she peeked into the guestroom where she discovered two blond heads together on her sister-in-law's pillow, Kate's arms wrapped around Daniel.

Making her way along the hall and down the stairs, she picked up her purse and keys in the foyer and then headed to the home's connected garage, her steps lightened by the knowledge that, at least for a while, those she loved more than life itself wouldn't miss her as she pursued the career that enriched her.

CHAPTER XXIX

In his dream, Chase was stretched out on the beach behind their Cape Cod house, Adrianna beside him, the fingers of their hands intertwined. Boats floated past, their white sails unfurled, and gulls called to one another overhead. Although he couldn't make out precisely which boat it was, he somehow knew that his deceased cousin Jack was steering one of them – happy and free.

Then, everything shifted, and he realized he was lying in the tower suite's half-tester bed, his eyes closed and his wife in his arms. Breathing in the scent of her hair, he floated in a state of semi-consciousness, content to remain as he was since his first appointment at the firm was scheduled for eleven.

Max let out another subdued woof in his oval bed on the hearth, and his owner realized that this must have been what had disturbed his sleep, the dog probably reliving in his own doggy dream a squirrel chase he had pursued the previous evening in the walled kitchen garden.

Slowly, Chase's mind reviewed the weekend that was now in the past, as always much shorter than he would've wished, glad that Adrianna enjoyed entertaining in their home as much as he did. Although why she had worried about fifteen being too large a number, he didn't know. Montgomery House could certainly manage more.

For a minute, he remembered the effect Daniel's words had had on his older male cousin, Larry's face flushing with embarrassment as Kate had glanced quickly at his friend, concern clearly written on her face. Fresh from her successful bringing together of Susan and Jack as a couple, Adrianna, of course, was sure the two of them were now an item, although he wasn't so sure. A complimentary comment made by himself to his friend later in the evening about Jack's sister had only received a curt nod from Larry in return, and once the meal had ended Kate had divided her time between Jim, Paul and the other women.

Arthur and Edwina now, his wife could claim victory there. Who knew that quiet, elegant Arthur had it in him to pursue Edwina? And the older woman hadn't seemed to mind when the artist had held her hand most of the evening. Well, more power to them.

Both Larry and he had let Jack know that they had something they wanted to discuss with him. Count on Jack to immediately ask them all for dinner at his place. It was exactly this open, friendly aspect of the author's nature that made him a perfect pick for the soon-to-be vacated ad hoc city councilman position. Jack had seemed interested before the paparazzi had shown up at his door. Hopefully, the episode with the photographer wouldn't adversely affect his willingness to run for office.

Thank goodness Julia and Adrianna had seemed to get along well. Pete Marlborough had done a marvelous job renovating Sheffield Place and turning it into the inn it now was, but he would not have forced Adrianna to work with a designer she didn't like. Part of him couldn't wait for them to get started on the upgrades to Montgomery House, and part of him wasn't looking forward to the mess.

Otis had agreed with his ideas for the third floor and had promised to organize the installation of a home elevator for them, while Penny had thanked him again for his suggestion that they install a skylight over the kitchen island during the initial work that Adrianna had done to the house. His wife had been right about the Plunks, too. They were so much more than employees. They were family.

How lucky he was that Adrianna had found her way to him when she did. The previous years of mindless overwork had left him more jaded than he had realized, but her shy smile and warm heart had soon softened his hard edges. His aunt's early death, while not something he would've wished for, had forced him to reevaluate at the same time it had provided him the time and space in which to do so.

Thank goodness as well that Susan would be back at the firm today, although he knew it would be hard for her to leave Jack and Daniel behind. He'd barely been able to tear himself away from Adrianna the first day he had returned to work after their honeymoon period, and he had taken off four weeks as opposed to the two Susan had opted for. She had indicated an interest in talking to him privately after dinner the previous evening, and he wanted to run some things past his law partner as well.

Maybe a luncheon meeting at Montgomery's would be a good idea, as long as it didn't set any Captain's Point tongues wagging. They would have to be more conscious of that now. There had been a time in high school when everyone had seen them as the perfect couple, their class even electing them prom king and queen.

Good friends they had always been, yes, as Susan had tagged along with Larry and him wherever they went, but boyfriend and girlfriend, not so much. Each had always assumed they would accompany the other anywhere that required couples to form, as much as anything because they weren't as comfortable with anyone else. The one time they had agreed to try kissing one another, they had both cracked up, recognizing it was like kissing a sibling.

Still, memories and misguided gossip in small towns lasted a long time, and he wouldn't want anything the two of them did in the course of their work to upset either his Adrianna or her Jack, now that they had found them. He'd suggest lunch out and see what Susan thought. They could, after all, order in, and lunching at Montgomery House wasn't out of the question.

Next to him, Adrianna stirred and opened her eyes, surprised to find him awake and looking down at her. "Good morning." She sent him a smile, and he drew her closer as his lips brushed her forehead.

"It's always a good morning when I awaken to find you in my arms," he replied.

"I'm glad you feel that way," she teased back, "because I'm not planning on waking up anywhere else." She rolled away and threw back the covers, but he reached out and caught her hand, where she sat on the edge of the bed.

"Hurry back, wench," he sent her a leer. "I've decided on a roll in bed with honey this morning in addition to my cup of tea."

"Silly!" She giggled, even as she placed the palm of his hand against her cheek. "At least, let me release Max, so Penny can let him out and give him his breakfast."

"So the canine comes before me." He attempted a hurt look that his wife patently ignored as she opened the suite's door, allowing Max to head downstairs and stay on schedule.

"Cook says we're all out of rolls," Adrianna teased when she returned to the half-tester a few minutes later. "You'll have to settle for a wedge of dry cheese."

"Not on your life, my pretty maid." Chase grabbed her and nuzzled his stubble-covered chin into her neck, again causing her to giggle. "You're mine to pleasure myself with for life. Don't forget I won you fair and square in a duel."

At which, Adrianna stilled and opened her dark eyes wide. "All I ask, sir, is that you be gentle," she played along with her new husband's game, surprised when the soft look that he reserved only for her filled his eyes.

"I love you, my queen," he forced the words past the lump that had filled his throat at this turn in their love play.

"I always will." And then, without further ado, he drew her close and gently lowered his lips onto hers, all thoughts of the firm and the day ahead pushed from his mind.

CHAPTER XXX

In his spacious apartment over The Cove's former carriage house, Larry set aside the blow dryer and laid down his comb before stretching his half naked body this way and that, pleased to find that he didn't need one of the heat patches today. If Kate had been here with him, he could've told her, but she wasn't.

Still, it had felt nice the evening before, when she had checked to make sure he was okay after the episode with the photographer. Not that he hadn't had people around him who cared for him all of his life. He had, but Kate wasn't a family member who felt they had a duty to do so in the strictest sense of the word. After all, their relationship existed only through marriage.

Daniel had certainly taken his new aunt under his wing, now making sure her needs were met right along with his mother's. Thank goodness that photographer hadn't been much more than a kid himself. Jack had been right in his estimation, when the author had told the intruder to watch out. Normally non-violent by nature, he believed he would be capable of doing serious injury to anyone who harmed his short cousin.

With a start, he realized he felt the same way about Kate. How tiny her waist was. And, after her fall on top of him, no one knew any better than he did that she was light as a feather. A woman like that could hardly protect herself, as even Susan had recognized when she had described to him some of the apartments they had located in Captain's Point.

For a moment, his mind filled with imagined pictures - an unescorted Kate carrying sacks of groceries towards a condo door, her purse slung trustingly over her shoulder, Kate walking across a parking lot in the dark, and Kate pumping gas by herself at night. Hopefully, she would follow through on her promise to call Glenda and make an appointment to go over her portfolio with him, giving him an opportunity to learn more about what she was looking for in possible housing. He would need to see her appropriately settled if he were to have peace of mind going forward.

At least, for the time being, she was safe at Blue Wolf Manor. No one would look after her any better than her brother, and even Daniel and his mini-pack would protect her in a pinch. He smiled at the memory of the little guy standing his ground against the photographer.

In the meantime, he was tempted to research the length of the separation period required for a Virginia divorce, since he was obviously beginning to have feelings for this woman and Kate had already indicated she was uncomfortable about still being married from the standpoint of dating.

Unaware that she was on his grown cousin's mind, Kate held a bright blue Chester's sweatshirt steady in Daniel's bedroom, so that her new nephew could slip his arms into it. "Do you need help with your shoes?" she asked.

"No, Mama taught me how to tie them before we moved to The Cove." He bent to the task. "Can you tie yours?"

"When required to do so." She held the corners of her mouth steady, not wishing to hurt his feelings.

"What will you do all day while I'm at preschool?" He straightened, his eyes filled with worry.

"Actually, I'm going to have lunch with Edwina's grandson's wife and great-granddaughter." She watched as he hoisted his open-weave pack over his head.

"That's good." He took her hand and pulled her towards the stairs. "I wouldn't want you to be lonely. Jack's promised to pick me up at three, and then you could help us throw the Frisbee to the dogs if you're here."

"Sounds like fun, if I'm back in time." She noted her brother's Mercedes SUV pulling along the drive from the garage as they reached the foyer and held the front door open for Daniel. "One star pupil ready and raring to go," she announced, as Jack lifted his stepson from the porch and prepared to belt the boy into his child seat.

"Thanks for the help," he threw over his shoulder as he rounded the vehicle. "That phone call with my publicist lasted longer than I thought it would."

"No problem." She remained on the porch, blew a kiss to Daniel as they started off and then waved as they turned from the drive onto the main road.

Left alone, she hurried inside, the November breeze off the ocean carrying with it a damp chill, and stepped into the home's library where she turned on her laptop and searched for Chesterton and Chesterton on Main Street, entering the address and number into her phone.

"This is Kate Sinclair, Jack Jefferson's sister," she introduced herself to Glenda a minute later. "Larry indicated I should contact you for an initial appointment sometime tomorrow to meet with him in regards to my portfolio."

"Mr. Chesterton has an appointment outside of the office in the morning," his secretary responded. "Would three o'clock work for you?"

"Three would be fine," Kate agreed. "I'm looking forward to getting Mr. Chesterton's opinion."

The call terminated, she turned off her computer and shifted in place, so as to take in the view of the front lawn, even as her mind wondered what it would be like to go over her finances with Larry. Hopefully, he wouldn't think she was an idiot if the fool that the Sinclairs had relied on had placed all of her money in the wrong securities. A quick glance at the list along with a brief internet search had led her to believe that she wasn't too badly positioned, but then what did she know? Her degree had been in accounting, not finance, and she had taken even those courses several years ago.

But then, she recalled Larry's eyes smiling at her as they had sat on the banquette at Montgomery's, and her concerns left her. How sensitive he had been to her predicament, and how understanding of her divorce. Certainly, there was no need to worry. She was sure he would be kindness itself, and according to her brother, his advice could be relied upon.

Letting out a small sigh of relief, she rose from the couch, now looking forward to placing at least this small part of her wellbeing into the care and keeping of Larry Chesterton's capable hands.

CHAPTER XXXI

Walking over to Montgomery House later that morning, Jack spotted Otis, obviously heading to the same destination, and quickened his pace.

"I wanted to thank you again for taking over the food and keeping the gals calm, when we had our spot of bother last evening," he said when he caught up with the older man.

"Glad both to have been some help and that everything turned out okay," Otis replied. "Adrianna said you two were going to meet about the marina for a while this morning. When you're done, why don't you stop by my office, and I'll show you some of the roses I'd recommend for the garden you're hoping to put in for Susan."

"Sounds like a plan." Jack opened the door into the walled kitchen garden and headed up the path to the home's rear entrance, not bothering to knock, but rather calling out that he was there as he entered through the mudroom.

Adrianna glanced at the retro cat clock. "You're right on time," she greeted him, along with the aroma of freshly baked molasses cookies. "Would you like to sample my wares along with a cup of coffee while we talk in the breakfast room, or is this strictly a business meeting?"

"We could stretch the boundaries to include a couple of those as long as Penny won't tell on us." He winked at Otis's wife, who rolled her eyes before replying, "You men are all alike."

"By which I'm taking you to mean that we all have good taste." He accepted a mug of coffee prepared exactly as he liked it from the hand of his employer and then followed her into the breakfast room.

"I'm glad you suggested this meeting." Adrianna put a plate filled with the warm cookies in front of him, once he was settled, and then took a seat herself. "I've been meaning to touch base with you to see if there was anything that you needed from me, but I've been knee-deep in some planning that Otis and I have been doing for a new project we've started."

"Hold that thought," he replied, "because you may not be all that pleased with what I have to suggest, but before we get started, is your new project anything I'd be interested in?"

For a moment, Adrianna continued munching on a bite of cookie as she considered her answer, and he waited patiently, perfectly aware that this was her way. "The simple answer is that I'm not sure, but your question has started my mind spinning."

"Why don't you tell me what you two are up to, and then we could think things through together," he suggested, pleased when he saw the worried look leave her face.

Briefly, Adrianna proceeded to fill him in on the basic plan for Otis and she to take on various renovation projects in Captain's Point's historic district. "As you know, I've made a number of changes to Montgomery House and its surrounding properties since I inherited my aunt's estate," she finished, "but there hasn't been time for Montgomery Properties to build up any sort of meaningful cash reserves. Larry says that financially the plan is viable, and Chase was nice enough to agree that we could lend the company starter funds from our personal assets for this new project."

"I doubt that he had any trouble making that decision," Jack stated. "Otis and you are proven promotables, and Chase has been interested in preserving the integrity of Captain's Point for some time."

"Thank you," she said. "The thing is I've set a ceiling on what I'm willing to draw on from our personal money, even though Chase has stated that the sky's the limit." Her dark brown eyes once again filled with worry.

"I see," he stated, even as he wondered if every intelligent, talented, beautiful woman in this small town underestimated their worth as much as Chase's wife and his Susie seemed to do. "Would you consider taking on other investors such as myself and, I'm willing to bet, Larry?"

"I'm so glad you suggested it first." Relief filled her face. "I wasn't quite sure that was what you had meant. My only real concern for our success, beyond the obvious ones, has been whether or not we can improve the area, investing in only one property at a time, as rapidly as other properties lose ground. It won't do our final outcome any good, if the property values are going down around our renovated houses. Do you really think that Larry would be interested as well?"

"Yes, I do." He thought it best not to tell her that Larry had already indicated an interest in being part of the new venture should the opportunity arise, thinking she would get much more pleasure from finding it out for herself.

"We're having a sort of brainstorming, organizational meeting this afternoon at four o'clock," she continued. "Would you be able to join us? You're welcome to bring Daniel and his coloring book along."

"I'll be here for sure." He reached for another cookie. "Especially if you'll be serving refreshments, but I'll see if Kate is available or if Courtney would be willing for me to drop Daniel off on my way here. If not, then I'll take you up on your offer. Why don't you give Larry a call now and ask him if he can join us as well, so he won't schedule an appointment if he's free?"

"Otis will be pleased when he hears about this." She picked up her phone. "Glenda? This is Adrianna Montgomery. Is Larry available?" She sent her marina manager a thumbs up as he stood and went into the kitchen in search of a refill for his mug.

"We'll see you then," she concluded the call as he returned, reminding herself as she did so that she would need to call Chase and ask him if he could attend the meeting as well, now that things had morphed in this direction.

Jack retook his seat, and her attention shifted back to him. "So what did you want to discuss with me?" she asked.

"I hope you'll believe me when I say that I had every intention of remaining as your marina manager for quite a while when I accepted the position, both to get me out of the house and as a source of new characters for my stories," he began. "Then I fell in love with Susan, we married, and I find now that it's really cutting into the time I want to spend with my family."

"I can't say that I'm surprised," Adrianna stated. "Chase and I had wondered if you would want to continue in the position."

"Before I simply did my writing around it," he explained, "but now, I've committed to overseeing Daniel's transportation to preschool, I want to be there for him when he returns home, and I want to at least have dinner started for Susan on her work nights. Evenings, of course, I want to spend with the two of them."

"Of course," she repeated, nodding her understanding, "and I want you to know that I appreciate all that you've done in the time that you have managed the marina. From what you've been able to show me, it had suffered under Captain Reb's management, and you've turned everything around and implemented some much needed improvements in a very short time."

"My pleasure," he accepted the compliment. "Would you appreciate a recommendation from me as to a replacement?"

"Definitely, is it someone I know?"

"You've met him, certainly, but I'm not sure you're aware of how qualified he is for the position," Jack answered. "Do you remember Andre Necaisse, the young man we hired not too long after I started in the position? We brought him on first for evening security, but very quickly began using him in more varied roles, everything from handling general repairs to the property to filling in for me during my honeymoon."

"Yes, you've spoken highly of him in the past," she agreed.

"What you probably don't know is that Andre has a degree in mechanical engineering, was downsized from a supervisory position at a large firm in Atlanta, and only recently returned with his family to Captain's Point, so they could sell their home before it went into foreclosure," he filled her in. "His father has fished these waters all of his life, and Andre loves being on and around the water as much as I do. He's every bit as knowledgeable as I am about boat and building repair, has management experience, and is disenchanted with engineering as a career, even if he could get another position in this economy. The staff loves him, and he did a wonderful job while I was gone."

"How long of a transitional period were you envisioning?" Adrianna asked.

"Given that Andre has a wife and two children and I don't need the salary, none at all." Jack sent her a grin. "He's been doing the job for two weeks. As far as I'm concerned, you can back pay him as marina manager for those weeks and keep right on going. You and I can pop over and tell him now, or I can tell him for you. I'll fill him in on the purchasing and reporting gaps in his knowledge and generally be there to answer any questions he has over the next weeks, and I'll be glad to let him know that he can call me any time for direction when you're not available, if that would be of help to you as a friend going forward. Otherwise, I'll bow out and leave it to you two at the end of two or four weeks, whichever one you prefer."

Adrianna laughed. "In the corporate world that was my home until just a few months ago, what you've suggested would be considered treasonous. Here in Captain's Point, it makes perfect sense on every level."

"Glad you agree." He lifted his mug in a toast and tossed back the remains of his second round. "So do we tell him together, or do you prefer to leave it up to me?"

"Given that I still have some things I'd like to do in preparation for this afternoon's meeting, I'll leave it up to you today, but I'll make it a point to stop by and congratulate him tomorrow," Adrianna said. "Please tell him that we'll review his new salary again at the end of ninety days. With the improvements you've made to the bottom line, we should be able to work in an increase at that time. I'll count on you to fill him in and keep an eye on him during the next two weeks, and I'd be grateful if you'd be available as backup whenever Chase and I are out of touch."

"He's going to be both pleased and relieved." Jack rose. "I'll leave you to it now and see you again around four, although…" He pointed to the now rather depleted plate of molasses cookies. "I would recommend that you place any of those you might serve during the meeting as far away from me as you can."

CHAPTER XXXII

At precisely eleven-thirty, Kate arrived at the red brick ranch house that declared itself on its mailbox to be the Fosters' home. Stepping onto the porch, she discovered the front door to be slightly ajar and a note taped to the doorframe that told her to, *"Come on in!"*

"Ginny?" she stage-whispered once she was standing in the foyer.

"I see that you've found us without any problem," her hostess appeared in an archway opposite the front door, which proved to lead into a large kitchen and family room combination. "If you don't mind, we probably should go ahead and eat since Lucy's taking a nap."

"What a lovely, open space," Kate commented as her eyes took in the gas fireplace flanked by book-lined cases, comfortable seating and a well-appointed, modern kitchen.

"We like it." Ginny's face beamed with pleasure. "Jason prefers a less formal lifestyle, and this room in particular works well with Lucy." She busied herself with setting a plastic-wrapped plate of mixed sandwiches and a bowl of fruit salad on the wide granite counter. "I'm so glad you could come."

"I was thrilled to be invited," her guest shared. "Yours was my first personal invitation to visit in a Captain's Point home, although Jack and Susan's friends and relatives have all been wonderful about including me in their invitations."

"Help yourself." Her hostess handed her a plate. "Would you prefer iced tea, lemonade or ginger ale?"

"Iced tea would be fine." Kate spooned some potato salad next to a helping of the fruit salad and then reached for a tuna sandwich. "You have a nice view of your flowers from the table here." She set her plate at one of the place settings that were readied on the dining table that separated the two parts of the room.

"I enjoy gardening, when I have the time – something that's been missing since Lucy's arrival." Ginny joined her. "Most of what you see I put in before she was born, and of course, I like to grow my own herbs whenever possible. I'm still learning what will grow well this close to the ocean, though."

"I saw you at church yesterday," Kate pointed out, "so you must know Otis Plunk. You should ask him for advice. They have everything from a large kitchen garden to a full rose garden at Montgomery House, and the plants are well-tended."

"Believe me, I've already bent Otis's ear several times." Her hostess laughed. "And Jeff Stuart's, too."

"Jeff Stuart…" Kate considered. "Would that be the blond-haired college student who helps my brother with his yard?"

"Quite possibly," Ginny confirmed. "Jeff's father owns a landscaping concern, so he's been raised in the business. I know he helps out at Montgomery House."

"That's a lovely sweater." Kate reached over and lightly fingered the tiny cable that ran up the outside of the sweater's sleeve. "Did you knit this one yourself?"

"It's the only garment I knitted for myself the entire time I was pregnant." Her hostess laughed. "I couldn't even wear it when I finished it, because I was so huge."

"You're lucky to be so talented." Kate played with a piece of pineapple on her plate. "Thanks to my brother, I was allowed to develop musically, but I envy your having something to do with your hands while you watch television or wait at the dentist's office." Perhaps, she thought, Ginny would teach her how to wield a pair of needles once they got to know each other better.

"I'm about to take my knitting and sewing to the next level." Something in her hostess's tone drew her close attention. "Edwina has convinced me to rent the retail slot next to Arthur's on the Montgomery House property, and tomorrow I'll begin setting up my new yarn and stitchery shop that I'm calling Needles & Thread."

"How wonderful!" Kate exclaimed. "I know you're excited. Will you be able to keep Lucy with you?"

"Most of the time, yes, and Edwina and Arthur have both promised to lend support if I need it."

"Support from family and friends can really make a difference, can't it?" Kate didn't wait for a reply. "I never realized how much it could mean, until I came here to Captain's Point. Back home, everyone was caught up in their own selfish endeavors, and except for Jack and me, our family has never been close."

"I wouldn't have dared to dream about an undertaking like this one, if it hadn't been for Jason and Edwina's support," Ginny agreed. "So how is your house hunting going? Have you found a place yet?"

"Not yet, but I'm keeping my eyes open." Kate set her fork onto her now empty plate, trying hard to hide her disappointment that Ginny would no longer be available to fill the role of weekday friend.

"Don't get discouraged." Her hostess sent her an earnest look. "You'll find something, and it always takes a little time to feel settled into a new place. Is something else bothering you?"

Kate hesitated, not really sure that she wanted to share her innermost feelings with someone she barely knew, no matter how sympathetic they seemed, but then she remembered that this was Captain's Point, where everyone she had met had been friendly, helpful and welcoming.

"I'm a little worried about what I'm going to do with myself once I move out of Jack and Susan's home," she admitted. "Right now, I can always help with Daniel, practice music with Jack or work out in their home gym with Susan. The time's coming, though, when I'm going to be on my own for the first time in my life."

"It sounds to me like your answer is simple," Ginny stated. "Get a job. Not only will your weekdays then be full of purpose, but you'll be introduced more quickly to a wider circle of people with whom you can make friends."

"Someone else suggested the same thing," Kate shared, as she remembered the disappointment that had filled Larry's eyes when she had pushed his suggestion aside. "I'm beginning to think that both of you are heading me along the right track."

A squawk emitted from the baby monitor that had been strategically placed where the kitchen peninsula attached to the wall, and her hostess immediately rose and began gathering their dishes. "Her Majesty calls," Ginny joked as she gestured towards a plate of homemade oatmeal raisin cookies. "Help yourself to dessert, while I change her diaper."

Two hours later, Kate returned to Blue Wolf Manor, where she discovered her brother in his home office, staring at the flames in the gas fireplace. "Working?" she asked.

"Sort of." Jack sent her an absentminded smile. "I'm trying to figure out a rather complicated plot series, but Anderson seems to have other ideas. It probably would be best if I took a break until he decides to be somewhat more reasonable. By the way, would you mind watching Daniel for a while around four while I attend an organizational meeting Adrianna is holding for her new investment venture?"

"Not at all." Kate let out a small sigh.

"Did your luncheon with your friend not go well?" he asked, as always quick to pick up on her mood.

"Actually, I enjoyed myself immensely," she filled him in. "Ginny is interesting and fun, and I really enjoyed playing with Lucy."

"Then why the long face?" Jack gestured for her to join him on the couch.

"I've realized how much time I'm going to have on my hands, once I move out."

"Ah… You're beginning to take some upper level classes offered by The School of Hard Knocks, such as the infamous Sophomore series How to Negotiate Life in the Real World."

"Ginny and someone else have both suggested that I might want to seek some sort of employment," she shared. "What do you think?"

"I think you could do worse." He threw his arm around her and drew her close, dropping a kiss onto the top of her head. "You're a smart woman, Sis, and you were given those brains for a reason. It won't hurt anything to bring them out, dust them off, and see where they can take you."

"The whole idea seems rather daunting," she admitted. "I've never really held down a job, and I don't have any references, unless one of my old acquaintances would be willing to admit to all of my efforts with the charity groups."

"You may find in a small town like Captain's Point that a personal reference from Susan or Adrianna or even Larry or Paul Lynch would go a long way towards securing a position," he pointed out. "I doubt that most employment opportunities even make it into the Captain's Point Gazette."

"Will you help me put together a plan of attack, once I'm ready to begin a serious job search?" she asked.

"Sure."

"You're the best of all brothers, you know." She smiled up at him.

"And don't you ever forget it, Peanut." He tapped the tip of her nose with his finger and then rose. "I'm heading over to pick up Daniel. Want to ride along?"

"No, I'd better get changed." She let out a small laugh. "I have reasonable expectations of being called upon to toss the orange Frisbee here and there as soon as he gets home."

"A favorite aunt's job is never finished, is it?" Jack pulled his keys from his pocket.

"No," she agreed, but then continued, "and I wouldn't have it any other way. Being part of that little fellow's life is now one of my greatest joys."

CHAPTER XXXIII

As the four o'clock hour approached, Adrianna felt herself growing more and more nervous. "There's really no need to stand on much ceremony, is there?" she asked Penny as they unfolded a table protector in the dining room, the meeting's new venue due to the increased number of expected attendees. "Do you think we have enough cookies and brownies?"

"Given that we also have an assortment of cheeses and crackers for those who don't have a sweet tooth, I'd say that we're bordering on overkill." The housekeeper partially unfolded a dark blue tablecloth and then sent one corner of it in her employer's direction.

"I'm a little unsure of the lines here in Captain's Point," Adrianna admitted. "Everyone who is coming is a friend as well as a potential coworker or investor, which is a far cry from the corporate world in which I'm used to holding meetings."

"Your Aunt Martha would've said that it never hurts to present a generous and welcoming face." Penny hugged her employer, not even questioning whether or not it blurred the lines of propriety. "You know Jack, Larry, Jeff and my Otis will all enjoy the spread, and I imagine the others will be more than glad to follow suit."

"I just wish I could get in touch with Chase." Adrianna led the way into the kitchen, where the two of them began assembling a coffee, tea and water service along the large island. "It isn't like him not to return my calls."

"Have you rung Bridgette?"

"No, I don't want to disturb him if he's in the middle of an important conference, and I've left two voicemails." Adrianna set out sugar and sweetener packets in small bowls.

"Anything we can do to help?" Otis asked as he passed through the doorway to the mudroom, Jeff Stuart following close behind, both men wearing uncustomary dress shirts and ties and receiving an approving look from Max, who greeted them warmly.

"Two handsome men coming through," Larry's strong voice announced Jack's and his arrival from the front foyer. "Hopefully heading in the direction of the kitchen."

"See?" Penny raised an eyebrow in her employer's direction as she headed into the other room with the last plates of refreshments in tow.

Noting that Larry was wearing one of his Armanis and Jack had changed into a shirt that sported French cuffs, Adrianna was glad she had chosen to wear a sweater jacket over a silk suit blouse and dress pants that would hopefully strike a balance between the meeting's attendees.

"Julia and I are right behind them," Pete Marlborough's tenor called out. "We're looking forward to finding out what this is all about."

"Help yourselves to drinks, and then we'll meet in the dining room," Penny stated as she returned.

"If she's serving the molasses cookies she was baking this morning, make sure you grab one," Jack said as an aside to Larry and Jeff, even as he sent a grin in their hostess's direction.

Checking her phone one more time, Adrianna was disappointed not to find even so much as a text of regret from her absent husband, since a glance at the retro cat clock on the kitchen wall made it clear that it was time for her to convene the meeting. Grabbing a bottled water and a napkin for herself, she made her way to the head of the dining room table, not surprised when the others began choosing their seats – Penny taking the place to her immediate left and Otis dropping into the second chair down on her right, leaving the one next to her free should Chase arrive.

A stack of legal pads sat in front of her position at the head of the table, and pens had been provided at each place. "I'll start by passing these out," she began as she handed several of the pads to Penny on her left, reserved one each for Chase and herself, and then gave the rest to Otis.

Disembarking from his SUV, Chase hurried along the vine-covered arbor towards the door into the kitchen garden, berating himself for not having remembered to charge his cell phone the previous evening. Hopefully, Adrianna wouldn't mind if he barged in unannounced.

Max leaping to his feet from where he had been seated by her chair in hopes of a handout from the cheese platter and heading into the kitchen, Adrianna brought her explanation of their development plans to a pause as her husband appeared in the room's doorway, looking extremely handsome in his double-breasted, blue suit.

"Chase!" She resisted the urge to stand and greet him in the way she normally did. "We saved you a place in hopes that you could make it."

"So I see." He took the seat beside her and patted her knee beneath the table, relieved by her effusive greeting, but concerned by the tension he felt emanating from her.

"I was giving everyone a brief outline of the overall plan we want to put into motion," she filled him in before recommencing. "Pete and Julia, we're hoping that you'll be willing to assist us on a contract basis with planning and locating historically correct features during construction as well as overseeing the staging of finished properties."

Adrianna noticed both that the designer glanced sharply at the architect and that he raised a questioning eyebrow in her direction, before returning her own gaze. "It would appear that we would both be willing to take that on as part of our obligations," Pete responded, "and I'm sure I speak for Julia as well when I say it's an honor to be asked."

"Absolutely!" the designer agreed. "Am I understanding correctly that it's your intention to either flip or rent these properties, depending on a number of variables?"

"That's correct," Adrianna confirmed.

"Will you want us at Marlborough and Company to provide the furniture, lamps and other items needed for staging, or will you stock your own supply of appropriate basics and only rely on us for the items that would add a bit of flair?" Julia asked, receiving a nod of approval from Pete, who leaned forward in his chair.

"That's a good question," Adrianna gave herself a moment to think through her answer. "Initially, it would make more sense for us to rely on your inventory for everything. Over time, though, it might be more financially sound for us to invest some of our proceeds in a few basic furniture arrangements in neutral colors, around which you would then create an atmosphere that would allow us to best show each individual property."

"We could utilize what's now an unfinished area above the new garage for storage, if it was needed here on the property," Otis interjected.

"That's true," Adrianna agreed, even as she noted that Chase had written on his tablet, removed the page and surreptitiously slid it to where it now rested face down by her pen.

"Are you talking as much as two thousand square feet?" Pete asked, and as Otis and the architect debated the merits of the space, Adrianna calmly lifted the corner of her husband's note, closely observed by him, and read:

Do you know how…you are when…?

Finishing the words in her mind, she sent him one of her shy smiles as she entwined for a moment her fingers with his beneath the hanging folds of the tablecloth's corner, not displeased that he found her sexy no matter what she was doing, even heading a serious business meeting.

Sorry when his wife retrieved her hand from his, Chase was nonetheless pleased that his note had served its purpose and had left her more relaxed, even as he wondered if she had any idea how proud he was of her.

"Penny has joined us today, because she has agreed to provide us with her expertise when it comes to kitchen and bathroom design and flow," Adrianna filled them in, "and at this juncture, Larry and Jack are lending us their rather substantial financial and business expertise. We'll be calling upon Maureen Brownley for assistance whenever we're in the market for a new property. Chase and Susan's law firm will handle all closings and matters pertaining to the National Register of Historic Places."

"I'm glad you're planning to go that route," Pete spoke up. "It's a little more work, but if part of your goal is to maintain Captain's Point's historical heritage, then I would want to be on record as having said that it's the right way to go."

"Jeff, we've asked you to attend today because of your long association with Montgomery Properties," Adrianna stated. "Otis and I wondered if you might be ready to take a next step. Each of these new investment properties will need at least some sort of landscaping upgrade, if not a complete redo. I don't expect you to give us an answer here and now, but we would like for you to consider taking on this responsibility on a contract basis, either through Stuart's Landscaping Services or as a separate business concern of your own. Would you be willing to meet with us separately to discuss this offer more in detail?"

"I'd welcome the opportunity to discuss it further," Jeff stated, his tone purely professional, before he quickly glanced in Jack Jefferson's direction and received a sharp nod of approval in response.

"Our main purpose for today was to provide you with an overview and determine your level of interest," Adrianna pointed out, "so unless anyone has further questions, I believe that takes care of everything. Feel free to help yourselves to some more refreshments and discuss anything that interests you more informally."

CHAPTER XXXIV

Shortly after Adrianna adjourned the more formal meeting, both Pete and Julia rose from their chairs and approached her.

"I'm afraid we have an appointment with a prospective client that requires us to cut this short," Pete said. "Before we leave, though, I wanted to clarify that you would be satisfied if at times we two merely oversaw the work that was done on your projects."

"Certainly," Adrianna relieved his mind. "Otis and I could hardly expect you to drop everything at a moment's notice to deal with what will only be our on and off needs, although we're hoping to develop a good working relationship between our two firms over a long period of time."

"I'll get in touch with you shortly about your wishes in reference to your renovations here at Montgomery House," Julia promised, and then followed behind Penny, who had risen from her chair and was waiting to show them to the front door.

Seeing that Otis had now joined Jeff at the far end of the table, Larry and Jack each picked up a plate of refreshments and switched places – the former taking a seat on Chase's right and the latter dropping into Penny's vacated chair.

"I've been wondering why you've allowed this riff raff to crash your meeting," Chase addressed his wife as he looked down his nose at the other two men. "Neither of them has done anything, except munch on your delicious refreshments ever since I arrived."

"Ah, but we've come bearing gifts, haven't we, Jack?" Larry sent his partner in crime a grin and then popped a small sandwich comprised of a square of cheddar cheese and a round of pepperoni snuggled between two buttery crackers into his mouth.

"That we have," the author agreed, flashing his dimples for everyone to see as he reached for yet another molasses cookie.

"Jack suggested to me this morning that both of them might want to buy into our development plans," Adrianna explained. "Did you get my voicemails?"

"No, I came strictly on my own volition in case you had need of any legal advice," Chase replied.

"Well, it worked out the same." Adrianna patted his fingers where they lay on the table, not surprised when he took her hand in his, given that her meeting was now over. "It's an idea I had considered, but I wouldn't want to allow just anyone to invest, my concern being that we would share a common vision for Captain's Point."

"Are you two thinking of this as a long term, committed investment with voting rights, or are you merely offering Adrianna and Otis venture capital?" Chase addressed the two men.

"I would prefer a long term commitment," Jack made his position clear and then glanced towards Larry, who merely nodded his agreement, his mouth currently filled with herbed cream cheese that had been liberally spread upon a rye cracker.

"Then I would suggest that you separate this business entity from Montgomery Properties and incorporate it, which would allow you to issue shares based on the amount each partner had invested," Chase advised his wife. "By limiting the number of shares being offered to these two trouble makers at inception, you can continue to maintain a controlling interest."

"You could set it up so that each investor was a board member, and you could also pay Otis and you salaries that reflect the time and effort you will both put into the project," Jack suggested.

"Or you could pay Montgomery Properties LLC on a contract basis for your time, in the same way that you'll be paying Marlborough and Company and Stuart's Landscaping, whichever works out best for you tax wise," Larry pointed out.

Jack glanced at his watch, surprised to see that it was already after six o'clock. "I'm afraid I'd better be going." He stood. "Daniel and the ladies are probably holding dinner for me."

"Given there are organizational decisions that still have to be made, why don't you all come to my place for soup and sandwiches Thursday evening at five-thirty, and we'll work out some of the details then?" Larry rose from his chair as well, sending a sorrowful but quick glance towards a lone brownie that remained on the plate in front of Jack before raising his eyes and continuing. "Bring Susan as well, if you want."

"Sounds like a good idea to me," his cousin-in-law agreed, "although Susie may arrive late, depending on her last appointment."

"Fine with us," Chase accepted based on the wordless communication he had received from his wife, as he escorted their friends towards the foyer.

"I'll stop by tomorrow after class and discuss your offer further," Jeff promised as he helped Adrianna by gathering the pads and pens from the other end of the table.

"All that I need to know is whether or not you're interested and committed," Adrianna informed him. "If your father and you feel that this would be handled best through Stuart's Landscaping, that's fine, but if it would work better for you to set up your own firm, then I want you to know that we're prepared to help you make that happen. You've proven your value to all of us here at Montgomery House over and over again, and we all agree that it would be worth a small monetary investment on our part now to have you onboard with this project long term."

"That ups the ante a bit, doesn't it?" Jeff's face dissolved into a broad grin, but then sobered. "There are a number of things that will be affected by this decision – the pace at which I can move forward with my degree, needs my dad may have for my time, and something else that's a bit more private." A pink tinge filled his cheeks, and Adrianna's matchmaking antenna immediately went into overdrive as a vision of a beautiful young girl with eyes like dark pools and long flowing hair, who had exchanged meaningful glances with the young gardener in the recesses of the tunnels beneath Montgomery House throughout one special afternoon, filled her mind.

"I'll be here all day tomorrow." She kept her thoughts to herself as she led their way into the kitchen, her hands filled with used napkins and empty water bottles, as he followed behind her carrying a load of refreshment plates and a fistful of coffee mugs by their handles.

"See you then." He deposited the dirty dishes in the sink and disappeared through the mudroom, as Otis cleared his throat beside her.

"Would you have a moment?" her property manager asked.

"Sure." Adrianna glanced around to find Chase and Penny already seated at the kitchen table.

"Jeff, Pen and I couldn't help but overhear what you were discussing with Jack and Larry," Otis began, "and it's given Penny and me an idea. If you think it's out of line, just stop me."

"I doubt that either of you is capable of having an out of line idea," Adrianna reassured him, sensing his uncharacteristic discomfort with whatever he wished to say.

"The thing is Otis and I have put aside a fairly tidy sum for our retirement with the help of Anders Chesterton over the years," Penny stated. "Then your great-aunt left us a hundred thousand dollars in her will that neither of us had expected. What with your wedding and the renovations here on the Montgomery properties, we haven't had a chance to discuss investing it with Anders, so it's currently waiting in a certificate of deposit that's giving us a return of close to nothing."

"The long and the short of it is that we wondered if you would consider allowing us to buy into this new venture as well," Otis put all of their cards on the table. "We fully understand that there's risk involved, but we were never counting on this money in the first place."

"Of course, you're welcome to join us," Adrianna declared without a moment's consideration, but then she glanced sharply at Chase, who merely sent her a proud smile. "I had no idea when I started this ball rolling that so many people would be interested in my idea."

"You've come to Captain's Point at a critical time," Penny filled her in. "Larry and your husband, as well as a few others on the council, have worked hard to maintain what's so good about our small town for a number of years now, but there are those who would like nothing better than to sacrifice everything we have for a quick profit before they retire to somewhere else."

"You may find that, when you file your incorporation papers and buy your first property, you will also be drawing a wide, dark line in the sand as far as those on the other side see it," Chase advised her.

"Which makes the venture even more risky." Adrianna's eyes widened.

"Which makes it even more important that we get started, the sooner the better, in as big a way as we possibly can," Otis made his position clear, his voice firm. "Pen and I have known for a long time which side of the fence we're on."

"It also takes Jack and Larry's offers to participate to a whole different level." Chase's tone matched that of their property manager. "Among the three of us, we've already managed to stop one group of developers. Your idea, though, will be seen more as an offensive move."

"It's a little overwhelming, isn't it?" Adrianna met Penny's warm gaze. "I feel a bit like I'm starting out on a difficult journey."

"Yes," her housekeeper agreed, "but you'll be okay because, like your great-aunt, you're a Montgomery through and through."

CHAPTER XXXV

His stomach alerting him that it was now time for supper, Chase invited the Plunks to stay and threw together a light repast of Salad Nicoise and crusty French bread that everyone agreed was exactly what they had needed as the conversation shifted to the upcoming holidays.

Thanksgiving and New Year's Eve would both be spent at The Cove, and Susan had already made it clear that Jack and she were expecting all four of them at Blue Wolf Manor for Christmas dinner. Still, there was Montgomery House to decorate for the season, and the programs at their church had been filled with requests for volunteers.

The meal consumed and the dishwasher running, Chase locked the front door behind Otis and Penny, set the alarm and then rejoined his wife in the library, pleased to see that she had flipped on the gas logs in the fireplace and had prepared them each a mug of hot chocolate.

Adrianna had barely set their mugs on the coffee table and turned around to face him, when she felt herself swept into his arms, where he kissed her with a fierce passion that surprised her, even from him.

"What brought that on?" she asked, once he allowed her up for air.

"Seeing you standing there in the soft light, so beautiful and welcoming." A warm look filled his eyes. "Do you have any idea how much I treasure you, our home and our routines?"

"I have some idea, yes," she replied, "because I treasure them and you as well."

"Decorating this place for Christmas is going to be quite a job, isn't it?" Chase took her hand and drew her down beside him on the couch. "We have Martha's old decorations to choose from, as well as my aunt's if you want to look through them. Have you given the whole thing much thought?"

"Not really," she admitted, "because I found it all rather intimidating."

"Then let's do it together," he suggested as his eyes took on a faraway look. "This place has always been magical at Christmas, and Penny can guide us as to how Martha would've begun and any resources upon which she generally called. If we start planning now, we can accomplish some of the decorating the day after Thanksgiving."

"I've never gotten to enjoy much of a traditional Christmas," Adrianna shared. "Often my parents and I were on a site in the middle of nowhere."

"Christmases at Sheffield Place weren't all that great either." Chase twirled a lock of her hair around his right index finger, kissed it and released it. "Which is all the more reason for us to make our first Christmas together in this wonderful old home really special."

"I'm starting to look forward to it all now." She smiled up at him. "By the way, you were right about Jack's not wanting to continue on as marina manager now that he's married. He turned in his notice this morning, recommended his replacement and volunteered to continue acting as a backup if we should ever wish to be unavailable."

"That's just like our Jack, isn't it?" Chase handed her a mug and then secured the other one for himself. "Taking care of every detail and then some."

"He's certainly left the marina in much better shape than the way he found it," she agreed.

"I've made some changes in my working arrangement today as well," he informed her. "Susan and I discussed the firm in detail over lunch, and both of us agreed that while we wish to remain actively engaged, we also want more flexibility going forward. I'm going to retain only the firms oldest, most valuable clients, which will lighten my load, and I'll be working from home on Tuesdays and Thursdays. Wednesday mornings, we hold our staff meetings, of course."

"You and I enjoyed working together in here during our honeymoon," she pointed out, "and once the renovations are completed, this will be even more of a functioning office."

"I hope you don't mind that I crashed your party, so to speak." He studied her face. "It's the sort of thing I would be able to do more of now that Susan and I have made our changes."

"Not at all." She sent him one of her special smiles. "In fact, I had wanted you to be part of it all along. The times I most enjoyed when Otis and I were implementing the first round of renovations on the Montgomery properties were those when you showed up and participated, and while I can make decisions on my own, I always value your input."

"I don't want you to feel like I'm trying to take over your sandbox," Chase pressed his point. "I merely want to tag along in my queen's footsteps, if she'll let me."

"Silly!" She kissed his cheek, but then her expression sobered. "I spent so many years working hard to achieve what I thought were my goals, and then my great-aunt's will forced me to journey to Captain's Point and everything changed. I found you, and a miracle occurred. We fell in love, and you asked me to share my life with you. The me who had worked so hard to develop a solo career path has discovered that sharing a team effort is much more fulfilling. Will you have time as we embark on our nontraditional life's path to be an equal partner in this endeavor as well?"

"Nothing would please me more than to spend at least a chunk of my productive work time with you, especially if we can spend our break times in even more pleasurable pursuits." Relieving her of her mug, he placed it on the coffee table, bent and kissed her neck, and then sent his lips downward in a firm way that set her whole body tingling.

"Chase, really...," she protested, even as she responded, giggling, "Again?"

And as he drew her to him and felt her press against him even further, he whispered into her ear. "I'm afraid you'll just have to accept, my queen, that this knight is well and truly addicted to you."

Later, as she waited in the tower suite bedroom while Chase let Max out for a final run, Adrianna stood and faced her many times great-grandfather's portrait where it hung over the hearth.

"Well, Jebediah, what do you think of us now?" she asked, glad as always that his eyes appeared to be twinkling back at her. "My simple idea has morphed, until now I hope that Otis and I are even up for the challenge. The good news, of course, is that Chase, Jack and Larry will be part of the mix, which makes us a very strong team going forward. I wonder, though, which side you would be on if you were here."

Drawing herself away from his friendly gaze, she strode across to the farthest window seat and closed the drapes, before moving on to the second and then third, where she paused. Beyond the gardens and the lawn, the sea spread before her, glistening in the moonlight that beamed down upon it, lights in the distance recording the presence of boats traveling northwards.

Suddenly, she closed the drapes over this bay window as well, before swinging around once again to her ancestor's portrait. "You'd be on our side, fair and square, wouldn't you?" Her dark eyes twinkled back at his blue ones. "You built this fine, old house and settled your family here, because you liked Captain's Point just as it is. Well, I'm going to fight for the Point and the values you stood for as hard as I can, so wish us luck, Jebediah, because we're going to need it."

Her husband choosing this moment to return and her heart filled with a desire for action, she flung her arms around his neck and drew his handsome face towards hers, kissing him with an abandon that this time surprised him.

Lifting her into his arms, Chase carried her once again to their bed, where he lost no time taking advantage of the moment, pausing only to whisper into her ear, "I cherish you, Adrianna."

CHAPTER XXXVI

"Are you writing?" Susan asked Jack as she picked up the remote from her bedside cabinet and turned on the gas logs in their bedroom's fireplace.

"No, just finishing off some emails." He hit Send, closed down his tablet and set it aside. "Were you thinking I might be working on another jungle scene?" He indicated the playful monkeys that were dancing around on her mint green pajamas.

"Courtney gave me these for my birthday." She made a dismissive gesture and sent him a half smile, as if that explained the change from the filmy nightgowns she had been wearing. "Do you mind if we talk for a few minutes before turning out the lights?"

"Not at all." He tossed back the covers on her side of the bed and pulled himself up straighter against the pillows, something in her tone alerting him to pay close attention even as she surprised him by sitting cross-legged, faced towards him, almost out of his reach.

For a minute, they sat in silence as she attempted to gather her thoughts and he searched through his mind for anything he could've done that might have upset her, but then, he caught sight of her trembling fingers.

"I'm going to amend what I just said," he spoke up, reaching out and taking her hands in his. "I'm willing to give you all the time that you need, but only once you're right here with me." He drew her up to where she could still sit facing him, but he could hold her comfortably in his arms if he felt called to do so.

"I'm sorry," she apologized, her voice almost a whisper. "I need your advice as my friend, a businessman and, most of all, as my husband, but I don't quite know how to put what I have to say into words." She looked up at him, her beautiful eyes sparkling with tears.

"Are you afraid for some reason that I'll be angry or upset by what you have to say?" he asked, finding it hard not to take her into his arms.

"Yes. No." She closed her eyes, but then immediately reopened them, trust warring with fear within them. "It's only that I can't seem to get my own mind around all of the thoughts I'm having right now, and yet, I believe it will be terribly important to us going forward that I get it right. Just when I think I have it all put into place, everything from the past rushes over me. I..." A single tear rolled down her left check, and he placed a finger to her lips, stopping her there, before he gently wiped it away with his thumb.

"I love you, Susie Chesterton," he said. "I really love you, deeply and completely. You do understand what that means, don't you? It means that you never have to be afraid or even slightly worried about approaching me with anything."

He expected her to utter a soft reply, but instead, she threw her arms around his neck.

"I love you, too, Jack Jefferson," she half-sobbed, "and I'm so glad I'm married to you and not..." Here she squeezed her eyes closed in an effort to hold back her tears.

"...and not to Bill," he finished silently in his own mind as he brought his arms tightly around her, thankful as he did so that he now had a handle on what was going on. "Shhhhh." He rubbed her back in large circles. "I'm glad that you're married to me, too, and whatever it is that's troubling you, we're going to work it out – calmly, quietly and so that both of us are totally happy with the outcome."

"I know." She snuggled her head into his neck. "That's one of the things that's so wonderful about being on my lifetime honeymoon with you."

"Well, as I've told you before, you're not going to be on one with anyone else." He reached into his bedside cabinet and removed a box of tissues. "Now let's get your eyes dried and see what we can do to settle your mind about whatever it is."

Susan accepted the three tissues that he offered her and then sat up facing him again, this time taking his left hand and cupping her face in it.

"You were fine when you left home this morning, so why don't you begin with what started you down this path," Jack suggested. "So far, all I know is that you want my advice from several vantage points in regards to something about which you would not have been able to approach your ex. Am I right?"

Taking a deep breath, she straightened, absentmindedly clutching his hand to her heart, which did nothing to help maintain his focus. "Chase and I took a two hour lunch at Montgomery's today," she began.

"In a public place in front of at least a hundred other people," he pointed out. "Was there French kissing involved?"

"No, of course, not." She managed a small smile.

"Then, since I've visited his wife alone in their house several times in relation to marina business, including this morning, I can honestly say that I'm neither angry nor upset at this juncture," he stated, at which she lifted his hand and kissed its palm.

"We wanted to discuss the future of the firm, somewhere away from the office," she explained.

"Is the firm in trouble?" he asked.

"No, not at all, but we are considering a general reconfiguring," she continued. "As you know, we've brought on three new associates – Gary Butler, Helen

Windom and Brett Vickers. Gary and Helen have already proven that they're partnership material, and Brett has local real estate connections that have allowed him to bring in a steady stream of closings."

"Sounds like you chose wisely from amongst the applicants during Chase's absence."

"He seems to think so," Susan admitted. "The thing is, now that we're both married, we realized as our discussion progressed that our priorities have changed." Again, she clutched his hand to her heart, this time her fingers pressing tighter. "This is where I don't want to go wrong."

"There is no wrong way for you to go, when we're both going down the same road together," he pointed out.

"There is if you're only going along the same road to make me happy because, in the end, you'll be miserable and then so will I." She held her breath.

"Ah… The world's oldest conundrum." He raised his hand and gently slipped one of her thick waves back into place. "I can't promise you that we won't trip occasionally as we travel along, Susie, but I'll be there to catch you and you'll be there to help me up if I fall, fair enough?"

"Yes." Her eyes filled with hope.

"Now why don't you come back over here and snuggle with me, because I really like that," he suggested. "Then you can run through your thoughts as they came to you today, and we'll try to make sense of them for the both of us going forward."

"You wouldn't mind?"

"I'd be relieved," he assured her as she slipped her legs beneath the covers and stretched out beside him on her stomach. "Now start at the beginning."

"Number one, neither Chase nor I need to work anymore." She glanced up sharply.

"Do you want to quit working?" Jack asked, trying hard to keep his tone even.

"Not exactly," Susan replied. "Both of us agreed that while neither one of us wanted to work the long hours we had covered before, neither of us wanted to hang up our hats either. Chase pretty much burnt himself out these past couple of years as you know. I've always wanted to spend more time at home with Daniel than circumstances would allow until now, and I can't tell you how hard it was for me to leave you in our bed and go into the office this morning."

"I'm never going to tell you to get up and go to work," he pointed out, "but then again, I'm never going to tell you to give up the law any more than I would expect you to tell me to give up my writing. They're both part of who we are."

"Exactly," she agreed. "One of the possibilities we discussed was that Chase would continue on as Senior Managing Partner, which he enjoys doing and I don't. He would retain only the firm's oldest clients as his own, and the rest would either remain with me or be parceled out to Gary or Helen at my discretion, since I know the current state of the files better at this point and have spent more time with the new associates.

"I would continue on as a Senior Partner, but any new clients I brought to the firm would be parceled out to either Gary or Helen, unless they were a relative or a particular friend that I wanted to retain. My workload would, therefore, be lightened as well. This way Chase and I would have way more flexibility as to both the number of hours per week that we worked and from where we chose to do so, while still flexing our legal muscles, so to speak. As a businessman, what do you think?"

"Strictly as a man of business, I think it makes sense," he replied. "Both of you remain actively engaged in the firm, so your clients will still feel their needs are receiving the value of your expertise, while at the same time your new associates will be able to see a clear chance at becoming partners in the future."

"As my friend, what do you think?" She again reached over and took his left hand in both of hers. "I worked hard for my law degree, and I enjoy the work. On the other hand, this would allow me more time with both Daniel and you. Do you think, as my friend, that I will regret doing this going forward?"

"As your friend," Jack repeated, still feeling as if he were standing on solid ground, "I think you would regret giving up the law completely at this point in your life, so this is a good middle ground, especially since it offers enough built-in flexibility to allow you to do more comfortably such things in the future as attending Daniel's school programs or teachers' meetings."

"I knew you would help me to set my mind straight." Susan beamed at him, her eyes filled with so much trust in his wisdom that it warmed him to the core, but then the muscles of her face, indeed along her whole body, tensed. "I know you've said you wouldn't mind my working from home before, but are you sure that it won't interfere in any way with your writing?"

"Only if you insist on playing high decibel, heavy metal music in the background or chomp loudly on oversized bags of chips while we work in our shared office space," he stated calmly, even as part of him was dancing a jig across his heart at the mere thought of spending more of their time in each other's company.

"And, as my husband?" She examined the back of his hand where his fingers remained intertwined with hers.

"As your husband, I want you to be happy in all things – your role as a mother, your home, your health, your social life, our love life and our marriage," Jack began, his mind searching desperately for the right words. "I want you to know peace and contentment and joy and, perhaps most of all, balance. I want you always to know that I love you. I don't ever want you to be worried or afraid like you were earlier this evening, especially when it involves asking me about something. I hope you will view me as your friend, helpmate, strength, protector and lover, and I want you to know without a shadow of doubt that I'm here for you in each of these ways whenever you need me."

"But what do you want from me?" she asked. "I feel as if I'm giving up part of what attracted you to me in the first place and that somehow I will bring less to the equation going forward. What should I do to insure your happiness as we travel along beside one another?"

"Like I've said before, all I need is your love." He repositioned himself so that they were now lying face to face and dropped a kiss on her lips. "I hope to deserve your respect as well, but your love will insure everything else that I need, because of who you are and how you love Daniel and me." He slid his hand under the back of her pajama top and began tracing gentle circles on her soft skin.

"We are going to have a wonderful lifetime honeymoon, aren't we?" She smiled at him, her beautiful eyes filled with love.

Before answering, he rolled her onto her back. "I'm thinking that we should seal that particular deal right now," he replied and then lowered his lips onto hers.

CHAPTER XXXVII

The next morning, Jewel Parkerson looked through the living room window just in time to see Stuart's Landscaping Services's worn truck pull up to the curb in front of her house and come to a stop. Stepping into the shadows, she watched for a minute as Herb Stuart, wearing a blue knit cap over his gray hair, disembarked, glanced up with a smile at the clear sky, and then went to work unloading a weedeater with an edger and a rake from the back of his vehicle.

Loneliness giving her courage, Jewel hurried into the foyer, swung open the door and stepped onto the front porch. "Do you have time for a second cup of coffee and a fresh-baked cinnamon roll before you get started?" she asked, surprised to see her breath exhibited as white mist in the air.

"Sure." Herb leaned his tools carefully against the front steps. "Let's get you back inside, though. You don't even have on a sweater."

Freezing, she hurried to obey and led him along the hallway to the kitchen at the rear of the house.

"Just hang your coat on the back of one of the chairs." Jewel nodded towards the oak table that dominated the center of the room. "You know where to wash up."

Lacing milk into a mug of coffee for herself, she set another of black coffee on the table in front of him, where he had now taken a seat. "It won't take me but a moment to whip up the glaze and drizzle it over these."

Settled, Herb breathed in deeply. "There's nothing like the aromas of coffee and cinnamon mingled in the air, is there?" he asked, not waiting for an answer. "Do you remember those cinnamon pinwheels my mom made from her leftover pie dough? The four of us used to wait for them to be pulled from the oven with our tongues hanging out."

"I still make those." Jewel set a plate with two of the warm cinnamon rolls in front of him, not needing to be told who the four children had been, and then nodded at the seat across from the one she took for herself. "Bruce sat right there in that chair, licking his lips and waiting for some, not two weeks before he…" She swallowed hard. "Not two weeks before he was gone."

For a couple of minutes, they munched on their pastries in the comfortable silence that surrounded them, each lost in their own thoughts of the two childhood friends who were no longer with them.

"Funny how an aroma can bring back a memory," Herb renewed their conversation, the first roll having disappeared from his plate. "I can't smell warm apples without seeing my Nancy standing at the counter peeling apples and then cooking them into her applesauce."

"Am I correct in thinking you had another job before you came here this morning?" Jewel changed the subject. "Eight-forty seemed like an odd time for you to arrive."

"I started at Mrs. Madison's big old Victorian across the marina road from The Cove at seven o'clock," he filled her in. "That woman's an enigma if ever there was one. One hour, she always tells me. One hour and no more, although I could easily take four working flat out to really do justice to her yard. I managed to get the front and the side by the portico cleared and edged this morning, but I stayed a half hour beyond, like I always do, in order to make it happen."

"I hope you charged her for the extra time," Jewel stated firmly.

"Never have, and I probably never will." He paused and enjoyed a bite out of his second roll. "The woman's in her nineties, and I've been scared of her ever since she stood at the head of our first grade classroom at the beginning of the year." A shy grin slid across his face, and a deep dimple briefly made an appearance.

"She was rather intimidating, wasn't she?"

"Anyway, that's why the odd time." He took another sip of his coffee. "The storm that went through night before last has left some small limbs strewn here and there around your yard. I'll haul them away, edge and rake the leaves while I'm here. Is there anything else that you need doing?"

"Nothing that I've noticed," she told him, "but I'll leave that up to you. I wish that you'd let me pay you, though."

"Now, Jewel, we've been over this before." He licked a last bit of buttercream glaze from his thumb. "Bruce was the brother I never had, and he would want me to see to these things for you." His expression sobered. "Besides, I need to be doing. That's one of the worst parts of Nancy being gone. Jeff and I stumble along okay, keeping each other company, but he's a man in his own right at this point and wouldn't want me to fuss over him. Still, I'm in the habit of taking care of someone."

"I know." She reached over and patted his hand. "It felt good to bake these rolls, knowing that you'd be here soon to enjoy the results, and Nancy would want me to watch out for you, too. I'm glad you were able to come this morning," she again changed the subject. "I went and saw Larry Chesterton last Friday, and I may need to rent out a room or two. He's offered to stop by later today and give me his opinion as to how I could best do it."

"This is a result of Bruce's investment in Gerald Tate's latest scheme, isn't it?" Herb's jaw tightened. "That man's a menace, and Bruce shouldn't have trusted the scoundrel. He was a snake and a bully back in grade school, and nothing's changed since. I think the only time your husband and I ever disagreed over anything was when we argued about Tate's so-called development idea. The whole thing's heading Captain's Point in the wrong direction."

"I take it then that you didn't put any of your money into Gerald's real estate consortium?"

"Not a penny," he replied, a firm tone underlining his words. "How deep did Bruce go, if you don't mind my asking?"

"Way more than he should have," she admitted. "He even borrowed against his life insurance. At this point, I'm relieved that he didn't touch the house."

"You still own it outright, don't you?" he asked.

"Yes," she assured him, before recalling a happier time. "That was a fun evening when the four of us went out to dinner and celebrated with champagne that we'd paid off our mortgages within a month of each other."

"Best move we could've made." He reached over and took her hand. "You know I'm here for you if you ever need anything, don't you? Anything at all."

"I know." She kept her eyes on their joined hands where they lay on the table, not sure she could keep her tears at bay if she looked into his gentle, gray eyes.

"I'd better get started." He withdrew his hand, tossed back the rest of his coffee and rose from his chair, then rinsed off his dirty dishes in the sink. "I'll check back with you before I leave," he promised as he shrugged on his coat. "Keep me posted about this rental business."

"Part of me is rather dreading the idea," she admitted, "but then another part of me realizes that I'm lonely knocking around in this big house by myself."

Herb paused in the doorway that led to the main hallway. "Bruce and I were brothers, just the same as Nancy and you were sisters, even though none of us were blood related, if you know what I mean. It might be that we should give a little more thought to that going forward, in the Biblical sense."

And then he was gone, his rinsed dishes and a tiny dead leaf on the floor beneath the chair where he had sat the only signs that he had ever been there. With a sigh, Jewel rose, picked up the leaf and carried her own dishes to the sink, where she stood as her shoulders silently shook and tears streamed down her cheeks. What exactly had Herb meant by those last words?

CHAPTER XXXVIII

"Do you have a few minutes?" Jeff Stuart asked Adrianna from the doorway into Montgomery House's library a few moments later.

"Sure." She smiled a warm greeting. "Why don't you grab something to drink in the kitchen, and we can talk in front of the fireplace in here."

Once they had settled into the facing leather club chairs, Adrianna sipped on the warm cider in her mug and waited for the young man in front of her to gather his thoughts, pleased to note that he seemed comfortable about approaching her.

"My dad and I had a long talk last evening after supper," Jeff began. "Frankly, for reasons of his own, your idea really appeals to him, and both of us would like to see Gerald Tate and his schemes for developing Captain's Point stopped in their tracks. Another facet of our discussion was the fact that Maureen Brownley and my mom had often talked about doing something to revitalize the historic district."

"I knew that Maureen had always been interested in the area, but I had no idea that your mother had seen its possibilities," she shared.

"Mom taught history at Captain's Point High until the cancer treatments made it impossible for her to continue," he filled her in, "and then, of course..." He shrugged and took a long drink from his mug.

"I'm sorry that I never met your mom," she said, giving him a moment. "Your family appears to have been very close, and I'm sure I would've liked her."

"Everyone did," he agreed wistfully. "She was smart and funny and caring all rolled into one. Dad and I both miss her terribly, even though there are times when it's almost as if she's there with us."

"Perhaps she's still watching over you," Adrianna suggested. "Sometimes, I feel strongly that my parents are."

"Anyway…" Jeff made a small gesture with his hand. "I had heard some of Chase's and your discussion with Larry and Jack, and I asked Dad's opinion about an idea that I'd had. Then he surprised me by taking the whole matter up a couple more notches. In the end, we were both bouncing ideas off each other."

"Sounds like you two had a fairly lively evening." Adrianna found herself more and more intrigued.

Her gardener took a deep breath, and for a moment, she was struck by how much more mature he seemed than when she had first met him.

"Mom had a life insurance policy that was left half to me and half to my father," he plunged into deeper waters. "Neither of us has felt right using it for anything up until now, since we were both uncomfortable with the idea of somehow feeling better off because she was gone."

"I can understand that," Adrianna stated, remembering how guilty she had felt when, after her parents' death, a small policy had paid out in time for her to meet a college tuition and dorm payment.

"The thing is your idea would've been right up Mom's alley," Jeff pointed out, "and the long and the short of it is that both Dad and I would like to invest in your endeavor." He held up the palm of his right hand as if to stop her from commenting. "I know this isn't what you had initially intended, and we discussed that as well."

"You're both welcome to invest in the new firm as long as you understand the risks involved, since you seem to be one hundred percent behind our ultimate goal, which is to help Captain's Point remain the wonderful place in which to live and raise a family that it's always been," she said, hoping to put his mind at rest. "We wouldn't have approached you at all, if we hadn't already believed that you felt the same way we did."

"That's super!" He beamed at her as she reached for her phone.

"If you'll give me a moment, I'd like to confirm something with Larry before we continue," she explained as she dialed the broker's office number.

Jeff disappeared once she was connected to Glenda and returned a couple of minutes later with his mug refilled to find his employer once again sipping on her cider.

"We're having a supper meeting at Larry's condo on Thursday evening to discuss the new company's organization," she brought him up to date, "and both your Dad and you are invited to attend as investors. Otis and Penny will be coming as well, since they indicated a similar interest after you left here yesterday."

"I'll be able to come, but I'm not sure about my father," he stated. "He has choir practice on Thursday evenings."

"Let me know as soon as you can, and I'll pass the head count on to Larry," she volunteered. "Now what did you two decide about our request that you handle the landscaping?"

"Dad told me last evening that he's been planning to bring me into Stuart's Landscaping Services as a full partner for some time, both as a reflection of the role I've played in helping to grow the business and also as part of his estate planning," Jeff explained as a crease furrowed his brow. "He had planned to tell me as part of my Christmas, but last night seemed like an even better opportunity."

"Why am I getting the impression that you're not entirely pleased with the idea?" Adrianna asked.

"Frankly, I'm not sure what I feel about it," he admitted. "Half of me is glad to know that he's recognized my contributions and thinks highly enough of me to make me a full partner, but the other half wonders how this will affect my plans to go into journalism. At this point, while I'm still working towards my degree, it won't make all that much difference, so I decided this morning after he left that I'll just take it one step at a time."

"Life has a way of pointing towards the roads we are meant to take," she voiced her opinion. "Look at me. I firmly believed that I was destined for a career in corporate management with one of the international firms that are home-based in Seattle. Then my Aunt Martha died, I journeyed to Captain's Point, met Chase and here I am – married, owner of one business and about to set up another."

"And career-wise you're happy the way things have turned out for you, aren't you?" he asked.

"Absolutely, on all levels," she assured him. "Sometimes, it's best just to flow until your ultimate purpose is revealed to you. If I were in your position, I'd keep taking my classes towards my degree and see how I felt when it was time to take the next step."

"Dad and I agreed both that we wanted to take on the landscaping required for your new properties and that we would do it as a division of Stuart's Landscaping Services, since it would keep the costs and tax implications under control."

"Welcome aboard then." Adrianna raised her mug in a toast. "To a long and fruitful partnership between our two firms."

"To our future success as a team." His blue eyes twinkled back at her, even as gratitude for his employer's faith in his abilities filled him.

CHAPTER XXXIX

A few minutes later, Kate hurried past the spot in the woods where only a couple of nights before Daniel and his mini-pack had kept the young photographer at bay, until the cavalry of men watching over him could arrive. The day had dawned bright and sunny, Daniel was at pre-school, Susan was at work, and her brother was writing in his library. Feeling a bit depressed by her idleness, it had seemed like a perfect time to get some fresh air and, perhaps, check on Ginny at her new retail location on the Montgomery House property.

Walking briskly, it took only a few minutes for her to cover the distance between the two locations. As she neared the window in which a neat sign proclaimed in white script set against a blue background that this was her friend's shop, though, she could clearly hear a baby crying through the glass front of the store and hesitated a moment before opening the door.

"Ginny?" She resisted the urge to shout as she paused inside the large area, which currently resembled a stockroom more than a retail space.

"Thank goodness it's you!" her friend exclaimed as she entered the room from the back, a screaming Lucy in her arms. "I was afraid it might be Arthur, and I need to nurse this one." She indicated her baby with a nod of her head.

"I'm sorry if I've caught you at a bad time," Kate responded. "I only stopped by to see how you were getting along and to offer an hour or two of my services, if I could help you set up. Why don't we pull this card table chair over here behind these boxes, so you'll have some privacy, and I'll keep an eye on the door?"

Ginny looking as if she might burst into tears herself at any moment, Kate grabbed the chair without waiting for a reply and thrust it into the shielded corner out of sight, pleased when her friend settled onto it and prepared to satisfy her baby's demands.

Once quiet surrounded them, the store's owner met her gaze. "I'm so glad you dropped by," Ginny stated as her worried expression relaxed. "Edwina had promised to help, but a light started flashing on the dashboard of her car last evening, so Arthur and she have taken it to the dealership. Are you really here to assist me?"

"I am," Kate assured her. "I love the carpentry you've had done." She eyed the white-painted, diamond-shaped cubbyholes that ranged along the walls above low storage cabinets all around the room.

What wall space was still visible had been painted a dark brown and receded from view. Waist-high cabinets had been placed beneath the large picture window at the front of the store, providing even further storage as well as display space that would be easily viewed by passersby. A large blue, green and brown braided rug remained rolled up as it pointed the way from the front door to the stockroom entrance at the back of the store.

"There's a little more method than madness to what you're seeing right now," Ginny explained. "The boxes are sorted by types of yarn and arranged in front of the shelves, where we felt they would be best displayed. I was hoping to unpack as many of them as possible while Lucy napped, but so far, she's refused to go to sleep in the playpen I've set up." She lifted her daughter onto her shoulder and began patting her back gently.

"I shouldn't have too much trouble unpacking the yarn." Kate again surveyed the boxes in front of her, her eyes alighting on a couple of matching box knives where they lay on a serviceable banquet table.

"Then you're hired." Her friend stood, Lucy having let out a loud burp. "I'm going to see if my little one will settle down now."

Left to herself, Kate approached the row of boxes that were lined perpendicular to the first shelves and cabinets leading off the front window, carefully opening each one of them before Ginny returned. "Have you given any thought to how you want to arrange the yarns on the wall?" she asked her friend.

"At this point, they're only sorted by type. Worsteds here…" Ginny pointed to the freshly opened boxes. "Variegated there, mohairs next, baby yarns over here. Do you have any suggestions for displaying them within their categories?"

Quickly, Kate reached into the series of boxes, removing one skein from each. "You could simply organize them by color groupings like this," she suggested as she placed one skein in the bottom V of each diamond-shaped shelf in the area designated for worsteds. "Or you could go a little fancier and use your neutrals to form a wave effect as the brighter colors worked their way through the rainbow." She grabbed several more skeins, rearranged the first ones, and displayed her idea.

"I hadn't thought of that." Ginny sent her a bright smile. "You have a marvelous sense of style. Why don't I open all of the boxes?" she suggested. "Then, if you would follow along behind me and place sample skeins where they should go to create the waves, my other helpers and I will be able to merely stock the shelves behind you."

Together, the two made quick work of the first long wall, but as they turned the corner, the baby yarns posed a problem, the quantities ordered being so much smaller in volume.

"What do we do now?" Ginny asked as she turned to Kate, her eyes clearly stating her faith in her friend's ability to solve the problem.

"How about filling the bottom of the diamond with one color and the top with another?" her volunteer suggested. "I can put a few skeins in each diamond like this to point the way. Eventually, you could even have dividers made from peg board material to separate the colors more efficiently."

"Excellent," the budding shopkeeper agreed, and the rest of the sample skeins were soon placed.

"I can stay a while longer, if you'd like," Kate informed her friend when they both stopped to view their completed design template. "Why don't I begin stocking the worsteds and you start filling in these beautiful heather-toned wools from Ireland along the opposite wall? That way, you'll see progress moving through the store from front to back."

"Sounds like a plan, if you don't mind staying longer," Ginny agreed and bent to the task, grateful for the surprise assistance she was receiving.

For her own part, Kate felt her spirits lifting as she worked, feeling energized by both the activity and the sense that she was making a difference in her friend's day.

Perhaps, this was what Larry had meant when he had asked her what she intended to do with herself now that she was here in Captain's Point. If so, he had been spot on in his assessment of her needing to keep busy. Now, if only she could find some sort of rewarding enterprise in which to immerse herself going forward.

CHAPTER XL

That afternoon, Kate turned right off Main Street into the large free parking lot a block along the road from the offices of Chesterton and Chesterton and headed at a sedate pace towards two free spaces ahead on her left, secure in the knowledge that she was a few minutes early for her appointment. But then, she felt a jolt and heard the screech of metal on metal as a red Mercedes backed from a space on her right and connected with the side of her vehicle.

Immediately bringing her own car to a halt, she took note of two things – the shocked look on a young blonde woman's face as she stood only a few feet away and the disgusted expression exhibited by a policeman so young he could only be a rookie, who was seated in the car facing hers. Grabbing her purse, she disembarked, but then waited as the young woman and the policeman approached.

"Gerald Tate…" The officer appeared to be about to spit on the pavement as he glanced towards the red Mercedes, but apparently thought better of it, clicked open his pen and began making notations on a carbonized sheet held within his clipboard.

"That man's a menace," the young woman stated firmly and then held out her hand. "I'm Sissy Stanton and this is Bubba Edwards." She nodded towards the policeman. "We'll both be glad to go on record in your defense. Gerald Tate may own the bank, but that doesn't mean he can go around damaging everyone else's property."

"Thank you." Kate shook the woman's offered hand and then glanced at her watch. "I'm Kate Sinclair, and on top of everything else, I'm going to be late for my appointment with Mr. Chesterton."

"You're Larry's three o'clock." The other woman shoved a large plastic container that appeared to be filled with chocolate-iced brownies into Kate's hands. "He'll want to know about this. I'll be right back, Bubba. Don't leave until I sign that form."

And with that, the blonde hurried towards Kate's destination, leaving her wondering as to why the man who had damaged her car hadn't yet disembarked and apologized.

Rolling his eyes, Bubba sauntered to the Mercedes' driver's door and tapped on the window.

"Can't you see that I'm busy?" the middle-aged man within snarled at him, once he had lowered the glass that had been separating them.

"So are we." The rookie stood firm. "This lady's late for an appointment, and I don't have all day. Now, I would appreciate it, sir, if you would join us, so that I can complete my paperwork."

"I understand you've had the misfortune to meet one of the few rude members of Captain's Point's supposed elite," Larry addressed Kate, glancing at the container in her hands as he approached her along with Sissy.

Kate handed the container back to her witness and attempted a smile. "I'm sorry you're having to wait on me," she apologized to the broker.

"Since I was supposed to be helping you at three o'clock, I'd say that we're right on schedule." In hopes of removing the worried look from her lovely face, he threw an arm around her and gave her a quick squeeze before he addressed the young officer. "I trust that you'll be making a full report as a witness, despite the fact this occurred in a parking lot, right, Bubba?"

"No problem there, Mr. Chesterton. This jerk of a banker has tied up a chunk of my aunt's hard-earned savings in some sort of development scheme of his, so it'll be a pleasure to see that he at least does right by Ms. Sinclair here." He turned towards Kate. "Now, if I could see your driver's license, ma'am."

While Kate was providing the required information over to their side, Larry again eyed the container in his employee's hand. "Am I right that those are some of the brownies that my aunt tells me are now a required component at any ladies' event in this city, Sissy?"

"Yes," she acknowledged, even as her gaze remained on the fair-sized container as if it were some sort of alien rocket debris that had found its way into her hand.

"Were you leaving us early again today?" Larry asked.

"Yes, sir."

"Are those designated for someone special?"

"No, sir." Sissy looked up, her eyes filling with hope. "I brought them in for everyone in the office to enjoy, but Glenda said she'd had about enough of my brownies."

"Our Glenda is more than a bit upset that you keep leaving her in the lurch and rightly so," Larry filled her in. "Why don't we make a deal here and now. I'll take that container and its contents off of your hands for my own consumption, and you'll keep your job, if you still want it, once we agree on the terms for a Chester's exclusive on those brownies going forward."

"I knew you were the nicest man in the whole world." Sissy threw her arms around her employer's neck at precisely the same moment that Kate completed her signature on Bubba's form and glanced Larry's way, raising one delicate eyebrow slightly as the broker's widened eyes pleaded for her to assist him.

"If Mr. Tate will sign Bubba's form, then I should be free for our appointment," Kate stated clearly, working hard to keep a straight face as she made her presence known to Sissy, who pulled back and thrust the container of brownies into Larry's hand.

"I'll have to turn in my notice, if you really want me to fill Chester's needs," his employee stated.

"You'll be our loss then and Chester's gain," Larry informed her and turned to the young officer, who was shifting his weight from one foot to his other, apparently unsure how to deal with the fact that the cause of all their troubles had once again raised his driver's window. "Let me have that clipboard, Bubba."

"Sure, Mr. Chesterton."

Not bothering to tap on the car's window, the broker opened the Mercedes' door and thrust the clipboard and its attached pen at the banker who was shouting into his cell phone loud enough that Kate and Sissy exchanged glances of disgust.

"Gerald, we've all waited long enough," Larry made his position clear. "I have a business to run, too."

"Call you back." The banker snarled and disconnected, before swinging his feet onto the pavement and leaning forward sufficiently to make eye contact with the victim of his reckless driving.

"I don't believe you've met Jack Jefferson's sister," Larry handled the necessary introduction. "Kate, this is Gerald Tate. Gerald, this is Kate Sinclair, who should not have to wait another minute for your insurance information."

"Jefferson's sister, you say?" The banker eyed Kate from head to toe in a way that made her uncomfortable. "I apologize, ma'am. I'm in the middle of closing a rather important deal. I'm sure your brother will attest to the fact that I'm not normally like this." He made a few quick scribbles on Bubba's form, signed it with a flourish and handed the clipboard back to Larry, who passed it on to the officer.

"Thank you." Kate sent Bubba a charming smile when he handed her a copy of the form. "And thank you, too."

She shifted her attention to Sissy. "Your securing Mr. Chesterton's help has made all the difference."

Then without giving the banker the slightest bit of attention, she made her way gracefully to the driver's door of her own car, turned the key in the ignition, and parked her scratched vehicle before rejoining Larry, who was waiting to accompany her back to his office.

"You're not hurt or anything, are you?" he asked as they began walking slowly towards their destination. "You car's received a nasty scratch, but the quarter panel isn't dented. Still, I wanted to make sure you're okay, before we go any further. Sometimes, it's a few minutes before the pain begins to set in."

"I'm fine, not to mention very glad that you offered me your assistance." She looked at him with eyes so full of gratitude that he was filled with an overwhelming desire to hug her to him and promise that he would smooth all of the bumps from the road for her going forward.

And, as he held the door that would admit his newest client to Chesterton and Chesterton's offices, Larry realized with no shock whatsoever that he had moved way beyond Chase's requirement that he put himself out there. Somehow, Kate Sinclair had found her way into his heart.

CHAPTER XLI

A few minutes later, Kate sipping on a restorative cup of tea and Larry placing a bottled water within reach, the two of them sat facing each other across the broad expanse of his executive desk.

"Thank you again for the way you took matters into your own hands out there," Kate said as her eyes filled with a level of adoration he believed would've been more in line with his having somehow flown to the moon and back on her behalf.

"You have to take someone like Gerald Tate firmly in hand." He brushed aside her comment. "Otherwise, they'll take advantage of you."

"You sound as if you aren't a fan of his," she pointed out.

"Can't stand the man." Larry's lips thinned for a moment, but then he continued, "There aren't many people I would say that about."

"Jack can't stand him either," Kate shared. "That's why I ignored him. My brother has a real talent for finding the good in everyone, so his dislike raises huge red flags as far as I'm concerned."

"Keep it under your hat, but your brother and I are about to invest in a new business venture of Adrianna's that's going to put a stick through the spokes in several of Gerald Tate's wheels." He reached for her file, opened it and leaned forward. "Now let's get started on what brought you to my humble office in the first place."

"I'm anxious to hear what you think of my financial position." Kate's eyes filled with so much trust that Larry automatically straightened his shoulders. "Jack and Susan have already told me that you're a genius when it comes to this sort of thing, but I would've trusted your guidance anyway, based solely on my own opinion of you as a person."

"To start with, you should give your father a big hug for having negotiated such a sizeable pre-nuptial agreement on your behalf," Larry began as visions of himself as a genius tried to find a home in his brain.

"My father wouldn't appreciate such a gesture," Kate responded reflexively as her expression hardened.

Surprised by such a harsh tone emanating from the soft-spoken woman before him, Larry sidestepped making a comment, even as he wondered what was behind her clear statement. "I know you were worried about the broker you had been using," he continued, "and I want to assure you that, for the most part, you aren't too badly positioned. Overall, I would say that about sixty percent of your funds are invested too conservatively, which surprised me, because I'm known as being fairly conservative myself."

"Jack said you wouldn't recommend that I do anything too risky." She nodded her head in agreement.

"If you were to leave things as they are now, you could live comfortably in Captain's Point on your investment income and probably accrue additional savings," he continued. "On the other hand, by reinvesting about thirty percent of your portfolio in some slightly more risky options, you could really begin to grow your wealth. There are those who would be more comfortable with the former, and others who would prefer the latter."

"Which would you recommend, knowing me as you do?" she asked.

"Given your age, I would consider reinvesting at least a portion of your overall assets," he stated. "As long as we are careful to diversify the new opportunities for growth, we should be able to minimize your total risk."

"I agree." Her beautiful crystal blue eyes drew him in as if he were a fish on a line. "Given what I've heard from both my brother and you, the first thing into which I would like to shift some of my funds would be Adrianna's new business venture."

Larry blinked. "I'm not at all sure that either your brother or I would consider that a wise investment for you," he stated. "For one thing, it's based on real estate, and real estate is more risky than I would normally recommend for you, especially since you've shared with me that you prefer not to work for your income."

"I've been thinking about what you asked me in regards to my seeking possible employment ever since that evening at Montgomery House." His client once again surprised him.

"What am I going to do with myself, once I'm living on my own, if I don't have a job to give some sort of structure to my time?" she posed his own question back at him. "Regular employment wasn't a part of the lifestyle that surrounded me most of my life, but my natural inclination has been to stay busy, which is why I've consistently volunteered in aid of various charitable pursuits in a way that clearly resembled what most people would call work. The only difference has been that I didn't receive a salary. The end result is that I've managed to maintain my computer skills and a good part of my accounting knowledge, and I've already spoken with Jack and Susan about helping me to put together a resume, once I've moved into a place of my own."

"Is it your intention to follow-up on your CPA?" he asked.

"Probably, although I have no idea what will be involved, since my prior steps along that path were all taken in Virginia."

"May I make a suggestion?" Larry forged ahead, not at all sure what his uncle would think of the move he was now making. "Sissy, who you just met, has turned in her notice, and the thing we will miss most will be her computer and fledgling accounting skills. Would you be willing to fill the vacancy?"

"You're offering me a position here at Chesterton and Chesterton?" Kate couldn't believe her good fortune, not sure if she was more excited by the prospect of spending her days in the presence of the man before her or by the realization that she would now be able to skip an initial job search.

"If you want it." He smiled back at her, forcing himself to breathe as he waited for her reply, not sure if he could handle her rejection if it came.

"I accept." She beamed back at him, and he took a deep breath.

"Wonderful! We'll fill Glenda in when you leave." He grinned. "How soon can you start?"

"Would Monday be soon enough?"

"Monday would be perfect."

Silence stretched as they gazed into the other's eyes, both celebrating the extraordinary thing that had just happened, each in their own way, but then Larry pulled himself together.

"Now, back to your portfolio." He made a note in her file on his computer. "Your being gainfully employed would make an investment in Adrianna's new venture more viable from a risk standpoint, since you would be in a position to recoup any losses you might experience up to a point. What percent of the funds you are considering for reinvestment would you want to risk in this particular area?"

"All of it." She surprised him once again, as he shifted his eyes from his computer screen to her. "If I understand correctly, Gerald Tate is leading folks along a road that will ultimately destroy all that's good about the Captain's Point I've already grown to love. If Chase, Adrianna, Jack, Susan and you all feel strongly enough about standing firm on the other side to invest your money, then I want to throw as much as I can into the pile, too."

Kate might weigh less than a feather and have the tiniest waist in the world, but no one could say that the woman before him didn't have spirit and courage. Larry's respect for his client rose another notch. At the same time, he found he wanted nothing more than to tell her he would invest some of his own funds for her in place of her own, in an effort to protect her from the risk she would now be assuming.

"I'll contact Adrianna as soon as we've finished here and ask if the option for you to be included as an investor is still available and at what level," he stated, "but I want you to promise me that you'll take advice from your brother on this one as well."

"I don't need to," she countered. "I trust you completely."

And with that Larry had to be content – part of him thrilled at his client's belief in him and part of him recognizing that Adrianna's new venture proving its worth had been added alongside Kate's being settled safely in a place of her own on his growing list of concerns about the woman before him.

CHAPTER XLII

As Larry stood on Blue Wolf Manor's broad porch fumbling for his key a couple of hours later, the door swung quietly open, revealing Daniel with a finger to his lips signaling for him to be quiet. Stepping silently into the house, he smiled his understanding as the poignant notes of Gabriel Fauré's Fantasy for Flute and Piano Opus 79 melodically drifted over them from the back of the house.

"I was watching for Mama and saw you coming," Daniel whispered.

"Let's listen to the music from in here," Larry picked up the boy and carried him into the breakfast room on their left. "Who's playing the flute?"

"Aunt Kate," his short cousin informed him. "She says Jack was right to turn her from ballet to an instrument, because her career would've been over and her feet ruined by her thirties, and this way she'll enjoy her flute all of her life."

"Smart gal, your aunt," Larry stated, as he once again realized how badly he had misjudged the woman who was more and more filling his days with her graceful presence.

The music ended and both of them stood. Surprised when they discovered Susan where she had entered from the attached garage and had been silently listening to the final bars in the hall that led to the parlor, Larry gave her a quick hug.

"Bravo!" He announced their presence as the three of them joined the musicians. "Fauré's music always speaks to me."

"I knew you were a romantic at heart," Kate teased him as she replaced her instrument in its case.

"Can you stay for dinner?" Susan asked.

"Actually, I came to steal your sister-in-law away," he replied as his gaze shifted to the flutist. "I have a lead on a rental opportunity. It's a bit out of the box, but there are aspects of it that may appeal to you, at least on a short term basis."

"How wonderful!" Kate beamed. "Let me get my coat."

"I'll see to it that we grab a bite to eat afterwards, so you three don't have to wait on us," Larry told Susan as an aside, then hurried to assist Kate as she slipped into her coat.

Left behind in the parlor, Jack rose from the piano bench, gathered his wife into his arms and lifted one eyebrow.

"Don't say a word," she whispered into his ear. "Little pitchers have big ears, and I wouldn't want to jinx anything that may be developing there."

"Nor would I." His expression sobered as the sound of the front door closing behind the other couple carried along the hallway. "Kate deserves the best the world has to offer, and he's one of the few men I know who meets that standard."

"Other than yourself, of course." Susan slipped her arms around his neck. "Otherwise, you would never have been able to break through all the defenses I'd erected after my divorce," she pointed out in her common sense way as she pulled his face closer to hers, pleased when he kissed her thoroughly.

"Being around you will always bring out the best in me," he promised as he guided her towards the front of the house. "Now you change into something more comfortable and hurry back down for supper, after which we'll put our

Daniel to bed and I'll spend the rest of the evening showing you just how much I love you in the best possible ways."

A few minutes later, Larry turned off his SUV in front of a fair-sized Victorian on Tuttle Avenue. "We are now in Captain's Point's historic district," he explained.

"The area that Adrianna's new venture is seeking to save in a way that will tap into Chase's and your successful efforts through the city council to reinvigorate downtown." Kate exhibited her understanding, much to his relief.

"Exactly." He disembarked and rounded the SUV, opening her door and guiding her up the sidewalk towards the welcoming porch. "One of my clients, Jewel Parkerson, owns this home," he explained. "Her husband Bruce passed away a few years ago, and, for reasons of her own, she is considering renting out a two-room, one bath suite for additional income. You may not have realized it as we drove here, but we're only six blocks from my office, so you would be within walking distance of work, the organic market, the post office, restaurants, and other amenities."

"I'm looking forward to seeing the space," she replied as he turned the old-fashioned doorbell.

"Welcome!" The pleasant-faced, middle-aged woman greeted them, as she swung open the door and indicated for them to enter. "I'm Jewel, and you must be Kate Sinclair. Larry was singing your praises to me earlier, and it's an honor to have you consider my house as your possible first home in Captain's Point."

"I'm drawn to your rental suite, because of its location." Kate shook the other woman's offered hand. "Have you lived here long?"

"My husband brought me here as a young bride," Jewel filled her in. "Now that he's gone, I find both that living alone in such a big house can be a bit lonely and that I would benefit from some additional income. This is the main parlor." She indicated a nicely proportioned room that led off one side of the foyer and was furnished with chintz-covered seating and antiques. "And this, of course, is the dining room."

"Antiques always seem so warm and welcoming, don't they?" Kate didn't wait for a reply. "My brother and sister-in-law have furnished their house in a similar fashion, and I've found myself feeling very comfortable in that type of surrounding."

"If you'll come this way, I'll show you the rooms I've planned to rent out." Jewel led them up the stairway that rose from the left side of the foyer. "As you can see, both rooms are large and are furnished similarly to the downstairs."

The first room, Kate realized upon entering, had been arranged as a comfortable sitting room and included a television and a desk that held a laptop and printer. Opening a door in the corner, she revealed a surprisingly large closet for a Victorian. Moving on to the equally large bedroom, she was even more surprised to find that it boasted a walk-in closet, part of each room having been sacrificed to provide storage space during an early remodel. Another doorway proved to lead into a large four-piece bathroom that had been renovated in an historically accurate manner that appealed to her.

"I plan to move the television and computer equipment to the sunroom downstairs," Jewel explained.

"I have my own," Kate assured her, "but since I don't have furniture, renting furnished rooms such as these would answer my needs perfectly."

Behind her, Larry let out a small sigh as the two women finalized their arrangement and discussed such details as kitchen privileges. Jewel's income needs would now be met, and he would no longer have to worry about Kate's safety.

A few minutes later, he shut the passenger door on his SUV, joined Kate, and headed them towards Montgomery's for dinner.

"I feel like a huge weight has been lifted from my shoulders today," she shared with him as he negotiated their vehicle's turn onto the main road. "I've found a home, settled my finances and secured a new position with Chesterton and Chesterton, all thanks to you. You have no idea how appreciative I am."

"I'm glad everything seems to be working out for you," he replied as he swung the SUV into a convenient parking slot. "You've survived a difficult time in the past, and I want your future here in Captain's Point to be different."

"With someone as wonderful as you to help and guide me, I don't see how it can be anything else," she assured him.

And as he disembarked and rounded the SUV, Larry felt somewhat amazed by how easily he fit into the role she had written for him. Chase had been right. Once he had settled his mind to it, finding someone to care for hadn't taken him all that much time.

CHAPTER XLIII

The next afternoon, Jack watched for the delivery van he was expecting to enter the driveway of his home momentarily, as the cold lump that had been forming in his stomach ever since he had discovered the notification email that morning hardened. He had faced a rampaging bull elephant, a king cobra rearing its ugly head and the dangerous frozen heights of one of the world's tallest mountains without blinking an eye, but now his knees felt like jelly.

Used to making split-second decisions, he had done so in Key West – first in the designer dress shop and later in the upscale shoe emporium next door. What had he been thinking?

Ever since both Adrianna and Susan had made their positions clear over dinner shortly after their return from Florida about Chase's and his predilection for giving them expensive gifts, he had realized that he had made a wrong turn, but there had been no way to wind back the clock. Now, he would have to face the music, not to mention Susan's anger, when she came home tonight – Kate's assurances to the contrary that his new wife would understand and be pleased having failed to convince him.

The van now making its way along the drive, he headed for the foyer, where he called to his sister, "They're here. Can you lend me a hand?"

"Sure," Kate responded as she hurried along the hallway from the parlor alone, since Daniel was still napping behind his closed door upstairs.

A few minutes later, the large shipping crate and a fair-sized box now taking up space in front of the fireplace in the master bedroom, Jack carefully opened the former with a box knife as his sister rejoined him.

"I purchased these this morning in case Susan doesn't have enough extras." Kate pulled three packages of oversized satin padded hangers from a large shopping bag. "Designer dresses deserve the best care you can give them. Are you planning to lay them out on the bed?"

"I hadn't really given it much thought, but that sounds like a good idea," he replied as he removed the first dress and its temporary hanger from a slot in the travel bar and handed it to his sister. "What do you think?"

"It's lovely," she breathed her appreciation as her fingers caressed the soft fabric. "I can see why you were so driven to purchase it for her. Susan will look gorgeous in this. It was made for her."

"Unfortunately, so were the rest of them." He sent her a wry grin. "I just hope that you're right and she won't kill me for doing this. Is it wrong for me to want her to have the very best that my money can give her?"

"No..." Kate sought for the right words. "Susan isn't like the women we grew up around, though, and it may take her a while to get her mind around the extent of your now joint wealth."

"It will if she doesn't take any more interest in it than she has so far," he agreed. "You know, she's never even asked me if I signed anything over to Daniel or her at the time of our marriage."

"May I ask you something?" Kate paused as he continued to remove one beautiful dress after another and then hand them to her to place on a satin hanger and display on the bed.

"Sure." He waited.

"Why didn't you hire people to help Susan, when you invited all those folks over for a cookout?"

"All the money Susan earns is hers to keep and do with as she pleases," Jack explained, understanding completely why his sister would've asked such a question, given their unusual upbringing. "She could've hired anyone she wanted to either help with the preparations or to cater the whole event. There's a great reward in doing things for others, though, and Susie and I both enjoy doing just that. It's one of the first surprise lessons that I learned after leaving home."

Kate let out a small sigh. "Sometimes I wonder if the transition from the life I've known to the one I seek is much larger than I first envisioned it would be," she acknowledged.

"Take it one day at a time, and you'll be fine." He broke down the large container for transporting downstairs and then opened the smaller box that had arrived from the shoe store.

"She will be glad that you purchased these, since you bought the dresses," his sister stated emphatically. "You can't wear designer gowns with any old kind of footwear. When will she have her first opportunity to wear one of these?"

Jack's shoulders slumped. "I hadn't even thought of that."

"Well, you should," she made her position clear. "At least, organize some sort of dinner party at Montgomery's for Saturday night."

"Good idea." He handed her the last shoebox. "I'll get in touch with Chase and Larry as soon as we're through here. Do you have something appropriate to wear?"

"I think I can come up with a little something that won't embarrass you." She chuckled.

"I'm so glad that you've settled here in Captain's Point." Her brother threw an arm around her shoulders as they both examined the finery that was now displayed before them. "If nothing else, you provide great moral support in my moments of self-doubt."

"Self-doubt? You?" Kate looked at him with surprise. "You always seem so self-assured."

"In most situations, I am fairly sure of myself," he admitted, "but love and marriage are two things I don't know all that much about. One thing I have recognized – the road to a successful marriage is filled with potholes, and I'm working hard to avoid them. Susie had an awful time with her ex, and I don't ever want to put her into similar positions, which places even more stress on me to get things right the first time around."

"Jack, please believe me." Kate turned him to face her. "Susan is very happy in your marriage. The love you two have for one another isn't that fragile. Anyone with half a brain can see that."

"Thanks." He gave his sister a quick hug. "I needed that. Now, I'm going to haul this trash out back and try to pull myself together before she gets here. Wish me luck."

"You're not going to need any," she sought to calm his fears, even as she wished she could wave a magic wand and insure that his generous gift would be received in the spirit in which it was being given.

CHAPTER XLIV

Completely unaware of what awaited her, Susan entered her home a short while later and headed straight upstairs to her bedroom in an effort to hide two shopping bags filled with toys that were destined for delivery to Daniel at Christmas from Santa Claus.

Aghast once he realized she wasn't going to join him first, Jack rose from the sofa in the library and hurried after her, only reaching the turn in the stairway before she shot from their room and called over the banister, "Jack Jefferson!"

"Yes, my love?" he responded as he took the last step, surprising her even further.

"What is the meaning of all that?" She pointed towards the room she had just left with the index finger of her right hand, her left hand firmly placed upon her hip, further signifying her displeasure.

"They're designer dresses," he stated the obvious, not sure in the face of her anger what to do.

"I can see that," she huffed. "Why are they here?"

"Susie, please don't deny me the pleasure of purchasing beautiful things for you during our lifetime honeymoon," he pleaded. "Please."

For a moment, they faced each other in silence, as along the hallway in Daniel's room both Kate and the child in her lap held their breaths.

But then, Susan filled with horror at what she had just done. How could she have put her intelligent, talented, wonderful husband into a position where he felt the need to beg her to let him do anything?

This man – who had taken her and her child under his wing, so he could love and support them – deserved better. Ever since she had accepted his kind, gentle, love-filled proposal, she had sought for a way to repay him, to show him just how much she loved him in return, and throwing his generous gesture back at him had been the best she could do? What was wrong with her?

"Oh, Jack…" Without thinking, she flung herself at him and threw her arms around his neck, even as she burst into tears. "I'm so sorry." She sobbed into his broad shoulder. "I'm so very, very sorry."

Neither happy with the turn of events nor understanding his wife's tears, Jack did the only thing that came naturally and held her tightly to him. "It's okay, Susie. We're okay," he sought to reassure her. "All I ever wanted to do was love and pamper you."

"I know," she wailed into the damp cloth of his sweatshirt. "You're nothing but goodness itself, and I've been horribly selfish. I love you so much, and now I've hurt you terribly."

"All it will take for me to get over it is for you to dry your eyes and give Kate and Daniel and me a brief fashion show," he advised her. "And then, I'm going to escort you, wearing one of your new dresses, to Montgomery's Saturday evening, where I'll be the envy of men for miles around."

"Don't be silly." She sent him a watery smile, and then whispered into his ear as she once again hugged his neck, "I'm so sorry, Jack. I should've known better. I'm simply not used to being spoiled at this level, that's all."

"Does this mean that you won't refuse me the pleasure of buying out the next jewelry store I enter?" he asked hopefully.

"I wouldn't go quite that far." She allowed him to guide her into their room, where he silenced any further objections by planting his lips firmly on hers.

"You do realize that I'm going to continue kissing you like this until you give in, don't you?" he asked once he let her up for air.

"But even you can't afford…" Again her words were cut off by a kiss.

"I can do this forever." His dark eyes twinkled down at her.

"But where would I…"

"I'm even enjoying it," he pointed out a minute later.

"Promise you won't get too carried away." She let out a small sigh as she pulled back slightly, even as her lips turned up at their corners.

"I promise I'll never risk our last couple of million." He gathered her to him again with his left arm, threaded the fingers of his right hand through her hair, and proceeded to kiss her thoroughly several times over.

Only silence now coming from the master suite, the eavesdroppers in the large room at the other end of the hallway began a whispered conversation of their own.

"My mama's mad at Jack, isn't she?" Daniel asked as he looked up at Kate.

"Not really," she said, trying hard to think of a way to explain. "Jack was downstairs, and your mom had just discovered something up here that surprised her. He'll explain everything to her, and she'll understand, because that's how it works when you love someone as much as she loves him and he loves her."

"So we won't have to leave our big, happy house?" His eyes widened with hope.

"Absolutely not!" Kate hugged him close. "Why would you even think that? Jack would never want your mother and you to leave here, unless the three of you were going someplace together."

"My real father wanted us to leave," Daniel pointed out. "He didn't want us."

"Well, my brother isn't like your real father." His new aunt ran her fingers through the boy's hair, straightening it. "Jack and your mom both know how to love – really love in a way that holds on and cares deeply, which is why you feel so warm and safe when you're surrounded by their love for you. They're filled with so much love for each other that there's even plenty for me, too."

"You're not staying here, though."

"No, but I'm leaving because I want to, not because either Jack or your mom has sent me away," Kate pointed out. "If I needed a place to live, both of them would tell me to make this my home forever."

"I would, too." Daniel reached his arms around her neck and hugged her hard. "I love you, Aunt Kate. Can you feel my love wrapping around you?"

"As much as I hope you can feel mine wrapping around you." She felt the prick of tears as she held him even closer for a moment. "Now let's see what that silly rabbit in this storybook of yours has gotten himself into."

And with that, she released him and reopened his children's book, wondering as she did so how such a little guy could have experienced so much pain and yet be able to show so much love for her at such a young age, something she was still struggling to learn how to do.

CHAPTER XLV

As Jack turned his SUV right onto the main road the next afternoon, Kate let out a small sigh where she stood watching him through the breakfast room window, thankful that she would report to work at Chesterton and Chesterton on Monday. Time was beginning to hang heavy on her hands, despite the warm welcome she had received in her brother's home. Even her move to Jewel's rental suite Sunday afternoon would only take an hour or two.

Crossing the foyer, she paused for a moment and breathed in the scent of the almost two dozen roses that still looked nice thanks to Susan's expert advice as to their care and feeding. With a smile, she recalled the three blossoms that were already drying between the layers of her sister-in-law's flower press.

How awful it would've been if her brother had married someone she didn't like. Instead he had chosen the first friend she knew she could trust with a secret such as her desire for a keepsake of Larry's gesture, and Ginny might soon prove to be the second.

Larry...

Did his heart beat as fast when they were together as hers did? Were his dreams as full of her as hers were of him? Did the scent of her perfume haunt his thoughts in the same way that she could recall his aftershave at a moment's notice?

She made her way to the library couch, retrieved her laptop from the coffee table, and flipped open its lid, just as her phone announced an incoming call. Checking the number, she recognized it only as local before she answered.

"Help! I need help, woman!" Larry's strong voice sent her pulse racing. "If I stop by there on my way home in a few minutes, can I kidnap you as an assistant, so I can pull everything together in time for this supper meeting that I volunteered to hold at my place in a mere two and a half hours?"

"Feel free to kidnap me, but I'm a fledgling in the kitchen," she admitted. "According to Susan, though, I'm a quick learner."

"If you have two functioning hands and a willing spirit, then you're all that I need," he assured her. "I've already commissioned Marissa at Sheffield Place Inn to make a pot of her broccoli cheese soup and a platter of her empanadillas – half of them filled with chicken and the other half with cheese laced with fruit. Adrianna and Penny have promised to bring dessert, so that only leaves the chili I'm throwing together and a couple of large salads."

"We should be able to handle that," she agreed. "How long do I have to get ready?"

"I'm walking to my car now, but I'll let myself in and wait in the library until you come down."

"I shouldn't be long," she promised as she headed for the stairs, glad that she had showered after working out in her brother's gym an hour before.

Thirty minutes later, Kate found herself in the upscale elevator that led from the first floor of the refurbished carriage house at The Cove to her companion's condo above. Now that she had seen the interior square footage of the bottom level, she realized that her expectations needed to be revised. Unless much of the second floor space was undeveloped, the home above was quite large – the carriage house having proven to be much deeper than it appeared from the outside.

"I really appreciate your help," Larry was saying as the elevator came to a halt. "The size of our guest list has almost doubled since I extended the original invitation, and between work and some council duties, I haven't had much time for preparations. Thank goodness, Thursday is Maggie Daniels' morning at my place."

"Oh!" Kate stepped forward into a wide foyer sporting matching antique, carved Moroccan doors at each end that she assumed hid two fair-sized closets.

Through the broad archway ahead, the home's living room lay before her. Although large, its warm ambiance welcomed her, primarily due to the rich leathers, fabrics and woods that had been used to decorate it. Expansive windows on the side facing the Atlantic provided plenty of light, and fine artwork that decorated the walls proclaimed both the good eye and excellent taste of the home's owner.

"Do you like it?" he called over his shoulder as he moved past her, and she hurriedly followed him through a lovely formal dining room and into a large, sunny kitchen, where he placed Marissa's soup on the stove.

"It's wonderful!" she breathed, her eyes taking in the French country décor of the room in which they now stood, even as she ran her fingers along an oak sideboard.

"I mixed my styles a bit when I was throwing it all together over the years," he pointed out. "Basically, I drew on what I liked when I toured Europe after grad school, and then there were pieces I fell in love with along the way that had to be included as well."

"It's the eclectic arrangement of the rooms that gives it the warmth," she sought to reassure him.

"Would you like a tour of the rest?" he asked, and for a moment, she was reminded of Daniel as the same eagerness her nephew often exhibited filled his older cousin's face.

"Sure, if we have the time."

He gestured her through a doorway and into a hall that ran from the back wall of the living room, past the dining room and kitchen to where four bedrooms lay beyond.

"This is the powder room." He paused for a moment. "And I use this bedroom as my study and home office because of the view."

She caught a glimpse of another larger-than-expected room that reminded her of her brother's library.

"Then we have two guest rooms, because I'm sometimes called upon to accept overflow from The Cove, and this whole back portion is the master suite." He entered the massive space and began throwing open doors revealing two walk-in closets and two full baths as well as a small room that contained a treadmill and a weight bench.

"Obviously, I only use the one closet and bath, but I went ahead and planned for a female resident at some point to maintain resale value," he explained. "Do you think a woman would be happy living in a place like this if she could redecorate?"

"Any woman with half a brain would love living in a home like this." She turned her sparkling blue eyes towards his. "Personally, I wouldn't change a thing."

"Really?" The eager look once again filled Larry's face.

"Really." She stepped forward and paused in the doorway of the massive walk-in closet. "Jack jokes about all of my clothes, but I couldn't even begin to fill this." She gestured towards the room's empty shelves and shoe cubicles.

For a moment, they both stood and faced each other in silence, as Larry fought to hold his tongue and Kate hoped for him to say the words she most wanted to hear. Then, the large grandfather clock in the living room chimed the hour in its deep tones.

"We'd better get a move on," Larry stated as they both stepped towards the hallway, and he signaled for her to go first.

"What can I do to help?" she asked.

"We're really expecting eleven, but there could be twelve total, if Herb Stuart can join us," he filled her in. "There are some hunter green napkins in that drawer on your right, and the silverware is in here. If you could roll a knife, fork and soup spoon into each one that will get us started."

Quickly applying herself to the task, Kate couldn't help but marvel at the fact that Larry kept referring to the party as theirs.

"I thought we'd set up buffet style here on the island," he explained as he began sautéing ground beef and chopped onions. "If you'll open the cabinet to the right of the island's sink, you'll find a set of rustic dinnerware that should do for us – twelve plates and twelve soup bowls, plus twelve dessert plates."

The whir of the electric can opener cut off conversation as he began opening the beans that would soon be needed, and she watched with envy as he moved assuredly around the space.

"Let's use these two wooden salad bowls," he suggested, lifting them down for her. "I bought pre-sorted packages of Caesar salad and the makings for a basic tossed one, plus a selection of dressings, if you want to unpack them from the shopping bags."

Relieved that so far she had known what to do, Kate organized the buffet area, and then set out the dressings. "We could go ahead and mix the lettuce, grated carrots and chopped tomatoes for the salad we're putting together from scratch," she suggested, "but we probably should wait until the guests begin to arrive before cutting into the avocados and mixing the dressing into the Caesar salad."

"I agree." He sent her a grin as he began washing out the empty bean cans and then tossing them into an under-counter recycling bin. "I'm beginning to think that, with your help, we're going to pull this off." He threw his arm around her and gave her a quick hug, before reaching for the chili powder.

Kate leaned against the counter and waited until he finished. "What about drinks?" she asked.

"There's beer in the refrigerator drawer to your left." His elbow pointed her way as he stirred the chili that was now sending out a wonderful aroma. "Wine's in the wine fridge. There are some sodas in the main refrigerator, and I mixed two pitchers of lemonade before I left this morning."

"Glasses?"

"In here." He opened a door that led into a surprisingly large butler's pantry.

"Where does that one lead?" She pointed towards a companion door to his left.

"Food pantry." He began placing glassware on the counter, but as she reached to pick up some wine glasses and carry them to the island, he took her hand. "I want to ask you something before everyone gets here." He surprised her by drawing her back to the stove where he turned down the heat under both pots and then stirred the contents of each one in turn, while still retaining his hold on her.

"Yes?"

"It's about the meeting this evening." He set down the second large spoon and turned to face her, taking her other hand in his. "Chase and Adrianna are going to want to retain control of the company, so they'll probably issue a limited number of shares in denominations of twenty-five thousand dollars each. I believe that Pete and Julia will both take on a share. Herb, Jeff, Otis and Penny would buy eight more shares between them, according to what I've heard. Your brother and I have already committed to half a million dollars each. Chase is willing to put in whatever it takes for Adrianna to retain a controlling interest and have enough funds available to be viable."

"Do you want me to back out?"

"Not at all," he stated firmly. "While there's risk involved in a venture like this, I understand and admire your desire to pitch in. We had discussed your reinvesting half a million. If you limit your investment in this venture to a quarter million, then Chase and Adrianna can throw in two million even and maintain a comfortable margin of control, which would leave you with another quarter of a million that you could diversify amongst some slightly less risky options. From my perspective as your broker, I would call that a win/win."

To his relief, she sent him a slow smile that reminded him of her brother's. "I'd be a fool not to accept the advice of a genius now, wouldn't I?" she asked as a three-note chime announced that the elevator was lifting the first contingent of guests to the upper floor.

"Bread and butter!" He dropped her hands and hurried towards the pantry, while she threw open the main refrigerator's door.

And, as he quickly displayed an assortment of crusty rolls in a large bread basket and she unwrapped sticks of butter, he basked in the look of trust that had once again filled her eyes as she had agreed to his suggestion, and she filled with contentment at being allowed to work beside him as his helpmate in his beautiful home.

CHAPTER XLVI

Friday evening surprised the owners of Blue Wolf Manor with even more quiet time alone, the first day of their working at home together having already gone well. Daniel had been tucked into bed for the night, and Kate had announced she was meeting someone for dinner without giving the name that they had both hoped to hear.

Each carrying a mug of hot chocolate, the newlyweds had found their way to the couch in their library, where Jack had sat at one end pounding the keys on his laptop for the last hour while Susan had read through a women's magazine at the other end.

"Done!" He hit Save and looked up. "I don't believe I've ever seen you reading a magazine before. Books or your ereader all the time and the newspapers, when they arrive, but never a magazine."

"One of my clients finished it while she was waiting for her appointment and left it with me to enjoy," she explained.

"And have you enjoyed it?" he asked, intrigued.

"Some of the articles, yes." She flipped back a few pages. "The makeup tips are pretty much lost on me, but there's one thing outlined here that I thought we might like to do." She turned the first page of an article towards him.

"*How to Strengthen Your Marriage*," he read the title aloud as he felt a cold knot form in his stomach. "Do you think we're in trouble already?" He closed his laptop and laid it on the coffee table, attempting a nonchalant look.

"Of course not." She tossed the magazine on top of his computer and joined him at his end of the sofa. "It's more about adjustment and communication. Some of it doesn't apply, because it's things like sharing a bathroom, which we don't do. The basic premise is that you should set aside times when only the two of you are present, during which you can have open forums of conversation and discuss whatever either one of you suggests."

"You mean things that are bothering you?" Her husband's face filled with concern. "Have I done something wrong?"

"No, you've done everything right." She took his face in her hands and kissed him until she felt him relax and bring his strong arms around her. "It isn't something we need to do. I just thought it might be fun, you know, something like typical newlyweds do. It was silly of me, especially when you can offer me something much more pleasurable as soon as we go upstairs where we won't be disturbed." Once again, she brought her lips onto his, guilt filling her for the worried look she had unintentionally brought to his face.

Several minutes later, Susan exited her dressing room, expecting to receive the aforementioned pleasure from her husband. Instead, she found him propped up against the pillows, reading her magazine that he must've gone back downstairs and retrieved.

Sensing her approach, Jack glanced up. "No nightgown again this evening?" he asked as his eyes took in her pajamas that were designed more for warmth than for pleasurable excitement, their gray bottoms and pink waffle-weave top decorated with kittens, her thick blonde hair held back in a ponytail.

Rounding the bed, she picked up the remote from his nightstand and turned on the gas fireplace, then perched on the edge of their bed. "Would you like me to change?"

She ran the back of her fingers along his cheek. "I'm sure you can keep me warm enough in your arms."

"Don't be silly." He pulled her down onto him, planting a firm kiss on her lips, even as the end of the magazine's spine was pricking her exposed lower ribs. "You look perfectly delectable, just as you are."

"So, which article did you find most interesting?" Susan teased, once he let her up for air again. "The one about this season's fashion in cocktail dresses or the one about the new shades of eyeshadow?"

"Neither." He reached for the slick pages, his dimples showing. "I was reading *Keeping Your Man Healthy* if you must know."

"And did you learn anything?" Her expression sobered. "Anything I should do?"

"Not a thing." Jack grinned. "I should be healthy as an ox, since I already follow everything they suggest and have done for years."

"That's good, isn't it?"

"Yes, and I think we should do what you suggested as well," he informed her. "I can see where good communication skills could benefit a marriage over the long term."

"So what do we do first?" she asked as he passed her the magazine, and she relocated the article. "Okay, it says that we should sit cross-legged on the floor, facing each other with our knees touching." She looked up at him, not sure what his reaction to these directions would be.

"It might be warmer if we just stayed on the bed," he suggested, his eyes twinkling.

"Good idea," Susan agreed. "Let's straighten the covers and get into position."

This proved harder to do, though, than either of them had anticipated.

"There's no way our knees can touch without my pulling a groin muscle," Jack pointed out with chagrin. "My legs are longer than yours."

"Why don't we just sit with our shins touching," Susan suggested. "I think the point is that we should feel a physical connection. We're supposed to lightly hold hands as well."

"Sounds good to me." He took her slim hands loosely into his strong ones as they each pressed their own shins against the other's.

"Now what?" Jack attempted to peer down at the magazine where it lay next to his wife.

"One of us is supposed to ask the other one a question, and then we continue along that conversational thread until we reach an end point," Susan explained. "It says we should attempt to complete four threads. Why don't you start?"

"I can ask anything I want?"

"Anything, and I'll answer whatever you ask me thoughtfully and honestly," she assured him as her beautiful eyes met his filled with so much love and trust that his mind went completely blank for a moment. "What would you like to know?"

Feeling completely unprepared, Jack fought to focus his thoughts, but then his face lit up.

"Yes?" Susan looked at him expectantly.

"No." He sent her a sheepish grin. "You'll think I'm not taking this exercise seriously."

"It says here that any question is to be taken seriously, because it may be drawing on deep-seated concerns." She looked up from the magazine and waited.

"Here goes then," he capitulated. "As a writer, I've wondered about this sort of thing for years – the motivation behind it and, in some cases, the desperation reflected within it. Frankly, my mother wasn't the kind of woman I could ask, and my sister was only a kid when I left home. It's about your toenails."

"My toenails?" Susan's eyes widened as she reflexively moved to hide her feet further beneath her legs.

"Not that there's anything wrong with them," he assured her. "Like everything else about you they're perfect, but I've noted all over the world, from jungle tribes to Mongolian herders to Captain's Point, how particularly women and sometimes men go to great lengths to embellish themselves with makeup or a stick pierced through their nose."

"I'm not sure I'm following you," she admitted.

"Your beauty is so fresh and clean." He studied her face, his own filled with frank admiration. "I honestly don't know what kind of makeup you use or even if you use any at all, except for occasional lipstick and your light perfume."

"My mother proved to me years ago that lighter was better on my type of skin, because heavy makeups stood out as opposed to enhancing my looks." To her surprise, Susan suddenly felt very shy sharing these intimate details with him – odd, she thought, since he certainly knew every nook and cranny of her body after the past three weeks. "I apply a little light cream foundation with my fingertip, add a dusting of powder and a touch of mascara, but none of that goes on my toenails."

"I'll have to remember to thank your mom the next time I see her." Jack leaned forward and dropped a kiss on the tip of his wife's nose. "So here's my question. You usually don't wear nail polish, but on our wedding day, you polished your nails – both fingers and toes. Then as soon as we arrived in Key West, everything went back to normal, but tonight I've noticed that you've polished your toenails again. What was your motivation to do that now, but not during our honeymoon trip? Why polish them for only the one day of our wedding?"

Susan laughed. "I'm not sure this is what the magazine editor intended, but here's your answer as far as I can deliver one. I normally don't bother with nail polish because between Daniel and the files I'm in and out of at work, it constantly gets chipped. As for our wedding day, Bitsy at Long and Short throws in a free manicure and pedicure when she does a bride's hair. Beach sand is not a pedicure's friend, so off it went once we arrived in Key West."

"And the pink toenails today?" Jack's eyes again twinkled.

Susan was appalled to feel warmth of a blush on her cheeks. "I was enjoying my lovely bathroom with the antique, painted tiles covered in roses that you had done up for me, and I wanted to feel pretty."

"I've traveled the world, and you're the most beautiful woman I've ever set eyes on." He held her gaze. "But I've got to tell you, Susie, between those pajamas and your pink toenails, you've morphed yourself into the cutest teenager that's ever existed and made me feel like one, too. You consider yourself free to give in to urges like these whenever you want. Just know that, when you do so, I may have trouble keeping my hands off of you."

"I love you, Jack Jefferson." She squeezed his aforementioned hands, the only thing she could do with their legs separating them as they were.

"I love you, Susie Chesterton, and your cute pjs, too." He leaned forward enough to drop a light kiss on her lips. "Now aren't you supposed to ask me some sort of question back, in order to keep the conversational thread going?"

"Yes," she acknowledged, even as she averted her eyes. "I'm not sure you'll thank me for asking this. We've never really talked about the question that came into my mind when you asked me yours, and you may find it impolite or even insulting."

"I can't imagine your being either one of those things."
It was Jack's turn to be surprised. "Isn't that what this is all
about, though, being able to ask one another absolutely
anything without fear of repercussions?"

"I suppose," Susan agreed, wishing now that she hadn't
mentioned the article while recognizing that she had no
alternative but to proceed. "It struck me when you said
your mother wasn't the type of woman you could ask and
Kate was only a kid. What about all of those other women
in your life? Why couldn't you have asked one of them?"

"You know how they say don't believe everything you
read or see on the internet?" Jack was relieved to finally
have an opportunity to explain to his new wife what this
part of his life had actually been like before he had moved
to Captain's Point. "Well, you shouldn't believe
everything you read in one of my novels either. The fact is
that over the years Jack has been a rather dull boy. I'm not
going to lie to you, when I was in college and my hormones
were racing, I spread my fair share of wild oats, but then I
joined the Navy and having casual sex with colleagues or in
ports of call really wasn't my thing."

"What about when you were at Harvard?"

"There were one or two occasions, sure. On the other
hand, I wanted to get my MBA as fast as I could, so I took
heavy course loads at the same time I was under contract to
write *Drifter* and *Adventures*. Writing is by definition a
fairly solitary business, and I found myself experimenting
with the first Anderson detective story for diversion as
well. What spare time I had, I usually spent at some sort of
sporting event or in an athletic pursuit with one or more of
the guys."

"And when you were traveling or working as some sort
of guide or pilot?" Susan asked. "Your literary novels are
full of romantic encounters, and I've seen where you were
considered to be one of the World's Ten Most Eligible
Bachelors."

"The latter is primarily because of the novels, some good publicity provided by my publisher and what's now our net worth due to my business investments," Jack explained. "As for my books, I wrote *Jungle Places* when I was in a pup tent alone on the side of a frozen mountain – not in some gorgeous woman's arms."

"But surely a man as handsome as you didn't have any trouble attracting women," Susan persevered.

"Not at all," he agreed with a wry smile. "Once my novels began selling and attracted some media attention, there were any number of females who were perfectly willing to fall into my bed one night and then sell the story to some gossip rag the next day."

"Oh, Jack…" She squeezed his hand as she noted the pain in his eyes.

"For several years, when I spent a good bit of time in Europe, there was one woman with whom I had a relationship on the occasions when we were geographically near enough to each other to do so," he kept the thread going.

"A serious relationship?" she asked, not really sure that she wanted to know.

"Not in the way that you mean." He sent her another twisted smile. "She was five years older than me, and her husband was twenty-five years older than she. He had been in an accident, was wheelchair bound, and had suffered a head injury. She still loved him and didn't want to divorce him, even though he no longer knew her.

"We were good friends, and we both had needs we could meet for each other. She knew she could trust me with her secret, and I knew I could trust her with mine. We were never in love, though, neither one of us, although we did enjoy some good times. Eventually, he died, and she married a rich widower, which ended things between us. We still email on rare occasions. She tells me about her children and keeps me up to date on common friends. I share news about the writing, which she always supported, and I let her know about our marriage. If we're ever near enough to do so, I'd like to introduce you to her. She's very happy that I've found someone to love, too."

"And after she remarried?"

"For the most part, I was either here visiting with Uncle Ivan as his health was deteriorating, in some remote locale with no real opportunity, or meeting the demands of writing to the point that months would go by without my seeing anyone socially," Jack filled her in. "One of my fears is that Kate is going to miss out on love for as long as I did.

"Then my uncle died, I decided to make this house and Captain's Point my permanent home, and the next thing I knew I was saving the most beautiful damsel in the world from losing her purse on the boardwalk at the marina. You'll never understand how much it meant to me that Daniel and you allowed me into your lives simply because you liked me as a person and not because of the level of fame I had achieved or the amount of money I had."

"Oh, Jack..." Susan breathed. "You're going to have to bend closer so I can give you a hug."

"Not on your life." He tossed the magazine onto the floor and drew her to him. "I'm making a rule here and now that in this house we only discuss one conversational thread per night, thereby leaving plenty of time for other joint ventures."

"I love it when you're masterful." She giggled as he nuzzled her neck.

Sometime later, as they lay snuggled against the pillows watching the flames dance in the fireplace, Jack kissed the top of her head. "You know, Susie," he said. "That exercise wasn't such a bad idea after all. I don't believe anything could make me love you any more than I already do. Still, somehow I feel like sharing those things with each other has drawn us even closer by adding another layer to our mutual understanding, and I'm glad I had an opportunity to dispel some of the rumors about my supposedly rampant sexual activities here, there and everywhere all around the world."

"I'm glad, too," she agreed. "I've been afraid I would never measure up to all those other women."

"Measure up?" He lifted her face, so he could see her eyes, his own filled with honest surprise at her concerns. "Don't you know that you're head and shoulders above the rest?"

"Honestly, I've tried not to think about it," she admitted.

"Think about this then." His mind rapidly thought through the best way to state his case. "It's true. I went to bed with other women during the twenty odd years before I met you, but you're the only woman in the world that I've ever felt this way about or shared this kind of relationship with. Truly making love to a woman like I only have with you and being loved in return takes everything to a whole different level - one that's way more rewarding and fulfilling than anything I've ever experienced before. That's special in my book, and frankly, I can't get enough of you and don't believe I ever shall, especially if you keep coming to our bed in those kitten pajamas."

And with that, Susan felt a wave of relief wash over her, a little more secure as to her place in her wonderful husband's overall life.

CHAPTER XLVII

"Thank you for doing this," Jack said to Larry as the two walked up the steps of Blue Wolf Manor together the following evening, the former having just dropped Daniel off for a sleepover at his grandparents. "Kate doesn't know that I've arranged for you to drive her this evening, but I didn't want her to get all dressed up and then feel like she was going to dinner on her own."

"My pleasure," Larry assured him, not quite believing his good fortune as a whisper of fabric on the upstairs landing caused both men to glance up.

"Beautiful!" They uttered the word simultaneously as Susan and Kate made their way downstairs – the former wearing the dark blue cocktail dress she had originally picked out, embellished by her pink diamond necklace, and the latter having slipped into a lighter blue creation partially hidden beneath a matching outerwear stole that set off her crystal blue eyes.

"How nice of you to join us," Kate stated, her eyes filled with warmth as she approached Larry.

"Actually, I came to escort you, so that you wouldn't have to climb in and out of a backseat," he explained. "I hope you don't mind."

"Not at all." She slipped her hand into the crook of the arm her escort had offered her, but then her attention shifted to her brother as she sent him a knowing smile. "I feel very cared for by both of you."

"That's the idea," Larry stated as he held the front door open for her.

"I never thought I would see you looking as beautiful again as you were on our wedding night, but in this dress you certainly come close," Jack whispered into his wife's ear as he helped her on with her dress coat.

"I had to work extra hard on my appearance this evening, since I'll be sitting next to you." She lifted her face to his, pleased when he kissed her tenderly.

"I love you, Susie Chesterton," he told her as they made their way to the porch.

Larry opened the passenger door of his SUV, but then turned Kate towards him. "I would be remiss if I allowed you to go one step further without hearing me say that this evening you are without a doubt the most beautiful thing I've ever set eyes on."

"You look very dapper yourself." She ran her fingers along the lapel of his suit jacket and then lifted her face to his.

For a moment, he searched for a sign in her eyes, but as he leaned towards her the door behind them opened and, turning, Kate took her seat in their vehicle.

"I love you, Jack Jefferson," Susan stepped through their front door and then waited while he set the home's alarm. "Don't get too excited, but I have to admit that I've never felt any prettier than when I slipped on this designer creation in the dressing room you had constructed especially for me."

"Does this mean…" he began, only to have her place a fingertip on his lips, effectively cutting off what he was going to say.

"No, it doesn't." She laughed as Larry's Mercedes turned right onto the main road, and she allowed her husband to steer her towards their own SUV.

Two properties away, Adrianna sent Chase a smile as he took up a position in the doorway to her dressing room. "I may need some help with the clasp on my necklace," she pointed out.

"That's why I'm here, as well as this." He presented her with a Tiffany's gift bag. "I held this back for a special occasion, and when you told me you would be wearing a black dress this evening, I decided the right time was now."

"Oh, Chase, I love it!" She pulled a dainty, black satin evening bag from the folds of tissue and gently fingered the emerald on its side, where it had been embedded in filigreed gold that matched her necklace. "It's perfect, just like you. We'll appear even more like a couple this evening than we usually do," she acknowledged the care her tall, lean husband had taken when choosing his black suit, white shirt, and black and emerald green striped tie.

"Lift your hair for me." He removed the more delicate of the two necklaces in her emerald set from its box and fastened it around her slim neck, dropping a kiss where the latter joined her shoulder before turning her so he could get a look at his beautiful wife.

"Do you like this one?" Adrianna twirled slowly around, showing off her new dress.

"It's a good thing you wore my old favorite the first time I took you to Montgomery's," he stated, his eyes somewhat glazed. "I would've embarrassed myself by not being able to keep my hands off of you if you'd worn this one." He took in the scalloped V-neck that plunged low enough to tease as it pointed towards a fitted waist, from which folds of fabric swirled softly to just below his wife's knees. "Consider yourself warned that I may still embarrass myself this evening."

"I doubt that." She slipped a tube of lip gloss and two folded tissues into her new purse, pleased to discover that it already held a small mirror, edged and backed in gold, and a miniature comb.

"Do you have any idea how sexy you are in that dress?" Chase's hands found her waist as she snapped the purse closed and pulled her towards him, where he proceeded to kiss her in a way that left no doubt as to the depth of her effect on him.

"One more of those, and we won't make the dinner," she breathed into his neck.

"Don't tempt me." He let out a sigh as he deliberately turned her towards the doorway, so they could set on their way.

"It seems that somehow I always do," she giggled as they headed downstairs.

"Jack has insisted to both Larry and me that we are to provide the Montgomery table and Larry is to escort his sister, the meal being his treat," Chase told her. "As much as I'm enjoying the idea of spending an evening with you looking like this, I'm thinking the six of us should make it a habit to dine this way once a month, alternating who pays."

"So you think of Larry and Kate as a couple, too." She smiled at him as he headed his SUV along the drive. "Susan says we shouldn't even think about it, so we won't jinx anything."

"They seem to make a good team." He completed their right turn onto the main road. "This is another time when I hope your matchmaking plans come to fruition."

CHAPTER XLVIII

A few minutes later, Adrianna slid along the banquette that surrounded the Montgomery table, placing herself next to Kate, thus allowing Chase and Jack the two ends that provided them with slightly more room in which to stretch their legs.

"I must say that this is one time when I wish a member of the paparazzi could be here," Jack stated. "We three men would be the envy of the entire world."

"And none of us would ever know another moment's peace," Chase reminded him. "There's no way that they wouldn't want more pictures of three such beautiful women."

"I agree," Larry spoke up. "All three of them have done us proud down to the last detail, including these tiny little purses that match their outfits."

"Shoes and purses are essential to a woman," Kate stated firmly, even as her eyes twinkled, "and you men are just as bad. I bet each one of you filled your pants' pockets with all sorts of unneeded things, despite the fact that you were only escorting us to a fine restaurant."

"Absolutely!" Susan backed her up as Adrianna nodded her agreement.

"A man never knows what he may need," Larry objected.

"Okay, let's see what you three felt was essential to be brought this evening," Kate insisted, and Chase whispered to their waiter to give them just a minute before taking their appetizer order.

"I brought my wallet." Jack obliged by placing a rectangle of soft black leather on the white tablecloth in front of him, watching as the others followed suit.

"And keys." Chase added to his pile.

"I always carry my pocket knife," Larry stated as both Chase and he added well-fitted red Swiss army knives to the pile, neither one surprised when Jack slipped a much more complete, black model onto his.

"And this is the Krugerrand that Uncle Augustus gave me when I graduated from Yale." Larry placed the gold coin on the table. "I carry it for good luck."

"What do you carry?" Kate looked to her brother, who obliged by placing a half of what appeared to have been a wooden disk on the table – its edge jagged, the initial J burnt into its surface.

Adrianna felt her husband stiffen by her side, as both Susan and Larry sucked in their breaths.

"Tell us the story behind it," Kate said.

"You'll recognize bits and pieces of this from *Leaving It All Behind*," Jack began, "but where that was fiction, this is the real life incident. A green recruit, this took place on my first voyage with the Navy out of Norfolk. In the novel, the other man's and my birthdays were the same. In real life, we both were named Jack."

"How neat!" Adrianna sat forward in her chair.

"The other Jack was a few years older than me, but we shared a love of music and became friends, often putting on spur of the moment shows in the evenings," their host continued. "Frank Callahan nicknamed us Jack Be Nimble and Jack Be Quick, and the names stuck.

"One evening I was enjoying the fresh air out on deck, and Jack joined me," he continued as his face sobered. "He told me that Callahan and he were going on a mission in about an hour and he didn't feel good about it. 'I've enjoyed getting to know you,' he said, 'and I want to give you this. It's brought me good luck so far, and I want you to have it going forward.'"

"This being the disk?" Kate confirmed.

"Yes." Jack nodded. "I told him I'd give it back to him the next morning, but he wouldn't be shaken from his belief. In the end, it turned out he was right. Neither Callahan nor he returned, and I've carried the piece with me ever since so as to keep Jack's memory alive. He told me that if I ever found the other half, I would've found my truest friend."

Without a word, Chase reached into his pocket and then placed a similar piece on the table – this one fitting exactly into the jagged edge of the first and forming a perfect circle, the initial C burnt into its top surface.

"Your friend's name was Jack Stanford," he said. "He was my cousin, and he made the disk in shop class when he was in high school. The C stood for his girlfriend Carolyn when he made it, but she broke up with him before he showed it to her. He gave that half to me before he left for the Naval Academy. I was still a kid, and he said it was to remind me that he would be thinking of me wherever the Navy sent him. I've carried it with me ever since, for much the same reason as you've carried your half."

Adrianna glanced at Susan, who she saw was also blinking back tears as Jack slid from the banquette and stood, Chase following suit.

"I never expected to see these two halves reunited." Jack placed his left hand on Chase's shoulder and held out his right hand. "Words fail me, except to say that all those years ago Jack spoke of you as his cousin, loved you and did his best in the circumstances to make sure that you would always know that."

"Thanks, friend." Chase took the offered hand and then did one better, throwing his left arm around Jack's shoulder and giving him a quick guy-hug. "I'm glad it was you who brought this full circle." He reached forward, once again separating the halves by pushing the one bearing the J towards the story's teller and reclaiming the other for himself. "I think my cousin would want us to leave things as they were, don't you?" he asked.

"Definitely," Jack agreed as both men retook their seats, all three women dabbing their eyes with tissues retrieved from their tiny purses, "although this does explain the sense I've had ever since I interviewed for the manager's position at Adrianna's marina that I knew you from somewhere. There's some family resemblance and a couple of similar mannerisms now that I know the truth. Your cousin's been gone for a number of years, so I didn't connect the dots. He sure could play a piano, though, just like you."

"He played well enough to have gone professional, according to Edmund, who was his teacher," Chase filled him in, referring to the elderly gentleman who now managed the Sheffield Place Inn that had once been his own childhood home.

"Edmund was Jack's piano tutor?" The author relaxed in his seat and stretched out his long legs. "Amazing!"

"Marissa was originally hired as his nanny, but when he got older, my aunt kept her on as a cook/housekeeper and Edmund eventually filled the role of her butler and general factotum," Chase shared. "As you know, they married, and then after my aunt died, I offered them the opportunity to move to Captain's Point and manage the inn, which is primarily furnished now with things from my aunt's Beacon Hill home that they lived in for so many years."

"And Larry and you recognized the piece when I set it down," Jack addressed Susan. "I sensed both of you reacting to it."

"More I thought I recognized it," his wife explained. "I knew that Chase had carried something similar when we were in high school, but I wasn't sure it was the same after all these years."

"What's really amazing is that Chase's cousin gave it to you of all people," Adrianna pointed out.

"Possibly not as much as it might seem," Jack responded. "I may have mentioned that I had an uncle in Captain's Point, because I'd visited Ivan here just before I reported to the ship in Norfolk, and he may have thought there was a real possibility that Chase and I would meet at some point in the future."

"Either way, I'm glad that you were with him near the end," Chase stated.

"So am I," their host's face again sobered. "Jack was a great guy, and I know from things he said that he thought the world of his younger cousin."

"I used to spend summers with my aunt and cousin on Cape Cod," Chase filled the brother and sister in a few minutes later as they all enjoyed a round of appetizers, "and that's the house Adrianna convinced me we should buy on our honeymoon trip up the coast. You four will have to come with us when we go there next time. It's where I learned to sail, and you would enjoy the area."

"We can all fly up in the Lear, if you're game," Jack offered. "I have friends near Harwich that I'd like to introduce to Susan and Daniel before too much time passes."

"You have a Lear?" Larry asked, one eyebrow raised.

"Actually, I have access to several." Jack made a deprecating gesture.

"Spill it, Brother," Kate again made her desires clear.

"This all started on the same voyage," Jack began his new story. "One evening, some of us had played a couple of rounds of penny ante poker. A guy named Seth Cox and I were putting away the cards and chips, and we settled in to finish our beers. Time passed, and he shared with me that he felt he was at a pivotal point in his life but wasn't sure what to do.

"He'd managed to save ten thousand dollars, which back then represented more than it does now, and he had promised his wife that they would use half of it as a down payment towards their first house when he returned. Now, though, his brother had patented a new oil drilling mechanism, and the two of them wanted to go into business, each of them putting in ten thousand dollars as startup cash. Needless to say, he was torn."

"What did he do?" Adrianna asked, fascinated.

"I had just inherited the farm in Virginia, which I had arranged to be leased, as well as some money from my grandmother, and I had saved a large portion of each of my paychecks," Jack explained. "In the end, I offered to throw in five thousand of my own money and go in as a silent partner. I didn't have any family, would still have what I needed for grad school, and he was a good friend. Over the years, the company's done rather well, both overseas and stateside, and I can call on the Learjets whenever I need one of them, which is why the one thing Gerald Tate and I have agreed on is that the runway at the local airport needs to be lengthened to better accommodate Lears. The only reason I didn't use one for our honeymoon was because I thought Susie and I might want to do some island hopping."

"Why didn't I know this?" Susan glanced his way.

"You've never asked." He shrugged. "I've started to tell you about some things I've set in motion for Daniel since you accepted my proposal, and you've shifted the direction of our conversation each time. I figured at some point you'd become curious enough to ask, and we'd go over things then. In the meantime, Chase and Larry will back me up that I've insured both Daniel and your needs will always be taken care of."

"That you have," Chase agreed. "I met the same reluctance from Adrianna after we were first married."

"I kept telling him that I didn't care what he'd brought to our marriage," Adrianna shared as her husband signaled for their waiter to take their orders. "I would've loved him regardless, and I meant it."

Two hours later, back at Montgomery House, Chase returned from letting Max out, expecting to find Adrianna waiting to discuss their evening with him. Instead, she surprised him when she rose from one of the Queen Anne chairs by the fireplace in their bedroom, looking lovely in a short, silk kimono covered in black and green swirls that set off her hair and eyes, the glow from the logs the only light in the room.

"Let's not talk until tomorrow," she approached him. "Are you okay? That was a bit of a shock about your cousin this evening."

"I'm fine," he assured her as he drew her to him, not at all convinced she was wearing anything beneath the kimono now that he held her. "Thanks to you, I only felt relief when I learned that someone as nice as Jefferson had been with my Jack during those tough moments."

"I'm glad." She lifted her hand and placed it along his cheek. "But still, this evening I feel the need to celebrate that you're here with me – alive and strong and capable of making love to me in the way that you do."

"Do you have any idea how much I adore you," he whispered as he bent his head towards her.

"I have a vague one," she breathed as he dropped feathery kisses along the side of her neck. "Why don't you show me more specifically?"

At which, he lifted her into his arms and laid her onto their waiting bed. "As much as I love you, this may take quite a while." He smiled at her once he lay stretched alongside her, his eyes gazing down at her softly, and then, he lowered his lips onto hers as his fingers found the kimono's ties.

Two houses away, Susan exited her dressing room to find the master bedroom empty and one of the French doors to the balcony beyond left slightly ajar.

"Jack?" she called softly into the darkness and then recognized his form leaning against the railing next to one of the posts. "Are you okay?"

"I'm fine," he assured her as he crossed the space between them and hustled her back inside. "I wanted a breath of fresh air, but the wind's picked up and it's cold out there."

"Get into bed," Susan commanded as she turned on the gas logs in the fireplace. "You're an icicle. Whatever possessed you to go out there at this time of night?"

"Your view of the ocean I suppose," her husband replied as she slipped into their bed and pressed her warm body against his. "I was a jerky green kid when I knew Chase's cousin. I wish now that I'd done a better job of saying goodbye."

"You may have been a kid, but Jack Stanford obviously saw your potential," Susan pointed out. "The same potential that you've now filled and I love so much." She pushed him onto his back, so she could look down at him, automatically running her fingers through his hair to straighten it. "You're the kindest, gentlest man I've ever known, and if I knew I only had a few more minutes to live, I'd want to spend them with you."

"And I would want to spend them with you." Her husband's arms tightened around her as he kissed her and then hugged her to him. "Do you know what a great gal you are?" he asked.

"No, but you can feel free to give me a demonstration." She kissed him again.

And, as his Susie showed herself ready to accept him some minutes later and he slid inside the innermost warmth and love of the woman in his arms, Jack recognized that in this bed in this way, he would finally be able to release the fear and pain that he had carried forward with him from that earlier time and place.

"Thank you," he whispered into her ear as he held her tightly to him, once he had brought them both to their goal and their breathing had slowed. "Thank you for opening your heart and loving me the way that you do."

CHAPTER XLIX

"I'm glad that you were here to help with the last of the large boxes, Arthur." Ginny caught her breath a few days later, yet another shipment of merchandise now sitting in the middle of her new retail space. "I really appreciate it."

"It's the least I could do." The artist sent her a smile. "We're neighbors now."

"I couldn't have a better one," she stated. "I still can't believe that Edwina convinced me it was the right time to start this venture."

"Edwina has a good head on her shoulders and a keen business sense," he responded. "She certainly helps me with Artful Soul. Be prepared for new-owner jitters and doubts, but don't let them get the best of you. Thanks to my son and daughter-in-law, I've realized that you should act when opportunity knocks and no one is ever too old to begin anew."

"Wise words." Ginny began unpacking one of the new boxes. "Would you like to come over for dinner Saturday night? With my grand opening on the day after Thanksgiving fast approaching, I'd love to learn a few final words of wisdom from you and also show my appreciation for all of your help. Edwina will be there, of course."

"That sounds lovely." Arthur's face beamed as he thought about the woman who had grown to be such an important part of his life. "Let me know what time, and I'll arrive with bells on and Edwina by my side."

"I'll talk to her and let you know." Ginny began placing skeins of yarn in the appropriate cubbyholes, as a vision of Arthur decked out in bells danced in her head.

Thinking that she was alone at The Cove two properties away, Elizabeth Chesterton glanced up sharply from the essay she was grading a few moments later, when she heard a tap on the doorframe of her home office.

"Jack!" she greeted her daughter's new husband warmly.

"Do you have a moment, Mother-in-law?" he asked.

"Certainly." She gestured for him to take a seat in one of the visitor's chairs, surprised by the nomenclature he had used for her since he had comfortably referred to her as Mom ever since his engagement to Susan. "How are things going over at your place?"

"Great overall." He sent her a grin, and for a moment she had a glimpse of the happy teenager that he could've been, but, she realized, he probably never had been, given the circumstances of his upbringing. "Kate's settled into her new digs and enjoying her position with Chesterton and Chesterton, thanks to Larry. Daniel comes home from pre-school every day with a happy smile on his face, and Susic and I are both benefiting from her lighter schedule at the firm."

"So, to what do I owe the pleasure of your visit?" she asked, settling back in her chair, even more concerned as she watched his expression sober.

"We may have a problem with our Susan," he began. "I need to tap into your expertise as her mother and possibly ask for your help going forward, if you and I can jointly work out some sort of plan."

"Whatever you need," she assured him, on the one hand used to being approached for advice by younger members of her family and on the other hand recognizing full well that the capable, confident man her daughter had married wouldn't have bothered her, if his concerns weren't terribly real.

Later that afternoon, Arthur looked around him at the plethora of autumn leaves that had fallen from the tall oak and maple trees that proudly stood on the Stern's property and now covered the Victorian's front yard in a blanket of red, yellow and orange. Always welcoming a chance to breathe in the fresh sea air that blessed Captain's Point, he systematically began raking nature's fall gifts into neat piles at the roadside. In a few years, he thought, Edwina's precious great-granddaughter Lucy might play in a similar pile he had collected, truly something to look forward to seeing.

His pleasure in Edwina's company growing daily and Thanksgiving, a time of family and togetherness, almost here, this might be the right moment for him to organize an opportunity during which she and his family could get to know each other better.

Getting up the nerve to invite Edwina and her family to dinner wasn't the problem. That would be easy, but his new living arrangement with his son and daughter-in-law in what had originally been his house alone might present one. He had never envisioned having to awkwardly ask permission to invite his special friend and her family to dinner in what used to be his own home.

Nonetheless, Edwina was too important a part of his life to let a little formality stand in the way of his pursuing their relationship, especially with his most honorable of intentions for their future.

As the sun began slowly sinking into the late afternoon sky, he glanced up and noted his daughter-in-law checking on him through the living room window. Family was everything to him, and his Sylvia would want him to include Edwina and her family in this year's Thanksgiving celebration. Waving to Laura, the nervousness that had plagued him slowly dissipated as he took in her smiling face.

Gathering his last leaf pile into bags, he admired the blanket of lush green grass that he had unearthed. Tonight he would insure an invitation for the Fosters. This year, Edwina, Jason, Ginny and Lucy would enjoy Thanksgiving dinner in the Stern home.

CHAPTER L

"It's nice of you to have us over, so that Jack can enjoy watching the game with Chase this afternoon," Susan stated the following Sunday as Adrianna and she settled in for a chat in front of the fireplace in the former's library, their husbands happily occupied in the top floor room of the tower and Daniel asleep on the morning room's sofa. "I never have been much of a football enthusiast."

"Me either," Adrianna admitted, "probably because I didn't grow up around it."

"I'm done with the magazine, so just pass it along when you're finished." Susan nodded towards the spot on the coffee table where she had placed the women's magazine Jack and she had enjoyed.

"You know Chase. He's always game for a new activity," her hostess pointed out. "It'll be fun to see how he reacts to this one." She took a sip of warm cider from her mug. "Is something bothering you? You seemed somewhat lost in thought after Jack mentioned that he wondered what Kate was doing this afternoon."

"I know I can count on Chase and you to keep this to yourselves," Susan began. "Kate made me think about Larry, and I'm worried about him."

"In what way?" Adrianna asked, both intrigued and concerned.

"You may not know this, but Larry was badly hurt by his high school sweetheart," Susan explained. "He was truly in love with her and planned to ask her to marry him at Christmas during his senior year at Yale – had bought her a ring and everything. Instead, he discovered upon his arrival home that she had dropped out of college before taking her finals and had gone to L.A., seeking a career in the film industry."

"Poor Larry."

"He was devastated, and the residual scars run deeper than most people realize." Susan placed her empty mug on the coffee table. "Now he's met Kate, and you know how Jack and I feel about that. Even so, her divorce won't come through until the end of March, and like I did, she feels uncomfortable about dating until it's final. I can tell that Larry's drawn to her, but at other times, I sense that he's pulling back. Kate could be his last chance at real happiness, and I don't want him to miss out on it."

"So what can we do?" Adrianna asked, the matchmaker in her a willing volunteer.

"It might help if Chase talked with him and pointed out the value of giving Kate the time that she needs," Susan suggested. "Do you think he would be willing to do so?"

"I'll ask him in bed this evening, either before or after…" Her hostess was obviously uncomfortable discussing the timing of her assault on her husband.

"Perfect," Susan agreed. "The way to a man's heart may be through his stomach, but to work on his mind, you have to make your move when at least some of it is engaged elsewhere."

"Although you shouldn't take advantage of the power you've been given over him too often." The sides of Adrianna's mouth twitched.

"Not more than twice a week." Susan's face filled with a grin.

"Or at least not more than once every three days." Adrianna chuckled.

And this having been settled to both of their satisfactions, the two women turned their attentions to the more serious concerns of the season, such as decorating their homes and shopping for Christmas gifts for the first time since their marriages.

Later that evening, Chase was surprised when he entered the tower suite bedroom to find his wife sitting on the floor in front of the fireplace, Max curled on her lap and a magazine opened beside her on the Aubusson carpet.

"Trying out a new meditation routine?" he asked.

"No, Susan brought me this magazine today and suggested that you and I might enjoy a communication exercise for couples she and Jack tried," she explained. "Apparently, they were both pleasantly surprised by what they shared with each other when they attempted it."

"I'm game." He took a seat in front of her. "Does our Max figure in it?"

"No, but he assumed that he did." She lifted the dog into his oval bed and handed her husband the magazine. "The article says we should sit cross-legged in front of each other, knees together."

Obliging as always, Chase shifted into the required position, but as Jack had before him, soon realized that his legs were too much longer than his wife's to accomplish the deed. "What if, instead of sitting cross-legged, we sit flat on the floor, bend our legs outward and bring our knees together?" he suggested.

"It's not quite as comfortable, but it does achieve the knee connection that the exercise requires," she agreed. "We're also supposed to hold hands."

"No problem there." He took her lovely hands in his larger ones.

"Now you ask me a question – anything that you'd like to know about me – and then I'll answer truthfully and completely with no fear of repercussions as we share and discuss along this conversational thread until we come to its end," she explained. "Then I'll do the same in reverse."

"I can ask anything that I want?"

"Anything." She looked at him expectantly.

"What were your Christmases like as a child," he asked, a serious tone underlining his words that surprised her.

"Strange from most people's perspective as I've mentioned before," she stated. "We were inevitably on a site somewhere in the world, often where it was sandy or hot or both. The first decorated Christmas tree I ever saw was at the finishing school I attended in Switzerland, and it was in the process of being dismantled when I arrived there."

"Did you celebrate at all?"

"We would go to church, if there was one, and exchange gifts on Christmas Day, and if there was a piano available, my parents would sing carols with me," she filled him in. "The food was always whatever was considered to be a company or festival meal in the country in which we were digging."

"No Santa Claus?"

"Never."

"Looking back, what would you have preferred those Christmases to have been like?" His voice now held a gentleness that told her he had sensed the sadness she carried as she reviewed her Christmas memories.

"Not having experienced a traditional American style holiday season, I didn't miss too much at the time," she explained. "On the other hand, I was surrounded by books, and I was enamored with the idea of a Dickens type of celebration."

"Anything else you would change if you could?"

"Because we moved around so much and often lived in other families' houses, I was never able to have a pet," she shared. "That's why I refused at first to release Max to you that day on the beach, when you came to our rescue."

"You scared me to death, when I saw that last wave crash against you." He lifted her chin and dropped a gentle kiss on her lips. "Even then, I knew you were destined to be part of my life."

"I scared myself," she admitted, "but I was very grateful to you for arriving when you did and cutting Max loose." She hesitated.

"And...?"

"I always wanted a dollhouse to play with," she whispered, surprised by tears that had suddenly sprung to her eyes. "Even here, where I had more toys than I did anywhere else, I never had one." Her mind shifted to the cabinet in her dressing room that still held the toys from her childhood visits to Montgomery House.

"Now it's your turn." She managed to add a bright smile to her face.

"What were your Christmases like as a child?"

"Lonely." Chase concentrated on their hands where they were joined. "We always attended church on Christmas Eve – my parents and I stranded in the Sheffield pew. I knew better than to awaken them, even as a very young boy, so I would get up the next morning, make a bowl of cereal for myself and wait for them to come downstairs. Usually, my mom would arrive first, and she would at least make an effort to overlay our conversation with a false gaiety as we continued to wait for my father. Once he arrived, though, things went downhill fast."

"I'm so sorry." She released his left hand and found his cheek with her freed one, pleased when he lifted his face and kissed her palm.

"That's why I'm so excited about our decorating Montgomery House," he explained. "This will be the first real family Christmas of my own that I've ever had. I was luckier than you, though. As soon as I could, I would run over to the The Cove, where Augustus always welcomed me. Generally, I arrived about the same time as Susan's family got there from the farm, and Larry was already in residence with his parents. Otis and Penny did little things for me casually during the season that helped, too, although looking back I'm pretty sure they had planned them."

"I'm glad they were there for you."

"The amazing thing to me as a child was that there were more gifts for me under The Cove's tree than there had been at my own house," he continued. "It wasn't until I was older that I realized Elizabeth must've seen to that, and when I thanked her as a teenager one Christmas, she pointed me to Augustus who had paid for them over the years. My life would've been very different if he hadn't chosen to mentor and support me until I could stand on my own."

"I only met him one time as a child, when he came to visit my Aunt Martha," Adrianna said. "He brought me a picture book and then stayed for supper. He was also very kind to me when I arrived here to attend my parents' funeral. I wish I had gotten to know him better."

"He would be pleased with our marriage," Chase stated. "The union of a Sheffield and a Montgomery would've appealed to him, and he would have found you as delightful as I do."

The mantle clock choosing this moment to chime the lateness of the hour, Adrianna released her husband's hands and rose, only to discover that her left leg had fallen completely asleep from being held at such a strange right angle from her body. "Oh, my!" She clutched at the arm of one of the winged-backed chairs to keep from falling.

Learning from her experience, Chase checked out his own limbs and then stood, at once gathering her to him. "We're going to have the best holiday season ever," he promised as he cupped her face in his hands. "Dickens never had it so good, and I'm going to get us started right now, by showing you in the best possible way just how much I love you and appreciate the home you've created for us."

Lying snuggled in the warmth of her husband's arms sometime later, Adrianna listened to his steady breathing beside her as she remembered the tenderness with which he had exhibited his feelings for her as he had taken her. What would make their first Christmas so wonderful, she understood deep in her heart, was the love that they shared for each other and the fact that, this time, they would celebrate the season together.

CHAPTER LI

As soon as Chase's SUV headed along the driveway the next morning, Adrianna fastened Max's leash to his harness and headed through the kitchen garden and along the vine-covered walkway towards the new stores that now inhabited much of her ancestral home's former carriage house.

The exercise her husband and she had completed the previous evening had generated some strange emotions within her, and as she reached the doorway of Times Past, the new antique and collectibles shop, she opened the door and entered to the sound of a tinkling bell overhead.

"Adrianna, what a pleasant surprise!" The slightly above-average in height proprietress approached her, dark hair swaying in a long braid down her back as matching eyes twinkled with genuine pleasure. "Would you mind coming into the back? I'd welcome your opinion as to which way I should go with a piece I'm refinishing."

"I have Max with me." Her landlady hesitated.

"Who is always a gentleman," Serena Mitchell stated, as if that covered any possible objections.

The two women having agreed that a darker stain would look better on the Rococo piece and Adrianna having claimed it for herself once it was finished, they returned to the main showroom a few minutes later.

"So, to what do I owe the pleasure?" Serena asked as she turned a café chair around and plopped on it as if it were a saddle.

"Actually, I need your help…"

At precisely the same moment, in his ranch style home a few miles away, Jason Foster appeared to be studying a pepper grinder in the middle of the kitchen table when, in reality, his mind was half the world away. Letting out a small sigh, he made a few quick gestures on the screen of his phone, hoping against hope.

"Dad, I'm glad I caught you." He heard the concern in his own voice. "I wasn't sure if you'd be on the ground or in the air with this new assignment you've been given."

"How are you, Son?" Hamilton Foster, Jr. asked. "Is everything okay with Ginny and Lucy?"

"We're all fine," Jason assured him. "It's about Gran…"

"Tara and I spoke with her two weeks ago, and she seemed fine over the phone – settling into her new life in Captain's Point and loving the friends she's made."

"That's just it," his son continued. "She's forming a close relationship with one new friend in particular. Gran acts like she's happy, but with some reserve, and I thought you should be aware of the situation sooner rather than later."

"I'm not getting your point."

"Gran is crazy about a Captain's Point widower and artist, Arthur Stern," Jason filled him in. "Ginny and I have met him on several occasions and like what we see, but things may be getting serious. Just how serious, we're not sure. We've all been invited to Thanksgiving dinner at Arthur's house where he lives with his son and daughter-in-law, and I'm hoping the time spent together will give us a good indication of what his intentions are towards Gran."

"Don't worry, Jason." Ham, Jr.'s tone was firm. "Things will work out. Mom and Dad had a great marriage, and I know she's been lonely these past years. I'm glad she's found someone pleasant with whom she can share common interests and do things. She's financially set for the rest of her life, and she should enjoy the time that's remaining. I don't think, though, that she'd want to begin a new marriage with someone at her age."

"That's exactly how I feel," his son informed him, "but Ginny believes that they're falling in love and planning a future together."

"You have enough to worry about with Ginny and Lucy right now." His father made his position clear. "I'll take care of anything that pops up. I may be back in D.C. in a few weeks for more briefings, and I'll plan for a side trip to Captain's Point while I'm in the country. I'll call you with the details once the trip and itinerary are finalized."

"I'm glad you'll be coming. I only want Gran to be happy and safe for the rest of her life."

"We'll definitely see to that," his father reassured him. "I can't wait to see Lucy again, and I'll make it a point to meet Arthur, too. Give my love to your ladies, but don't tell Gran I may be coming. I want to surprise her."

"You got it! Thanks, Dad. Have a safe trip."

"We'll talk soon. Love you, Son." Ham, Jr. disconnected.

"Who were you talking to?" Ginny walked into the great room holding Lucy's now empty juice bottle.

"My dad."

"How are your parents doing with the new Paris assignment?" Ginny continued to the kitchen area of the large room, where she rinsed the bottle and placed it in the dishwasher.

"Dad may be coming to Washington soon," Jason filled her in. "He'll let us know, but he wants to surprise Gran, so don't mention it to her."

Ginny plopped down on the sofa. "That sounds nice. Did you tell him about Arthur?"

"I did." Jason took a seat in his favorite chair across from her. "He's reserving judgment on the matter as usual."

"You men." Ginny sighed. "I think it's great. Your grandmother's happier than I've seen her in a long time, and I'm all for their relationship."

"Don't get Dad and me wrong," Jason defended the side. "We want Gran to be happy, too, but we also share a need to protect her."

"That's honorable, but you and your father need to realize that we Foster women know what we want and we recognize a good thing when we see it."

"I can't argue with that," he motioned for her to sit on his lap, where he proceeded to kiss her thoroughly once she had joined him.

Later that same evening, Chase returned home, the back of his SUV filled with plastic storage boxes of various sizes – the conversation of the previous evening having reminded him that right now Adrianna and he had Martha Montgomery's Christmas decorations and his aunt's. Going forward, he wanted what they had chosen to use themselves to be joined together and packed separately from the others.

Glancing along the sidewalk, he noticed a light was still on in the window of Drifters, the new store that had been opened by Cheryl and Michael Wolford. Entering the shop, he was pleased to see that Michael was the one who remained behind the counter.

"Do you have a minute?" he asked while still standing in the doorway.

"For you, anytime," his friend assured him. "I still owe you for saving Cheryl's life on the beach below Montgomery House when she was a little girl."

"That was years ago." Chase made a dismissive gesture with his hand. "Right now, I need to ask you for a huge favor if what I need done is even possible."

"Sure." The shop's owner crossed to the door and flipped a small sign so that it read Closed to those on the outside. "Why don't we adjourn to my corner of the back room, where we can share a couple of cold ones from my private stash in the fridge and you can fill me in on what this is all about?"

CHAPTER LII

Waking up before the alarm on Thanksgiving morning, Susan gradually floated towards consciousness, surprised not to feel the warmth of her husband's body beside her. Rolling onto her back, she slid her hand along the sheet and confirmed his absence.

"Looking for something?" He chuckled softly as he rejoined her, the strength of his aftershave announcing as he stretched out beside her that he had just completed his morning ablutions. "Can I get you anything? Coffee, tea, juice or me?"

"That depends on how cute me is," she teased, her eyes still closed. "I'm hoping for someone young and athletic, possibly that well-built, younger fellow who helps out with the yard here."

"Going to send a boy in to do a man's job?" her husband asked. "Perhaps, I should inform you that Jeff Stuart's heart is already taken."

"Really?" Susan's eyes flew open at the news that the college student who helped her husband with their property maintenance had found a girlfriend. "By whom?"

"Don't know exactly." Jack's words felt like a caress against her neck. "He asked me if I could offer any suggestions for an appropriate Christmas gift for a young lady."

"What did you tell him?" Susan raised her left hand and ran her fingers through his hair, straightening it where it had fallen forwards.

"I suggested that he should come up with three ideas of his own, and I would then offer my opinion on them." Her husband's hand found the soft skin of her stomach and began making slow, steady circles. "That way, he would learn from shopping for her himself, while at the same time benefiting from my experience."

"Good advice." His wife pulled him down for a light kiss. "And you have no idea who it is?"

"Now, I didn't say that I didn't have an idea," he teased her as his lips moved to a sensitive area on her neck. "At a guess, I would put Becca Tate's name up for a vote."

"I'm glad," Susan said. "Mom says both of her interns are really nice girls, and he did bid fifty dollars for her box lunch at the Animal Shelter's charity event. In his own way, that was as much for Jeff to bid as the thousand dollars you bid for my lunch and lemon meringue pie."

"Exactly." Her husband's hand moved again, igniting small sparks within her.

"I believe I've revised my expectations," Susan breathed the words. "Someone tall, dark and experienced would be just the ticket."

At which, Jack reached over and turned off the alarm, not wishing for any further interruptions as he proceeded to awaken his new wife in style.

Two properties away in Montgomery House's tower suite, Chase opened one eye and looked at the alarm clock, not surprised that Adrianna and he had slept slightly later than planned due to the storms that had interrupted their sleep all through the night.

Tightening his hold on his wife, he brushed a stray wave of her dark hair back from her temple and said softly, "Adrianna, it's time to wake up."

"So early?" she moaned as she snuggled against him.

"It's nine o'clock, and we still have to make the Indian Pudding," he reminded her. "Why don't you snooze a while longer, and I'll let His Majesty over there on the hearth into the kitchen garden, feed him and make us breakfast in bed. After all, you were up half the night dealing with his anxieties."

"You're spoiling me." She smiled, lifting her face to receive what she knew he would give her, even though her eyes remained closed.

"I wouldn't be so sure of that." His kiss, when it came, was more passionate than she had expected. "I may merely be buttering you up."

"Oh, I hope so." She let out a small sigh of expectation. "Hurry back."

A short while later, she heard her name being called through the dialogue that was streaming through her dream.

"Adrianna, Sweetheart, sit up, while the omelette's still warm."

"Chase?" His voice finally registered, and she made an effort to comply, half-opening her eyes and thrusting herself up against the pillows.

"Are you awake enough to put your mug on the bedside table and hold the tray steady while I get into bed?" he asked.

"Close enough, I think." She forced her eyes open the rest of the way and reached for her coffee, surprised to find that he had pulled back the drapes that flanked all three of the window seats, revealing a deep blue sky against which a few snow white cumulus clouds floated. "What a lovely day!"

"It's chilly, but the storms have certainly passed," he confirmed as he slid beneath the covers and then handed her a fork. "I brought a pain au chocolate and a plain croissant." He indicated the single plate, on which a large cheese omelette and the pastries presided, garnished by a fan of orange wedges. "I figured you for the chocolate one, but we can reverse if you'd rather."

"Chocolate is fine, or we can share," she made her wishes clear and then took a bite of the egg. "This is delicious – no surprise."

"Nothing but the best for my queen." He dropped a kiss on her cheek.

For a few minutes, they munched on the food he had prepared and sipped on their coffee in companionable silence.

"So much for your attempts to assuage our friend's angst." Chase finally nodded to where Max appeared to be asleep in his bed on the hearth. "You were forced to hold him each of the three times a storm passed over us last night. I must say that your humble servant is quite envious that the canine is so obviously your favorite."

"Don't be silly!" The twinkle in Adrianna's eyes belied the tone of her voice. "Whatever made you think such a thing, my liege?"

"Perhaps, it was the fact that for most of the time you were ministering to his needs, you were clutching him to your fair bosom." Chase sent her a knowing look.

"I would be glad to do the same for you, should you need me to, my knight in shining armor." She returned his gaze with so much love in her eyes that he immediately reached over the side of the bed and placed the tray on the floor, wasting no time before he gathered her into his arms and made his need for her clear.

Sensing that his humans' attention was now engaged elsewhere, Max silently rose, stretched and slunk around the half-tester bed to the plate that still held the remains of the cheese omelette and one-third of the plain croissant. Seconds later, he returned to his oval bed, satisfied, licking a last smidgeon of cheese from his whiskers before once again curling himself into a ball, content and totally thankful for the day as it appeared to be stretching before him.

CHAPTER LIII

Two hours later, Arthur extended his hand to Edwina as she stepped from his Buick, where he had parked in front of the home he now shared with his son Alexander and daughter-in-law Laura. How quickly his world had changed since he had met his Edwina. Knowing her these past months had returned the spring to his steps, he realized with a flush of pleasure. Love really did make the world go round.

Edwina gladly accepted his hand and stood. Noting the twinkle in his eye, she felt reassured as they faced this major step together. Knowing that Jason, Ginny and Lucy would be joining them for dinner calmed her nerves, too. Standing still, she took a moment to appreciate the classic Queen Anne Victorian before her, then allowed Arthur to escort her along the slate walkway towards the front door of the home that he had purchased with his late wife Sylvia.

Despite feeling at ease with him by her side, questions still loomed in her mind. Would his family like her? Would they accept her? Would they think Arthur and she had lost their minds as they considered another chance at happiness together? Maybe it was too soon to be spending Thanksgiving with his family.

"How are you holding up?" Arthur gently squeezed her hand as they approached the front door that was adorned overhead with a large, colorful wreath fashioned from intertwined fall leaves.

"I'm a little nervous," she admitted, speaking in a hushed tone. "When was the last time you brought a woman home to meet your family?"

"Only once before, and that was to meet my parents." Arthur took her other hand in his and looked her straight in the eye. "You'll do fine. Just be yourself. My son is exactly like me, and my daughter-in-law has been supportive of all my decisions."

"You're right." She felt herself relax as his faded brown eyes reassured her, filled as they were with his gentle spirit. "You always are."

"If you don't stop, I'll have a head so big I won't be able to put on my golf hat." He chuckled. "You'll fit right in, I promise."

As Arthur reached for the doorknob, Laura Stern swung open the door and greeted them.

"I thought I heard someone drive up." The forty-something redhead hugged Arthur, not allowing him to get a word in edgewise before she continued, "And this is the special woman who's captured my father-in-law's heart." She reached out, gently grasping the older women's hands. "It's wonderful to have this chance to get to know you better. We've heard so much about you."

"I feel the same way." A rush of excitement swept over Edwina, as the aroma of roasting turkey permeated the air along with an undercurrent of apples and cinnamon.

"Please, come in, and I'll take your coats." Laura indicated for them to enter the living room where Arthur's son Alexander joined them.

"Hello, Mrs. Foster." The dark-haired, brown-eyed younger version of Arthur extended his hand to hers.

"Please, call me Edwina."

"Why don't we all sit down and get comfortable?" Alexander gestured for her to have a seat on a blue damask sofa. "Jason just called and said they're on their way. In the meantime, Laura's whipped up a few yummy hors d'oeuvres for all of us, and I'll get the drinks. Name your poison."

But before she could answer, Arthur chimed in. "We'll both have one of your famous Chesapeake Bloody Marys. Make mine extra spicy," he added.

"Does that sound good to you, Edwina?" the younger man inquired.

"I must say your father knows exactly what I like." She gave him a nod of approval.

"You've still got it, Dad." Alexander chuckled as he headed for the kitchen.

Edwina surveyed the formal parlor of the old Victorian with its cozy fireplace accentuated by tall ceilings and original dark moldings. Built-in cabinets and bookshelves filled with leather bound volumes of the classics caught her eye, and a bay window, framed by velvet drapes and lace sheers, sported a comfortable window seat.

As Arthur's hand covered hers where it rested on the couch pillow, her eyes gravitated to a large, gold-framed oil painting of his that hung on the far wall. The entire room reflected his touch, as it generated an overall elegance of style that reminded her of fine Italian residences.

"Here we are!" Alexander approached holding a tray of drinks as Laura followed close behind him from the kitchen, carrying a silver platter filled with tiny hors d'oeuvres, including feta-stuffed mushrooms, endive leaves with crab stuffing and herbed cheese-filled cherry tomatoes.

"These look delightful, Laura." Edwina placed a small cocktail plate and napkin in her lap as she reached for one of the delicate bites she was offered. "Arthur tells me you're a gourmet cook, and I've already sampled your delectable sandwiches and salads as we've lunched together."

"Thank you." Her hostess took a seat on the matching sofa by her husband. "I do enjoy cooking."

"It was thoughtful of you to include my family in your holiday festivities today," Edwina continued in an effort to make polite conversation. "This will be Lucy's first Thanksgiving, of course."

"That must be them now." Laura rose in response to the doorbell's tone. "Isn't she the most precious thing?" Her greeting carried to those remaining behind.

Once the newcomers were also settled in the parlor, Alexander addressed Ginny, who held Lucy in her arms, "Dad tells me that you're opening your own shop in the space next to his."

"That's right," she confirmed. "I've always wanted a knitting shop of my own, and the timing seems right. While Lucy's still young, I can bring her with me sometimes, and Edwina has offered babysitting assistance."

"Will you be giving classes?" their hostess asked. "I've wanted to learn to knit for some time."

"Yes, and I can hardly wait. I'll email you a class schedule, if you'd like," Ginny offered as she noted that Beth's Buds had done a good job with the round coffee table arrangement that she had ordered to be sent on behalf of the four of them.

The oven timer announcing that the turkey was now ready, their hostess hurried towards the kitchen as Arthur and his son led their guests to the dining room, where a mahogany table was set for six with a high chair in place for Lucy.

"Our grown children couldn't be with us today," Laura explained as Alexander carved the turkey once his father had said grace. "Taylor is in her first year of grad school in California and is spending the holiday with friends. Our son Sam is a senior at Rice, and he's spending the weekend with his girlfriend's family in Dallas."

"I remember the first year that Ham, Jr., didn't come home," Edwina shared. "I prepared the same size turkey as usual, forgetting that our largest appetite would be missing, and his father said he didn't know if he should be sad about our son's absence or happy about having both turkey legs to himself."

And, as bowls of sweet potatoes, green beans and cranberry sauce were emptied, conversation flowed easily until, by the time desserts and coffee were served, Edwina found herself as totally relaxed with her Arthur's son and daughter-in-law as she always was with him. Nothing could've been any more pleasant than this Thanksgiving meal, she thought, and who knew? It might prove to be the beginning of a new Stern/Foster tradition.

CHAPTER LIV

"Welcome to our zoo," Anders Chesterton, Susan's Nordic god look-a-like father, greeted Chase and Adrianna when they arrived at The Cove, bringing with them a large casserole dish filled with Indian Pudding that was destined for the Thanksgiving table.

"What are all these dogs doing here?" Larry's mother asked as she paused on her way through the foyer.

From where he was seated next to his mistress's foot on the floor, Max somehow managed to look down his long narrow nose at the comment, the only male in the home who sported the collar of a white shirt as well as a blue and green-striped tie beneath his warm sweater, thus adding a certain sartorial elegance to the gathering.

"All of them are well-trained and familiar with each other, Gertrude," Elizabeth explained as she joined them. "I didn't want anyone to have to pop up and leave just to let out a dog."

"Never in my time," her sister-in-law huffed and continued on her way to the broad stairway leading to the second floor.

"Thank goodness, she convinced Anders' brother to retire to Florida." Elizabeth rolled her eyes as her husband took their guests' coats. "Now you two come with me. I've assigned you both to kitchen detail."

A few minutes later, Susan and her older brother Andy weren't surprised to see Larry being escorted from the kitchen by their mother.

"So soon?" Andy asked, attempting an innocent look.

"I cry foul," Larry announced as he plopped down on the other angle of the L-shaped couch next to Kate, passing his arm along the sofa's back behind her shoulders. "I only ate a couple of miniature marshmallows."

"How many?" Susan raised an eyebrow.

"And, even more important, had they already been arranged atop the mashed sweet potatoes ready to pop into the oven?" Andy added.

"They were already arranged," Larry admitted, "but there were more in a bag, and I planned to replace them."

"Don't be too upset." Kate looked up at him, her eyes filled with concern. "Jack told me that I wouldn't be much help and didn't even let me into the kitchen."

"Now that was unfair," Larry stood up for the side as he gave her a quick squeeze. "You were a great deal of help when we readied my place for the dinner meeting. I couldn't have done it without you, and we made a great team."

"Thank you." She sent him a bright smile as her eyes filled with so much gratitude at his compliment that he wanted to take her into his arms and claim her as his, wisely refraining as the vibrant tones of his mother's voice could be heard descending the stairs beyond the room's archway.

"Help yourselves." Adrianna approached the kitchen rejects with one of Jack's warm Brie cheeses drizzled with maple syrup. "Dinner will probably be another forty-five minutes. Courtney just called, and they're on their way with the collard-stuffed ham to go with the turkey."

"At least, we won't starve." Larry sent Andy a grin, as notes Edmund was coaxing from the music room's piano began drifting their way.

"No, and it's unlikely Courtney will get sick like she always did when we were little," his cousin agreed.

Three hours later found The Cove's Thanksgiving meal consumed, the leftovers packed away, the dishes done and the two youngest cousins napping upstairs.

The large family room gradually grew quieter as first Adrianna fell asleep in Chase's lap in a big comfortable chair by the fireplace, where he soon followed her example. Next, Kate's eyes sagged and finally closed, as her head drooped gently until it rested against Larry's upper arm where he lounged next to her on the couch, only moments before his own cheek found a home on the top of her head. Finally, Andy and his wife continued to converse in low tones, once Jack and Susan had excused themselves and joined Edmund and Marissa in the music room.

"There you are!" His mother's strident voice jerked Larry awake. "Don't you think it's time for you to go to Chester's and make sure Bill Graham isn't making a mess of things in your absence?"

Still half asleep, Larry's eyes narrowed, but then Kate let out a small moan in her sleep and snuggled deeper into his arm, reminding him of her presence in a way that took his reaction to a whole other level. "No, I don't need to go to Chester's and check up on a man who knows the business every bit as well as I do."

The calm, quiet tone in which his cousin spoke belied an underlying edge that Andy thought would've told anyone with half a brain that Larry was way past furious. But then, his Aunt Gertrude never had struck him as having much sense.

"Furthermore, I would appreciate it if you would lower your voice, Mother," Larry continued, if anything his tone firmer. "Some of us are trying to rest." And with that, he closed his eyes, signaling the matter to be closed – a dark, heavy line having been drawn in the sand.

"Well, I never! To think that I've lived to see this day!"

Andy watched as his aunt's face turned a vivid shade of red before she turned and strode from the room without as much as a backward glance.

For a moment, it seemed as if no one breathed, but then Larry's ribs moved in a deep, silent chuckle, Andy worked hard to hold back a laugh, and Chase opened one eye and sent his friend a thumbs up from his chair by the fire.

"She's luckier than she realizes that she's living to see tomorrow," Larry stated firmly. "I've had enough."

In response to which, before she snuggled deeper against his upper arm once again, Kate surprised him by patting the back of his hand and setting his spine tingling by whispering for his ears only, "I'm proud of you."

CHAPTER LV

That evening, Edwina unlocked the door to Montgomery House's dependency and turned to Arthur. "Would you like to join me for a cup of Irish coffee?" she asked.

"Sounds like a perfect ending to a perfect day." He followed her into the cozy home, where he took her coat to hang along with his in the closet while she brewed their coffee.

"Why don't we sit at the table," she suggested when he rejoined her. "Adrianna dropped off a magazine the other day in which there's a communication exercise that couples can do. Apparently, Jack and Susan tried it and found it beneficial, and Chase shared something that had given Adrianna some real insights into how to best build their Christmas traditions."

"I'm game for anything you think would be good for us," he agreed as he lifted the coffees she had prepared from the counter and carried them to the table.

Taking a seat, Edwina reached for the magazine. "Give me a minute to find the instructions." She turned the pages. "Here it is. We're supposed to sit cross-legged on the floor with our knees touching as we hold hands," she told him, a crease forming between her brows.

"I think we would be better served if we remained seated in our chairs," he pointed out. "If we face each other and move closer, our knees will touch quite comfortably, and we can still hold hands as well."

"The mathematical side of your brain does come in handy." She turned her chair around slightly as he stood and pushed his closer. "I would never have thought of that."

"I'm sure Chase and Jack did," he retook his seat, unaware of the very different solutions resolved upon by the younger couples. "Now what is our next step?"

In the master suite of Blue Wolf Manor, Jack lounged against the doorframe of his wife's dressing room and watched as she brushed her hair. "That was my best Thanksgiving ever," he shared. "Are they always like that at The Cove?"

"They have been ever since I was born." Susan set her brush down and approached him, leaning against him in a way that pinned him to the doorframe as his arms came around her. "Thank you for being so willing to share the holidays with my family."

"No need to thank me," he stated. "Kate and I both had the times of our lives. You have no idea how much it meant to the two of us to be included, and I would never want our Daniel to miss out on a gathering like that one. It's important for him to feel like he's part of an extended family."

"Are you sure you still want us to do Christmas dinner here?" she asked.

"Certainly, we need to develop some traditions of our own as well, and this house can accommodate it," he assured her. "I thought the three of us could begin looking through Ivan's decorations first thing in the morning, and then we'll know what we'll need to complete our collection going forward. I've already arranged for Stuart's Landscaping and Beth's Buds to do the outside work."

"I do love being on my lifetime honeymoon with you, Mr. Jefferson." Her blue eyes twinkled up at his dark ones.

"And I love being on mine with you, Mrs. Jefferson." He swept her off her feet and carried her to their bed, where he whispered into her neck once he was stretched out beside her, "Now prepare yourself for another glimpse of just how spectacular a honeymoon night can be."

Three properties away, Larry stood in the doorway of the empty walk-in closet off his bedroom and tried to imagine it filled with Kate's clothes. How right it had felt to have her snuggled against him. How much clearer his vision of his life's journey became when he included her in it.

In her furnished suite, Kate settled her head on her pillow as her face relaxed into one of her slow smiles. Never had she enjoyed a Thanksgiving more – family, friends, food, music and, most of all, Larry all forming into a perfect day. How delicious that Christmas and New Year's lay ahead, after which it would only be three more months until her divorce would be final.

A few minutes later, Chase entered the tower room suite, clad in his pajamas and carrying a fair-sized, gift-wrapped box carefully in his arms, only to find Adrianna seated in one of the wingbacks by the fireplace – Max sitting alertly next to her in the chair and a large, gift-wrapped box on the Aubusson at her feet.

"What's that?" She eyed the gift in his hands.

"I might ask the same." He nodded towards the one next to the chair.

"This is just something I thought we might use as part of our decorations," she explained. "Otis and Penny really got into it, and she insisted that we wrap it once he had brought it up here yesterday. I was afraid you would notice it stuffed in the corner of my dressing room, because I wanted you to open it this evening."

"We appear to have been two minds with but a single thought." He took a seat at her feet, setting his gift to her alongside hers for him. "So which of us should go first?"

"You should," she stated firmly, not surprised when a boyish grin spread across her fun-loving husband's face. "I can't wait for you to open it."

Ripping the paper off the box with abandon, he looked up at her with one eyebrow raised as the words FRAGILE and OPEN WITH CARE met him on the outside of the otherwise plain cardboard box.

"Use these on the tape." She handed him a pair of utility scissors from the wine table beside her chair. "Everything's fine. Just don't rock it back and forth."

Proceeding more slowly, Chase carefully cut through the tape holding down the flaps and then opened them to reveal a vintage HO scale model train set, complete in its original box and looking brand new, as well as a bridge, four wooden houses, a church, and a railway station.

For a moment, she was afraid that she had done something wrong as he sat perfectly still, his eyes averted. But then, she saw how stiffly he was holding his shoulders, and she slid onto the floor beside him, where she drew his head to where her neck met her shoulder and stroked his hair. "Is it wrong?" she asked as he squeezed her to him.

"No," he found his voice. "It's perfect. It just took me by surprise." He straightened, having pulled himself together. "Can we run it through the presents under our tree?"

"That's the idea." She sent him a smile. "Serena Mitchell pulled in a favor from a friend and got it for me. It's guaranteed to run like a top."

"Do you have any idea how sexy you'll look wearing the engineer's cap that I'm going to buy you?" he asked.

"Really, Chase!" She giggled, glad he was back to his old self and so obviously pleased with her gift.

"Now yours." He slid the present he had brought along the carpet towards her.

Adrianna pulled the gift card he had tucked into the ribbon out first and opened it. *"To my queen, the best wife in the world, on the occasion of our first Christmas together,"* she read in a whisper. "Thank you." She lifted her face and kissed him.

"You haven't even opened your present yet." His dark blue eyes smiled down at her full of love.

"Your gift can't be any more wonderful than your words," she told him as she took her time, wanting to keep as much of the beautiful paper intact as possible.

Finally, a heavy duty, beige box stamped with the word Drifters in dark brown came into view.

"Mike Wolford has worked a miracle," Chase explained as she pulled off the lid. "Here, let me help you." He shifted the creamy tissue paper inside and then removed a detailed replica of Montgomery House from the folds, the weathered driftwood from which it had been carved lending credence to the granite blocks that formed the building.

"Oh, Chase…," she breathed as he placed it on the carpet next to her. "It's lovely."

"There's more." He pointed to a gold hook on one side of the tower. "Open it."

With eager fingers, she pulled back the clasp at which the front of the house swung open revealing the interior rooms inside, complete with carved fireplaces.

"Cheryl says she'll be glad to help you furnish it from the catalogues they keep at the store," he told her. "Just let her know when you're free, and she'll come over with the ones she thinks you'll find most helpful."

"I can't believe you were able to do this for me." It was Adrianna's turn to blink back tears as her fingers ran along the smooth surfaces of the rooms' floors.

"I'm going to spend the rest of my life filling your days with laughter and joy." He lifted her chin gently with his index finger. "That's what you do when you love someone as much as I love you."

CHAPTER LVI

Three Fridays later, Susan made her way through the revolving doors of the Medical Professional Building that connected to Captain's Point General Hospital in a daze, barely aware of her surroundings as she made her way to her car. How could a routine annual doctor's visit have shocked her so badly? More to the point, how could she tell Jack?

Well, one thing was for sure. She would keep the news to herself until after New Year's, because Daniel and her new husband had been looking forward to both Christmas in their own home and New Year's Eve at The Cove ever since Thanksgiving. She would paste a smile on her face, attend the Tate's Christmas open house tomorrow evening, and somehow make it through the rest of the holidays, beginning with Christmas in the middle of next week.

Unwrapping a tuna sub for another lunch at his desk, Pete Marlborough glanced through the archway that connected what had once been the second parlor of an Italianate Victorian and now served as his office into the former music room where Julia Henderson sat working.

Who would have been able to predict the twists and turns of the past weeks? Ever since the organizational meeting Adrianna had held in the dining room at Montgomery House, the options filling his life had seemed to expand one hundred fold.

First, he had been offered the opportunity to enter into a new business venture with the Sheffields, Chestertons and Jeffersons. Then Julia had come to him for advice as to whether or not she should pick up the option as well, her faith and trust in his wisdom completely surprising him. Finally, Chase had called and explained that he would like to extend the renovations on his wife's ancestral home even further, to where they now included work on the expansive third floor.

Of the three, though, it was Julia's perception of him that had opened his eyes and shifted the kaleidoscope of his life. Now all that remained was for him to process the feelings for her that he now realized had been at the root of his irritation and to decide how he wanted to handle them going forward. Perhaps, the best solution would be to see how their working relationship fared under the stresses of both this new business venture and the renovations at Montgomery House.

Feeling unsettled, Larry hurried along the sidewalk towards the offices of Chesterton and Chesterton, as he faced yet another late Friday afternoon appointment that disrupted what was supposed to be his work-at-home day.

If he was truthful with himself, though, that wasn't what had gotten under his skin. It was working so closely with Kate that he was finding hard to tolerate as the months until her divorce would be final seemed to stretch forth as a never ending course of days filled with frustration as she remained so near and yet so untouchable.

True, both Chase and Susan had made it a point to tell him that the waiting would be worthwhile in the end, but experience had taught him that waiting had left him nothing but empty handed.

At least, Christmas and New Year's would provide opportunities for shared times similar to the Thanksgiving Day he had enjoyed so much, ending the past weeks of gut-wrenching denial and evenings filled with nothing but thoughts of the woman he loved. Never had he felt so alone as when he had gone Christmas shopping at the mall the previous weekend, where he had found himself surrounded by hand-holding couples and families with children.

In the end, he had done what might well prove to be the unforgivable. He had entered Captain's Point's most expensive jewelry store and had purchased a sapphire and diamond tennis bracelet for Kate. Now, all he had to do was present it to her in a way that his feelings for her could remain hidden between them and not interfere with her sensibilities about not yet being divorced.

At least, he had been able to take a stand when it had come to Gerald Tate, refusing to attend his Christmas open house this year on the grounds of his principles. Probably, no one would even notice that he wasn't there, but at least, when it came to this one thing, he could look in a mirror. Besides, Susan had told him that Kate had preferred to babysit Daniel over attending herself.

Swinging the door to his office open with more force than usual due to his frustration, he entered the reception room just in time to overhear Paul Lynch say to Kate, "I'll meet you there about five then," followed by her warm reply, "I'll look forward to it."

So…

Larry breezed past the two of them into his private office. It appeared that Ms. Sinclair's prohibition against dating only applied to him.

He dumped his briefcase onto the floor and plopped into his manager's chair, immediately turning it so as to face the window, only to be greeted by a view of scarf and knitted cap-clad friends and smiling neighbors passing in a steady stream that resembled a moving Christmas card as a few random snowflakes fell around them.

A moment later, a gentle tap on the doorframe behind him caused him to swivel around and discover Kate approaching, a small stack of papers that needed his signature held in her hand.

"Is something wrong?" she asked as she hesitated after placing the documents on his desk.

"No, you seem to have everything, including your plans for this evening, completely in order," he spit out in response, immediately regretting his tone as a hurt look filled her eyes.

"Mrs. Madison is here," Glenda announced from the doorway, allowing Kate an opportunity for a smooth exit.

An hour later, Larry escorted his elderly client to the building's main door, noting as he turned back towards his office that Kate's computer had been turned off for the weekend and her desk straightened as she did each day before leaving.

"Paul left you a flyer as well." Glenda handed him a white paper covered in green and red print that proclaimed the children's tree gift giving at church would begin promptly at five-thirty that evening – an event for which he knew Kate had volunteered her assistance.

"Thanks." He kept his tone even, as realization sunk in that yet again he had been way off base when it came to his thoughts and actions a short time before towards Kate.

How many times was the woman going to allow him to hurt her and then forgive him? What was it going to take for him to put the past behind him and move forward once and for all?

CHAPTER LVII

Once Jack and Susan had left for the Tate's open house the next evening, Kate heated a simple supper of fish sticks and French fries in the oven for Daniel and herself, but no sooner had the child taken his first bite than he began coughing.

"Are you choking?" she asked, relieved when he shook his head in the negative.

"Something's poking my throat," he whispered as if he was afraid to do more.

"Don't talk," she said, working hard to keep her voice calm as she hurried to the mudroom where she retrieved a small flashlight. "Now open your mouth really wide for me, and I'm going to use this spoon to hold down your tongue, so I can take a good look, okay?"

Wide-eyed, Daniel dropped his jaw and held his head back slightly, as Kate silently prayed for guidance, appalled when she spotted a slender fish bone that had penetrated her nephew's tonsil and was now sticking horizontally across the youngster's throat.

"Hello?" Larry's strong voice came to them from the foyer as the front door could be heard closing.

"Hold perfectly still and don't say a word," Kate told Daniel. "It's important that you don't move the muscles in your throat. I'll explain to your Cousin Larry what's wrong, and then, between us, we're going to make everything okay." She gave her young nephew a quick squeeze and hurried from the room.

"Thank goodness you've come!" She grabbed Larry's arm and drew him further from the kitchen, her eyes filled with hope and trust when they came to a halt and she looked up at him. "We have an emergency with Daniel," she quickly informed him about what had happened.

"Have you called Susan and Jack?" he asked.

"No, there hasn't been time," she explained. "I just determined what's actually wrong with him. There's a small fish bone sticking into the right side of his throat, but it's running straight across. If he moves or swallows too much, it looks like it could end up stuck in both of his tonsils."

"Is he in here?" Larry didn't wait for an answer, heading to the kitchen from which she had come.

"Don't move or talk," he, too, admonished his short cousin as he picked up the flashlight and spoon from the table and quickly confirmed what he'd been told, before he addressed Kate, striving to reassure her. "We can take care of this ourselves without ruining Jack and Susan's evening, but I don't have a child's seat in my Mercedes."

"Both of their vehicles are here," she filled him in. "Chase and Adrianna picked them up in Chase's SUV."

Larry reached into his pocket and withdrew his key ring. "This one is for Susan's car. It'll be an easier transition to slip him into the child's seat in it than to have to hoist him into the SUV." He lifted Daniel from the chair as Kate once again hurried from the room. "Pug and Bev will soon have you put back together again," he promised as he headed with the little guy towards the front door.

A few minutes later, they reached the emergency room entrance at Captain's Point General, where Larry quickly removed Daniel from his seat and carried him inside, while Kate parked the car.

"Are either Pug or Bev here?" he asked the reception clerk. "We have a bit of a problem."

"Bev?" The young woman rolled her chair back slightly and gestured with a nod of her head towards the waiting room.

"Daniel?" The head ER nurse sent the frightened boy a smile, when she appeared. "What kind of a mess have you gotten yourself into this time?"

"He has a small fish bone stuck in his throat," Larry explained as Kate rejoined them. "Is Pug here? We're concerned about what could happen if the bone moves even a tiny bit in the wrong direction."

"Bring him in here." Bev led the way into the treatment area, where she indicated for Larry to set her patient on one of the waiting gurneys. "He should be free in just a minute." She strode across to the reception clerk, said a few words and returned with the beginnings of a chart onto which she made a few notes.

"You again?" Pug Brownley sent Daniel a twisted smile as he approached them. "I can always count on you to fill our quieter moments here, can't I? Let me see, first I had to remove a plug of wax the size of a water buffalo from your ear, and then you managed to be struck by your stepfather's helicopter. What is it this time? I've been looking forward to making yet another entry about you in my soon-to-be-world-famous casebook." He took the chart from Bev's hand. "Ah... The classic fish bone in one's throat maneuver. Well, we can set you right quick as a wink, although I now understand why you've been so quiet."

"We thought it would be best if he didn't talk or swallow any more than necessary," Kate interjected softly as Larry reached over and took her hand.

"Probably right," Pug agreed as he took a look at the problem and then addressed Daniel, "I'm going to need you to be slightly braver than during the wax incident and less brave than after the helicopter fiasco. Now, let me see." He glanced around the open area. "Yes, this should do it."

He retrieved a straight-backed chair from a corner. "Larry, if you could sit here with Daniel on your lap, facing forward."

Larry lifted his cousin from the gurney and complied, while Pug selected a long pair of surgical tweezers from a drawer of sterilized instruments and held them behind his back out of sight as he took a seat on a rolling stool.

"Daniel, I want you to lean your head back against Larry's chest and relax," the ER doctor directed. "Then, if you can drape your legs over your cousin's like this, I can roll forward between his legs so I can have a good view of your throat."

Larry widened the space between his knees for the stool and its occupant.

"Unfortunately, this leaves our two gals here with nothing to do," Pug continued. "Kate, why don't you hold Daniel's right hand, so you won't be so scared, and, Bev, I'm sure our patient wouldn't mind if you held his left in order to earn your paycheck. Does anyone know if this little fellow can count to ten?"

"Daniel can count to at least twenty," Kate filled him in – her face, Larry noticed, drawn and white under the harsh fluorescent lights.

"Excellent!" Pug beamed. "Larry, if you'll hold your cousin's head tightly on both sides, let's everyone except Daniel count backwards from ten, and when we reach one, I'll slip this troublesome bone out."

Daniel's eyes widened as the group around him began the countdown, "Ten, nine, eight, seven…"

"Whoops!" Pug exclaimed. "Would you look at that? It slid out all by itself on seven, and it's a really nice specimen, too. I think we should send it home with the boy in a suitable container, so he can show his mother. Don't you, Bev?"

"Definitely," she agreed. "Jack and Susan will both be impressed. I'll get a bottle." She opened the door to a white metal cabinet that stood a few feet away as Larry lowered his hands and gave his cousin a hug.

"It's okay if he talks and moves around now, isn't it?" Kate asked from where she still stood holding onto Daniel.

"Absolutely," Pug confirmed. "Tell Susan that if his throat is sore in the morning, he should see his pediatrician about a mild antibiotic, but I don't anticipate that he'll have any real problem."

"Wow!" Daniel's face lit up with a grin as he accepted his bone in a bottle from Pug, who then gave him a high five and approved of his having been so brave.

"You'll need to stop by the receptionist's desk on the way out and sign her forms," Bev addressed Larry.

"Sure thing, and thanks to both of you." He lifted Daniel down from his own lap and rose.

The hospital paperwork signed and the short drive back to Blue Wolf Manor having been completed in near silence, Larry removed his now sleeping cousin from the child's seat and carried him upstairs to bed, while Kate returned Susan's car to the garage.

"Cousin Larry?" Daniel asked as the act of putting him into his pajamas half-awakened him.

"Yes?"

"Aunt Kate takes good care of me. She promised to make everything all better just like my mama would, and she did. She's never lived in the real world, but we're helping her learn. She's working hard at getting things right, and I'm being supportive of her. You'll tell her for me that we love her, won't you?"

"Of course, I will, Tiger." Larry tucked the little guy in, pausing only long enough to be assured that Daniel had dropped back to sleep, as he realized that even the child before him had a better grasp on how to love the woman who held his own future in the palm of her hand than he did.

With his small cousin settled, he hurried downstairs in search of Kate, where he looked with no success through the empty rooms before he discovered that one of the French doors to the wide porch that overlooked the ocean stood slightly ajar. Pulling it towards him, he caught a glimpse of her where she leaned against the thick column at the left of the stairs that led to the lawn, hugging herself for warmth as she stood coatless in the cold, night air.

Grabbing an afghan from the back of the armchair to his right, he hurried forward and slipped it around her, surprised when she exchanged the post for his chest and leaned into him. "What are you doing out here in the dark?" he asked, not sure that he wanted to know, even as he brought his arms around her.

"Thinking things through, so I can decide what to do." She looked up at him with eyes that glistened with tears.

"What you must think of me," he stated, hearing the anger with himself in his voice. "And, frankly, I don't blame you. I'm so out of practice, and I've made one stupid mistake after another as I've tried to make my way back. It's why I showed up here in the first place, so I could apologize."

"I don't understand." She searched his face for answers.

"What do you see when you look at me?" he asked.
"Good and bad."

"Honestly?"

"Yes."

"I see a man who's confident in himself and his abilities, who knows how to deeply love those he cares about and will sacrifice himself for them, perhaps at times more than he should like you did over Chester's," she began.

"I see a man who loves children and is loved by them in return. I see someone who cares about his community, a wonderful friend to those he's known since childhood, to his cousin Susan, especially when she really needed him after her divorce, and to my brother. I see someone who welcomed me to Captain's Point, the person who found me my apartment even though it wasn't in any way his responsibility, and the man who has encouraged me to press forward with my sidetracked career goals and offered support along the way."

"What about the bad? Don't you see me as mean, short-tempered, and a constant source of hurt?"

"No." Her face as he studied it clearly showed her confusion. "Do you want to know more?"

"Yes," he replied. "I need to know what you think of me."

"I see in you a man I can trust, whose word is his bond as old-fashioned as that may sound. I see a kind and gentle nature, a protector, a man who would take a fall for me to keep me from being hurt over a silly Frisbee." She reached up her hand and cupped his cheek, as her voice choked with the tears that once again filled her eyes. "I see the man whose arms I want around me, the one whose children I want to bear. I see the man that I love, which is why I'm going to leave Captain's Point."

"Leave Captain's Point?" He gathered her more tightly to him and spoke into her hair as her head rested against his shoulder. "Why? Because I've treated you so badly, been so hard on you and kept pressing you for more?

"That was all about me, Kate, about an old hurt that I'd pressed down for too long. Life's a journey, and I'd taken a wrong turn in the road. After a time, I'd even lost sight of the goal. When you came into my life, I realized where I had gone wrong, overcompensated and dragged you along with me as I swerved too far in the opposite direction.

"You didn't deserve any of it. Don't you know how wonderful you are? You're smart and beautiful and kind and generous and giving and loving…" Here he was forced to take a breath, and she raised her face once again to his.

"I've fallen for you, Kate, and I've fallen hard," he continued. "I haven't followed through like I've wanted to because you're still tied to what's his name and I didn't want to make you feel uncomfortable, but that's only for three more months now.

"As soon as that part of your life is behind you, I want to spend every minute of my day openly showing you how much better things can be for you here with me in Captain's Point. Please tell me that you'll find your way to forgive me, to give me another chance, to let me start over with a clean slate and none of the baggage I've been carrying with me for far too long, so I can prove to you that I can make you happy."

For a moment, they remained silent as they each searched the other's eyes, but then he brought his lips onto hers, lightly touching them as each experienced the feel of the other in this way for the first time. But then, his kiss turned into a question as he pressed harder before he drew back slightly, once again searching her eyes before he crushed her to him and took possession of her mouth in a way that left no room for doubt as to the strength of his feelings, pleased when he received her response.

"I think I could hang around a little longer," she breathed softly when they finally separated, his arms still encircling her as he gazed down at her with eyes filled with love. "I've always believed in second chances, and if I've been given one here in Captain's Point, then you're certainly due."

Which is why, when Jack and Susan quietly returned to their home a few moments later, they discovered his sister and her cousin locked in each other's arms in the dark on their back porch overlooking the ocean.

Coming Spring of 2014!

The Fourth Novel in the Captain's Point Stories Series

Love's Surprise

Does Larry succeed in his quest for Kate?

What was the news that shocked Susan so badly?

Will Edwina and Arthur find their way forward?

What new secrets will Montgomery House reveal during its renovations?

Can Daniel get through a novel without a visit to Pug?

Discover the answers to these and other questions posed by series readers in this next romantic women's fiction/family saga tale of true love and personal growth from Charlotte Kent.

A Special Treat for You!

From

Charlotte Kent

A Clue for Adrianna

Chase and Adrianna's Courtship

Chapter One

Viewing the tarmac beneath her, Adrianna Montgomery could see Chicago's Midway Airport's ground crew loading last minute luggage and truly relaxed for the first time since her arrival home to her condo in Seattle the previous evening.

"Is this seat taken?" a shy, cultured voice asked from the aisle to her right.

Turning, she found herself looking into a pair of worried blue eyes. Reflexively, she straightened the seat belt and lowered the arm that would separate them as she replied, "No, it's free. Help yourself."

"Thank you." The elderly woman joined her. "I don't often fly, and I've been dreading hours spent aloft beside a crying child." With the toe of a tiny shoe, the newcomer pushed a large patent leather handbag beneath the forward seat before fastening her seatbelt.

A light fragrance of honeysuckle wafted its way towards Adrianna, reminiscent of early childhood summers spent playing in the gazebo behind her great-aunt's seaside mansion, breezes blowing off the Atlantic lifting her dark curls. Despite her parents having left her behind as they had traveled the world in search of archeological treasure, those had been happy times.

But then, she had grown old enough to accompany them, and the summer visits had ended. As promised, she had written to her great-aunt of her travels, her childish script filling pages with stories of her adventures – a camel ride in Egypt, a mosaic at a dig in Turkey, a Minoan vase her mother had uncovered on a Greek isle – the list had gone on and on.

"My name's Edwina Foster." Her traveling companion broke through her thoughts. "I'm flying to visit my grandson and his wife."

"This trip is strictly business for me," Adrianna replied.

"Actually, it's more than a visit." The blue eyes now twinkled. "They're in their mid-thirties, and Ginny is expecting their first child. Jason has to attend a long conference in New York and didn't want to leave his wife alone this close to her due date. They've just moved to Captain's Point, Maryland, and haven't had time to make friends."

"Captain's Point?"

"Do you know it? I hear it's lovely."

"I haven't been there for any length of time since I was seven – almost twenty years ago, but I liked it back then. The town was full of little shops, but my favorite memory is of looking for shells on the beach."

With a start, Adrianna realized she had just lied. Her favorite memory had nothing to do with the beach, but rather with the wind-tossed woods behind the giant house.

One day during the early part of her last summer visit, she had found an old butterfly net stuffed between the croquet sticks and badminton racquets that were stored in a deep closet beneath the staircase. Not wanting to disturb her great-aunt's pre-dinner nap, she had gone outside to play with it, neglecting to tell the housekeeper where she was going. Happily chasing a bevy of yellow and white butterflies, she had left the manicured lawn and entered the cool quiet of the woods.

Other paths covered in pine needles had crossed, joined and then separated from the one that she had followed, and as the sun had set, she had realized that she was lost. A twig had snapped sharply somewhere behind her, and she had started to run, her way partially revealed through the leaves of the trees by a full moon rising overhead. Inevitably, she had tripped on a root and fallen to her knees, her right one striking the corner of a sharp pebble as she had let out a cry.

"Who is it?" A voice had called out up ahead.

"Adrianna," she had responded, forgetting her great-aunt's careful instructions about speaking with strangers.

"Stay where you are," the voice had commanded. "I'm coming."

A light rounded the bend ahead and came towards her, at first blocking her view of the boy who was carrying it. "What are you doing out here?" He had dropped a backpack onto the ground. "Miss Martha will be fit to be tied."

"You know my great-aunt?"

"Everyone knows Martha Montgomery." He had shrugged, calmly pulling a first aid kit from his pack and cleaning the cut on her knee with water from a Boy Scout canteen. "These woods aren't safe at night for a little girl."

"You're here," she had pointed out.

"But I'm older, and besides, I'm collecting specimens for my merit badge."

At the time, she hadn't known what a merit badge was, but it had sounded important. Silently, she had watched as he had applied an adhesive bandage to the cut by the light of his flashlight.

"I'll walk you back." He had held out his hand, and she had taken it gladly.

As the aircraft's engines roared to life, Edwina's voice broke through Adrianna's long ago memories. "I'm sure I wasn't the first person my grandson called on, but still, it's nice to be needed," Edwina admitted.

"I know they'll appreciate your help," she assured her traveling companion.

Turning towards the window, Adrianna watched as the runway flashed by, wondering if she had ever been needed by anyone – certainly not by her bright, shining parents, who had left her at a Swiss finishing school just two weeks before they had plunged to their deaths from one of the infamous curves along the Amalfi coast. And yet, here she was, flying from one end of the country to the other in response to two letters – one that had been more a command than a request and one that had broken her heart.

OTHER TITLES AVAILABLE FROM ANNIE ACORN PUBLISHING LLC

By Annie Acorn

Chocolate Can Kill

Murder With My Darling

A Stranger Comes to Town

The Young Executive

When to Remain Silent

On the Road

The Magic Sand Dollar

One More Christmas Past

One Last Gift To Go

A Haunting Christmas

Too Busy for Christmas

A Christmas Rescue

Christmas Shoppe Magic

Christmas Shoppe Magic Revisited

The Christmas Spirit of Starlight Cove

By Angel Nichols

Christmas in the Mojave

Christmas Love Exchange

By Billie Thomas

Murder on the First Day of Christmas